LAWS OF PHYSICS BOOK 3: TIME

PENNY REID

HTTP://PENNYREID.NINJA/NEWSLETTER/

COPYRIGHT

Caped Publishing

Print Edition, April 2019

ISBN 9781635763416

[1]
INTRO TO MODERN ASTROPHYSICS

Mona

I didn't know enough about spiders.

For example, what did they do during the winter when flies were scarce? Did they sleep/hibernate like bears? And what's the deal with hibernation? How does one get in on that action? Sleeping for long periods, as though time doesn't exist. *Then again—*

"Time doesn't exist."

"What?"

In the fuzzy distortion of my peripheral vision, I saw Lisa turn toward me. She'd been sitting at her square kitchen table, working on her laptop since I'd *meh-ed* all her suggestions for leaving the apartment today. I think she was relieved.

I sat in her living room, somewhat reclined on a big, brown leather couch that was too large for the space. It wasn't that the room was small, the couch was just too big, messing up the feng shui. Lisa had filled her apartment with fancy and colossal Williams Sonoma monstrosities, whereas what she really needed was some Ikea in her life.

My elbow bent, my cheek pressed against the underside of my forearm, I peered at the window.

"Time doesn't exist," I repeated, watching the spider in the corner of the glass pane as it did nothing. It wasn't dead, the web was too new, but it was completely motionless. "I need to read more about spiders."

"What does time have to do with spiders?" My sister's tone was uncharacteristically gentle, almost wary. I hypothesized that my bursting into tears with the smallest amount of provocation over the last three days had made her cautious. Poor Lisa. She'd invited me to stay not knowing I'd transformed from *not a crier* to *a crier*.

At first, she'd insisted we go out and, at first, I'd been happy for the distraction. However, no matter where we went, disaster struck. Abram's voice singing "Hold a Grudge" in the restaurant and at the movie theater. A poster of Abram and Redburn's album cover at L stations and street corners. A young woman wearing a Redburn T-shirt. He was everywhere and yet nowhere—no calls, no emails, no attempt at contact—and the combination made everything worse.

I figured, at least in Lisa's apartment I would be safe from the onslaught of Abram propaganda.

"I'm thinking about exploring the viability of human hibernation," I said through a yawn. If it was good enough for bears, need I say more?

"I don't think spiders hibernate." The sound of Lisa's chair lightly scraping against the tile drew my attention away from the spider. My sister stood, stretched, and her slippered feet made scuffing sounds as she walked. It was past 11:00 AM and we were still in our pajamas. "Do you want tea? Or coffee?"

"They should." Everyone should hibernate. "Why haven't humans investigated hibernation as an alternative to living through nonexistent time?"

"Mona. Do you want tea?" Lisa's tone wasn't impatient, but it wasn't patient either. Again, I didn't blame her. I'd been crying early and often, and I hadn't yet fully explained why. I couldn't, because every time I tried, I cried.

Which had me wondering, which came first: the try or the cry? *A paradox.*

"Yes to tea, please."

I zoned out as she moved around the kitchen and out of view. A short time later, a tea kettle screeched. Sometime after that, she set a mug on the coffee table. At some point, she sat next to me on the couch and placed her hand on my back. I didn't remember her touching me, only that one moment her hand wasn't there and the next moment it was. Straightening from where I half-reclined on the arm of the couch, I twisted to look at her.

Her lips were curved into a tight, small smile and she inclined her head to the right. "Your tea is ready."

"Thank you." I glanced at the mug, but I lacked the energy to reach for it. Therefore, I stared at it, willing it to move into my hands.

"What are you doing?" she asked after another vague span of time.

"You don't want to know."

More moments passed. Lisa's eyes were on my profile while I stared at the tea.

Eventually, she huffed, reached for the mug, and placed it into my hands. "You seriously need to snap out of this. What did he do to you? You've been here for three days and it's like hanging out with a ghost."

"WooOOOoooOOOooo." I made my voice shake, the pitch go up and down.

That made her chuckle. But then, for the hundredth time, she asked, "When are you going to tell me what happened in Aspen?"

I brought the mug to my lips because a sting of tears rushed to my eyes. I knew the contents within the mug were too hot to drink. I took a sip anyway. I burned my tongue. I blinked back the tears.

"Mona, come on." Her hand came to my shoulder. She squeezed it. She sounded concerned. "This isn't you. You're a mess."

"I'm not a mess." I was a mess. The logical path forward had abandoned me. Every road led to disaster. *The wolves are definitely on their way.*

"You *are* a mess. One minute you're giving me monosyllabic answers, and the next you're crying at the airport! I'm worried. I've never known you to be like this, ever."

I released a watery sigh, my eyes losing focus, the white mug and its dark brown contents swirling together to become a nebulous blur. "My display of emotion within the airport is self-explanatory."

"Yes. The large poster of Abram Fletcher in his underwear was difficult to miss." Once again, her voice gentled. "I'm sorry. I didn't see it on my way in, otherwise I would have walked a different way."

"It's okay." It was okay.

Martin Sandeke, Kaitlyn Parker's churlish fiancé, had mentioned the existence of the posters in passing last week. We'd been talking in the kitchen the day before Abram left Aspen, and Martin had said, *He just did that underwear modeling thing, soon there will be posters of the guy in his underwear everywhere.*

I hadn't given the statement extensive attention, instead focusing on the second part of Martin's claim, *That's not a guy who's changed. That's a guy who is just getting started.*

There he was. Abram. At the airport. Gorgeous. *Spectacular.* Hand over his heart. His eyes on the ground. A bright white background. Lust in my heart. His hair was down (I'd never seen him with his hair down since he'd grown it out) and he wore no shirt, just black boxer briefs that left very little to the imagination. Even worse, the advertisement for underwear had been life-sized.

I'd been warned, I should have prepared myself!

I wasn't prepared.

Martin had been right, the posters were everywhere, and *everywhere* included the baggage claim at O'Hare. I'd wanted to take it out of the plexiglass display, roll it up, and steal it, especially when I spotted two other women do a double take as they walked by. One of them elbowed the other and they shared a look.

They shared a look about my boyfriend . . .?

No.

Wait.

Is that what he was?

That would make you his girlfriend.

No.

Maybe?

I had no idea.

Anyway, I couldn't stop thinking about the fact that people in the airport had seen Abram with his hair down, shirtless, *in his underwear* before I had. And that gave me the sad. Would I ever see him with his hair down? Would I ever see him in his underwear?

Only time would tell, and time was being evasive.

Presently, my hand moved to the folded piece of paper I'd been carrying every day, now in my PJ pocket, and I rubbed my finger over the outline of its folded corners. I'd replaced my beloved letter—the one that Abram had burned in Aspen—with the poem he'd left me on my side table. The original letter I'd carried was thick, three pages of hefty hopes and dreams. This one was much smaller, which felt appropriate because it contained just one hope, *This is not goodbye.*

Then why does it feel like goodbye?

"Hey," Lisa said, pulling me out of my reflections. "You know, I almost cried when I saw the poster too." I could tell by the shift in her tone that she was trying to be funny, trying to cheer me up. "O'Hare should take it down, otherwise the arrivals area will be full of swooning, weeping women."

Ugh. "Not helping."

"I'm sorry. I'm just trying to—" Lisa's tone changed. "Listen, he's famous. Okay? He's famous, he's a rock star, and he's a model, and he's hot, and that means he's going to be a sex object, an object of lust for thousands of women. Those are the facts. You can't burst into tears every time you see a billboard of Abram Fletcher in his underwear."

My head whipped around to my sister and time slowed. "There are billboards?" My voice cracked, because of course it did.

She scrunched her face, and her response seemed to take forever. "Forget I said that."

"You've seen billboards of Abram in his underwear?"

Now she winced, again taking forever to respond. "Just two."

I set the mug away and covered my face, my elbows on my legs, and shook my head. "I can't do this."

"I'm sorry! I shouldn't have said anything." Lisa's fingers encircled my wrist. Just like when she'd placed her hand on my back earlier, I didn't flinch. Flinching had been instinctual for so long. I had no idea why the reflex suddenly stopped in some situations, with some people, yet persisted in others. But I couldn't think about that right now.

5

Removing my hand from my face, Lisa wavered for a moment, and then used her leverage on my arm to pull me forward into a hug. "Oh, Mona. I wish you would tell me what happened in Aspen. He hurt you? I'll make him suffer."

Heaving another watery sigh, I bit my bottom lip to stay my wobbly chin and clung to my sister. "He didn't hurt me. He was wonderful. So wonderful."

She made a sympathetic sound. "You miss him? Is that what this is about?"

I nodded.

"You two are together?"

I hesitated, because I wanted to be precise. "I think so."

"You think so?" An edge entered her voice and I felt her stiffen.

I pressed my lips into a firm line and endeavored to work through the jumble of feelings and thoughts and second-guesses cluttering my brain. Were we together?

Abram's words from that last night echoed between my ears, *Stop trying to put us in a fucking box!*

Sucking in a breath through my nose, I finally answered, "Definitely. Maybe."

I felt her chest rise and fall. "Maybe. What the hell does that mean?"

Scrunching my eyes, I leaned away, but kept hold of her forearms. "It means we love each other, and I told him I'd be open to seeing him whenever he wants to see me, and he—"

"What?!" She gripped my biceps and shook me until I opened my eyes. When I did, I was faced with a pissed off Lisa. "No. Oh *hell* no. You are not doing this. I will not allow it. You are not becoming one of Abram Fletcher's groupies. You are Mona DaVinci, world famous scientific badass, strong woman, brainiac, and role model to women everywhere. This is not happening!"

"It's not like—"

"I get it." Lisa gave me another little shake, her angry whisper like steel, her eyes flashing. "I get the insanity, I do. He's so talented, right? And sexy, and the sex is incredible, and he makes you feel special and alive, right? But, guess what, I guarantee you are not special to him."

6

"It's not like that."

"Mona, come on, you are so much smarter than this. You are a literal genius. You are no one's groupie."

"No, listen to me, we love—"

She let me go with a derisive snort. "Please. Love? He's known you for what? Two weeks total over two years? Bullshit. That's not love, that's sex and infatuation."

"Lisa, you're wrong. We haven't even had sex."

That had her straightening her spine, blinking her surprise. "What?"

"We've kissed, but that's it. You don't know what it was like when we were together that week here in Chicago. You don't know what it was like in Aspen. He—we—it's like, I don't even know how to describe it. I've never felt so . . ."

"Alive?" The question held a note of mockery.

"No. Comfortable. Effortlessly comfortable, being myself. He *knows* me, somehow, in a way I don't even know myself." I grunted, and then growled at the insufficiency of my words. "I'm not describing this correctly. The thing is, it's not about sex. Most of the time we were together, we just talked."

My sister's eyes narrowed into suspicious slits. "Seriously, Mona, this whole week, you don't even sound like yourself when you talk about him."

"Who do I sound like?"

"I don't know. Someone else. Someone not you." Her gaze moved over my face, like she was looking for the sister she knew within a stranger. "I guess, let me ask this, do you want to change? Do you like this person he's made you into? This weepy woman who can't leave the apartment without crying over a *guy*? Because—in my mind—this weak, sad, emotional person is not who you are."

Nibbling on my bottom lip, I dropped my eyes to my hands in my lap, absorbing her words. "I don't feel like I've changed. Much."

"But you have." Her hand closed over mine again, and this time I flinched, reflexively moving out of her grip. "Look. You're my sister. Obviously, I love you and want what's best for you. If you want my opinion—and you can take it or leave it—then it's this: Abram is not

7

good for you. I'm not just saying this because I'm worried about how twisted up and emotional you've been this week, I'm saying this because I have experience with guys like him."

"You mean musicians."

"Yes. Exactly. They're a different breed. They're leeches. He might say he loves you, but he really just loves himself and his music."

"He's not Tyler."

"Oh, really? Has he called you? Has he texted you since Aspen? It's been almost a week, right?"

I winced against the chilling stab of pain slicing through me. She already knew the answer to her questions. He hadn't called. He hadn't contacted me.

After several beats of meaningful silence, during which I worked to breathe around the ache, I glanced at her. "You know he doesn't have my phone number."

"Right. And he can't get it from Leo, like, anytime he wants." Lisa lifted an eyebrow, her tone heavily laced with sarcasm, her lips a thin line. "No, honey. You forget, I chased after the human trash bag Tyler for years. I've been you. I've made these mistakes. I know what you're thinking and feeling, and I promise you—if you'd just cut him out now and stop hoping for more—everything will be so much better. You'll go back to being the Mona we all know and love."

Thankfully, the sound of Lisa's phone buzzing on the kitchen table saved me from having to form more words. With an irritated huff, she let me go and walked to the kitchen. I swallowed several times and lifted my eyes to the ceiling, willing back another confounded wave of tears.

She was right. Abram hadn't called or texted or made any attempt at contact. But, even if he did have my number, he was on tour. One quick Google search two days ago also told me that he was giving nonstop interviews to media outlets, radio stations, and magazines. He was busy. Having watched my parents go through similar times in their lives, I knew how full his days were. Just like them, he (probably) barely had time to sleep, and just like them, he didn't have time for me yet.

You should call him.

This wasn't the first time the thought had occurred to me. It was an insidious little whisper, a prodding, pushing, haranguing voice, and it disregarded facts.

Fact one: I didn't have his number.

Fact two: I could call my brother to get it, but I had no guarantee he would give it to me. After my discussion with Leo in Aspen about Abram, how he'd warned me away, I doubted he'd want me calling his friend. Yes, I would probably be able to extract the number from him after many minutes—or hours—spent in hostage negotiations, but that was assuming I didn't start crying on the phone. If I cried on the phone, Leo would never give me the number. Since I couldn't stop crying, calling Leo would just have to wait until I was more "myself."

Fact three: I wanted to talk to Abram, more than anything, but he'd been the one who left this time. He was the one who'd insisted it wasn't goodbye. I had to be patient. I had to be practical. I would give him space. I would wait. But I promised myself, if a month or two passed and he still didn't reach out, then . . .

Then you will still want to see him.

GAH!

Was Lisa right? Was I becoming someone else? Someone pathetic? Over a *guy*? But Abram wasn't "a guy."

But is he "the one?"

I hated the term, *the one*. However, here I was, using it, because I needed to call him something relative to my feelings for him. And yet, he couldn't be "the one." He didn't meet the minimum requirements.

By his own admission, Abram had never thought of getting married. I wanted kids, a house, a picket fence, normalcy, consistency. My feelings for Abram hadn't made those dreams go away, they'd just shifted, settled around him. He'd now become part of that picture.

But what if he didn't want to be part of that picture? What if he didn't want any of those things? What if his picture was completely different than mine? What then?

I rubbed my chest with stiff fingers, massaging my hurting heart through my ribs, telling myself that it wasn't Abram who'd made me weepy, he wasn't the cause for my constant catastrophic crying. It was me.

I was the problem. Me and my quest for stability while falling in love with a *musician.*

"Yeah, come over and help me talk some sense into her." Lisa raised her voice, obviously wanting me to hear her phone conversation, and I glanced up. She was sending me a stony look, her eyes slightly narrowed.

I glanced at the phone in her hand. "Who is that?"

"It's Gabby. She's on her way, bringing over ice cream and wine, but also offered male strippers."

Ah, Gabby.

I reached for my tea. "No. No, thank you. I don't need the wine or the ice cream either."

We'd gone out with Gabby during my first two days in Chicago. She was an *excellent* distraction. Or rather, her constant gabbing, zaniness, and wacky stories were. I was glad she was coming over just for the distraction factor.

"Well, you're getting wine and ice cream because she already bought them," Lisa said to me as she meandered closer, and then to Gabby, "Tell Duke to stay on standby. Okay, see you in a little bit. Bye." My sister returned to her spot on the couch, leaving her phone on the coffee table.

Taking as deep of a breath as I possibly could, I decided it was time to explain the entire situation to my sister. The inability to speak without becoming a blubbering mess had been a major limiting factor. I would just have to get over it. I would accept the tears, rather than fight them, and I would tell her the whole story.

"I'll tell you everything that happened," I rushed to say before she could launch into another rant. "Truly, Lisa. Abram is not like that, he's not like Tyler. He's not like Mom and Dad either."

She gritted her teeth and released a humorless laugh, shaking her head. "He is exactly like Tyler—and Mom, and Dad—musicians and artists are all the same, Mo, especially the brilliant ones. They're flighty, selfish, and vain. They might be brilliant, but they only care about themselves, their ego, and their music. They will suck the soul right out of anyone who loves them, and they use it to feed their own brilliance until your light is extinguished, until you're left broken. And then they move on."

"Let me just tell you what happened, okay?"

"Fine, but if he doesn't call you soon, *groveling*, and begging for forgiveness for not making contact in *six days*, then I will junk punch him with my new taekwondo moves, and then break his femurs."

For the record, I didn't want Lisa to junk punch Abram, but for some reason her overprotectiveness warmed my heart and, you guessed it, made me want to cry. I blinked against the new onslaught, lifting my eyes to the ceiling.

"Okay, first, let me explain something." I cleared my throat and endeavored to recenter my thoughts. "You first have to understand, time doesn't exist. As such, I can't be angry at Abram for not calling me."

One of Lisa's eyebrows lifted, her gaze became a glare. "*Riiiiiiight.*"

"No, hear me out. We talk about people being deep, we talk about feelings being heavy. I've been thinking about this for the past week and it made me wonder: Do heavy feelings have more mass? Do they have their own gravity? Fields we cannot detect with any scientific instrument because they're calibrated for the physical world?"

"Mona—"

"Just listen. If time is the result of gravity shaping or warping reality—which it is, which is why clocks tick faster on a mountain than at sea level—then what impact do heavy, weighty feelings have on time? I hypothesize that sadness slows time, and happiness does the opposite. Make sense?"

She rolled her eyes. "Only you would overcomplicate something so simple. Forget about the rules of physics—"

"Laws of physics."

"Whatever! The rules of life, of society and engagement say that—if Abram was serious about you, if you were important to him—he would have called you *the very next day*. You can't tell me the weight of your feelings is at all responsible for the force of the mass of the gravity of fucking, selfish, shitty boys being shitty to you, blah blah blah." She waved her hands through the air, working herself into a frenzy. "He hasn't called you in *six days*. I don't care about gravity and feelings. In every universe, six days is a ridiculous amount of time."

"Yes. But—"

"There is no but! Stop making excuses for him!" Lisa's voice had lowered to a sharp whisper, and it was clear my attempt at using logic to explain my behavior was angering her.

"I'm not making excuses. You're right, okay? Six days is long, fine. But it's not really about Abram, is it? It's about me. What I'm saying is, I am heavy with unfamiliar feelings. All this crying, it's not because of Abram, not really. I've slowed time to an eternal crawl, and I'm overwhelmed. Therefore, me and my heavy, unfamiliar feelings are the problem. Not Abram."

I reasoned that, perhaps once I adjusted to this new time—Abram-less Agony Time—I'd stop being such a mess. Unfortunately, the only cure for Abram-less Agony Time was more time, and time was the problem in the first place, and time didn't even really exist! AH!

I need a nap. And a cookie would be nice.

Lisa gathered a deep breath, looking like she'd run out of patience and maybe needed a nap too. "Mona, I love you. But you are making me crazy. You can't accept responsibility for other people being assholes. I know you really like Abram, I know he said he loved you, but there's a reason people say, 'Actions speak louder than words.' I *totally* get it. He's hot. Talented. Charismatic. Something special. But if he doesn't treat you like a goddamn queen, then it doesn't matter how special he is, he's not worthy of you! And one more thing—"

The buzzer to the apartment cut her rant short and she frowned, looking mildly surprised. "Whoa, that was fast."

"Is that Gabby?"

"It must be." She seemed frustrated by the interruption. Lisa stood, walking to the button in her small foyer. "This conversation is on pause, but it's not over, okay?"

I nodded, frowning, feeling increasingly muddled.

Meanwhile, Lisa pressed the button, unlatching the main door at street level. She then unlocked and propped open her front door before shuffling to the kitchen and calling over her shoulder, "Prepare your-self for some serious day drinking. This is an emergency and the wine will help you relax enough to tell us the real story of what went down with you and Abram in Aspen. Think of it as medicinal."

"I thought you didn't drink anymore?" I straightened from the couch and stretched, walking aimlessly back and forth in front of the coffee table. Slowly, I turned toward the entryway. My brain was scrambled, but I figured I might as well be useful and help Gabby carry up her provisions.

"I don't drink anymore." Lisa appeared at the entrance to her kitchen holding two wine glasses. "But Gabby does, and she's a frequent visitor. She bought me these as a housewarming gift."

Despite the brain scramble, this data made me chuckle. It sounded so much like Gabby, buying someone a gift for their apartment because she would use it. Reluctantly, I admired how good Gabby was at looking after herself, knowing what she wanted, making it happen, and being unapologetic.

However, Gabby was also generous in completely unselfish ways too, like the wine and the ice cream.

"Here." I shuffled toward the door. "I'll go help her carry every thing up. Be right back."

"You're still in your pajamas."

I glanced down at myself, at my plain white T-shirt, and black and blue pajama pants. "Yeah?"

Lisa twisted her lips to the side, considering. "I guess, nothing. Go ahead. But if you see the cute guy in the apartment below mine, make it clear you're my twin sister."

"Oh. I see what's going on." I nodded, managing a small smirk, and backing up toward her front door. "You want me to say I'm *Lisa* and ask him if I smell. Do I have that right?"

A rueful grin pulled her lips to one side, and she opened her mouth as though to respond to my teasing. Her eyes then moved beyond me, her mouth snapped shut, and she flinched. "What the hell?"

I glanced over my shoulder and did a double take. My heart jumped to my throat. My hand flew to my chest. I stumbled back. Behind me, standing in the doorway, was Tyler.

And behind him was Abram.

[2]
ELLIPTICAL ORBITS

Abram

S tepping around Tyler, I walked directly to Mona. I saw only her, and her stunned expression gave me no pause. I wrapped my arms around her body, lifted her off the ground, and kissed her lips.

She was warm, and soft, and tasted like peppermint and honey. I bit back a groan.

God, she felt good. Great. Celestial. *Heavenly.* I may have surprised her, but she responded immediately, enthusiastically, twisting her arms around my neck, opening her mouth and welcoming the invasion of mine.

It wasn't enough.

It was a crumb, and I was starving. Desire—to tighten my hold, devour, take, keep, cherish, to never let her go—obscured thought and sight, and I slipped a hand under her shirt to touch the silky skin of her back, sliding my fingers upward until they rested under her bra strap.

Mona lifted her chin, breaking our mouths apart, and I kissed the point of it, the elegant line of her jaw, the tender spot beneath her ear, the hot skin where Mona's graceful neck met the slope of her shoulder.

I was so hungry for her, I couldn't stop myself from tasting every exposed inch.

"Abram," she said, her voice a breathless, disbelieving whisper, followed by a little laugh. Her fingers flexed at the back of my neck, pressing me closer. Every part of my body hummed and vibrated, unable to contain the immensity of now, of this divine feeling.

"You're here," she said, her soft voice full of wonder and happiness, soothing the ravenous panic holding me hostage for the past six days. It had been a peculiar kind of madness, not being able to reach her while pretending all was fine, pretending she didn't occupy my mind every second of the day. But receding now, it left a new kind of turmoil and urgency in its wake.

We had no time.

No, I corrected myself, *We have time. We have the rest of our lives.*

"I need your fu—your phone number." I spoke gruffly against her neck, squeezing my eyes shut and breathing her in, again and again, the heat and sweetness of Mona.

I'd missed her, and that was a gross understatement. I'd been speeding toward this moment for days and being with her now felt like the aftermath of a head-on collision. Stupefied, frantic, but determined to enjoy every shared second remaining. My hands were shaking.

We have time. Calm down. Calm down.

Mona laughed lightly, the sound melodic, beautiful, and she pressed a kiss under my ear. "Why didn't you just ask Leo? Or send me an email?"

Leo.

I worked to keep the darkness of my thoughts from showing on my face as I leaned away, letting her slide to the ground but unwilling to release her fully, fisting my unsteady hands into her T-shirt. "I couldn't find an email for you anywhere, and neither could Marie. She tried calling your department for me. They told her all media requests had to go through the PR department at the university and it would take two weeks to a month for a response."

"Ah, that's true. My email is on lockdown, otherwise it gets out of hand." She nodded contritely. "But what about Leo?"

"Leo." I forced my jaw to relax and I lowered my voice but

couldn't completely disguise the intensity of my wrath. "Leo wouldn't give me your number."

Mona's hand moved to my face, her palm pressed against my cheek, the pads of her fingers softly stroking my beard. "What? Are you serious?"

"Yes," I ground out. "He said he was doing me a favor. So I flew to LA."

"You flew to LA?" I felt her body tense, and the moment realization dawned, her beautiful eyes growing impossibly large as they moved over my face. "You must be so tired and—but I wasn't in LA, I was—"

"Here. Yes. I found that out yesterday when I stopped by your department at Caltech and they told me you weren't due back until Friday," I rushed to explain, multitasking, using the time to devour the sight of her, soak and submerge in the reality of being here with her.

Calm down. We. Have. Time.

"They said you'd be leaving for Geneva on Monday," I continued, willing my heart and speech to slow. "But that you were in Chicago, visiting your sister this week."

I left out the part about Mona's department secretary being a huge fan of Redburn, but not enough to give me Mona's email or phone number.

"What's he doing here?" Lisa cut in, sounding pissed.

I glanced at Mona's sister out of the corner of my eye. She didn't seem to be paying attention to us. Her stare was firmly fixed on some point behind me, I assumed Tyler.

"I also tried calling Gabby for your phone number," I continued, needing to tell the rest of the story before explaining Tyler's presence. "But her number had changed."

That caught Lisa's attention and her stare shifted to mine, held. "Yeah, well, that's Tyler's fault. He wouldn't stop harassing her last year, asking for my number, so she had to change hers." And then to him she said coolly, "You can leave now."

I spared a glance for the rocker, turning over my shoulder. "You should go."

17

The blond lifted his chin, his slate blue eyes flickering between me and his ex. "Don't forget what you promised."

I sensed Lisa's stare as it bored into the side of my face.

"I won't forget."

With a head nod and one more distracted glance at Lisa, Tyler turned and left.

As soon as the apartment door closed, Lisa spun on me. "What did you promise?"

Ignoring her, I turned to Mona. First things first.

I stepped back, pulled out my phone, unlocked it, and offered it to her. "Mona, will you please do me the honor of entering your cell number into my phone? And your email address."

"Absolutely." My beauty wore a small, genuine smile, but I also noticed she seemed tired, pale.

Before I could study her in greater detail, she took my cell, lowering her face and navigating to messages. She sent herself a text that contained her email address, handed the phone back to me, then her cell chimed from somewhere in the apartment. I took a moment to read her email address and number, repeating it to myself.

"It's so great to see you." Mona seemed to hesitate before hooking her fingers into the beltloops of my jeans.

I looked up from my screen. Her grin had grown, her gaze warm and hazy and happy, but now I could see her eyes were puffy, like she'd been crying recently. This discovery settled like a punch to my stomach, added a restless frustration to my sense of urgency, and I felt my eyebrows pull together.

This. Right here. This was the reason I'd been frantic to get here, to see her. We had time now, we had all the time in the world *now*, but I knew—I *fucking knew!*—the clock had been ticking on her faith in me. I'd told her it wasn't goodbye, I'd asked her to trust me. But without contact for days, she must've been thinking the worst.

Fucking Leo.

"Hey." I returned the phone to my back pocket, repeating her number to myself one more time, and cupped her cheek. "Are you okay? I honestly came as soon as I could. I promise, if I'd had your phone number, you'd be sick of hearing from me by now."

Mona pressed her cheek against my palm, her eyes drifting shut as her smile grew soft, dreamy. "Yes. I'm better than okay." She sighed. "Now that you're here, I'm awesome."

This was exactly the reassurance I'd needed. Relief didn't crash over me. It gradually settled, like a soft, warm blanket thawing the freezing panic in my bones. The terrible truth was, I hadn't trusted Mona to trust me. Technically, we'd known each other for over two years, but in reality, it had only been twelve days.

If I'd been her? I would've been irate.

Tilting her chin up, I kissed her again, softly this time, just a quick taste even though a sharp, throbbing pulse beneath my skin demanded I do more, take more, touch more.

We have the rest of our lives. Take your time.

"I missed you." Unwilling to cede any distance, I spoke against her lips. "I'm not here for very long, so we need to make plans to—"

"Hey!" Mona stiffened at Lisa's shrill interruption, her eyes flying open. My mouth landed on her jaw instead of her mouth as she gave the third person in the room her attention.

"Abram," Mona's twin demanded, "what did you promise Tyler?"

Unwilling to give Lisa my eyes—not while this woman I'd been craving was finally *right here*—I brushed my lips against Mona's temple and nuzzled the soft texture of her hair, answering Lisa distractedly, "He said he knew where you lived and would take me here, so I said I'd play Pirate Orgy's new single as part of our set during a few tour stops."

I didn't know why I was explaining myself. This was a waste of time. I was here, Mona was here, I'd been thinking about nothing else but hoping she'd still want to see me. And if she did, I'd been obsessing about what I would do to and with her body and brain.

Discussing stuff that didn't matter with Lisa—because it was already settled and done—was pointless.

"Which tour stops?" Lisa sounded obstinate, like she believed she had a right to the information.

"LA, Chicago, New York, and Miami," I mumbled, while pulling Mona forward and against me by the fabric of her pajamas. I smoothed my palm down the length of her arm, entwining our fingers together.

19

How many hours had I spent thinking about this? Hoping she would still let me hold her hand?

Too many.

We have time.

Mona, splitting her attention between me and her sister, whispered sweetly, "I missed you too." And that made me smile.

But Lisa made a sound of indignation. "LA? New York? Why the fuck would you do that?" And that made me scowl.

"Lisa." Mona's voice was beseeching, and I leaned away to study her profile. She looked fretful, unhappy. *Damn.*

Damn. Damn. Damn.

Curling my free hand into a fist, I gathered a steadying breath, filling my lungs before turning from Mona to face her twin. Never mind that I'd barely slept in almost thirty-six hours. Never mind Mona and I hadn't seen or spoken to each other in almost a week. Clearly, if I wanted to spend any time with Mona, the sister would have to be dealt with first.

"Let it go," I said, deepening my voice so I wouldn't shout. "It's done, and it has nothing to do with you."

Lisa seemed to clench her jaw at my statement, her lips tightening, but kept her eyes—shining with accusation—stubbornly pointed at her sister. "You know what he did to me. And now your boyfriend is going to launch his career?" Ignoring me and addressing only Mona, her voice had become softer, and yet definitely angrier. "Fuck that and fuck you! You know that's not okay. I'm your *sister!* Don't just stand there and let him—"

"Hey." A sudden and savage spike in temper, the single word erupted from me, sounding like a bark, and Lisa's startled glare cut to mine. "Back off."

Mona's sister angled her chin, her eyes narrowing into slits. "You don't tell me what to—"

"That's where you're wrong. I don't care who you are, no one talks to Mona like that. No one."

Lisa scoffed, sneering. "Oh yeah? You speak for Mona now? Give me a fucking break. She is one of the most intelligent, amazing, strong, capable people in the world. She's a *genius.* She doesn't need you intervening on her behalf. Mona can more than speak up for herself, and this isn't any of your business, *Abram*."

"No. This isn't any of your business, *Lisa*. You're right about your sister. She is amazing, strong, capable, but she also has a huge and sensitive heart that you don't seem to have a problem kicking around whenever it suits you. I see you're angry. I get why. But your anger isn't going to change a damn thing. Giving Tyler's song a spot was my decision. Mine. Bullying Mona isn't going to change my mind. You talk to her like the queen she is or shut the fuck up."

That made her flinch, her eyes blinking, a crack forming in her stony exterior as though I'd touched on a vulnerability, a fear. "I'm not —I'm not bullying her." Her gaze, now looking agitated, shifted to Mona at my shoulder. "I would never do that, I would never—"

"Yeah. You are." Some protective instinct had me stepping to the side, blocking Mona from her view. She didn't need this, especially not from her own sister. "She's not responsible for your screwups. No one is responsible *but you*. You don't like it? Too bad. You made the shit sandwich, now you have to eat it, all by yourself. Want to whine to someone? Call your brother. But back off Mona."

"Abram." Mona squeezed my hand, her voice—again—sounded beseeching, and my name on her lips, in her lovely voice, acted like a pin puncturing my swelling fury.

Turning, I stiffened at the sight of her conflicted gaze, and my stomach dropped. But I fought against the reflex to apologize. I was contrite, but I wasn't sorry. I'd never be sorry for defending her. Mona's sister—and her brother—they didn't know her, didn't understand how sensitive she was. They didn't take care of her or look out for her like she deserved, like she needed. They made assumptions that were unequivocally false, and it pissed me off.

I swallowed the reflex to say sorry, and I faced her fully. I brought her hand to my lips and kissed the tender junction between her middle and index finger.

"What can I do?" I asked.

Mona's lips pressed together, her steady stare looking no less conflicted, maybe even a little resigned. "Give me a minute to talk to my sister."

My hands tightened on hers and a jolt of alarm made it difficult to breathe. I wanted to deny her. I wanted to drag her out of this room and apartment. I wanted to bring her back with me to the West Coast for the rest of the week and take care of her.

I swallowed those reflexes too. Working my jaw, I nodded. I stepped forward and kissed her quickly. I pressed my forehead to hers.

And, with effort, I forced myself to say, "Whatever you need."

[3]

CELESTIAL MECHANICS

Abram

I waited in the room where Mona was staying, a small guestroom with a sleeper sofa and sparse furniture. Tearing off and tossing my outer layer of winter clothes to the dresser, I pushed my hands through my hair and fastened it back. It needed a cut.

Though the space was cramped, I had an uninterrupted span of nine feet and paced—back and forth—while studying her phone number and email until they were branded on my brain. I would never be without a means to contact her again.

You will see her again. After today, you can talk to her any time you want.

As much as I told myself we had plenty of time, I couldn't shake the notion that we had no time. In just a few hours, I needed to be on a plane. Despite acknowledging that this afternoon was just the first of many I'd be seeing her during the tour, purpose obsessed me, I was determined: we needed to make plans.

Definite plans. Commitments of time. Promises.

Unfortunately, after the shit-show with Lisa, everything I'd wanted to share and discuss and resolve with Mona had been eclipsed, muddied by her sister's breathtaking selfishness. I couldn't believe how Lisa spoke to her, and that Mona allowed it.

You shouldn't allow her or anyone else speak to you that way. You are so much more and better and worthy than you allow them to treat you.

The words rolled around in my mouth, souring my tongue. I wouldn't speak them out loud. They would undoubtedly lead to an argument and I wasn't here to pick a fight. But it wasn't just Lisa, her brother was just as bad. Even now, days later, the memory of my last conversation with Leo had me seeing red.

"You'll thank me," he'd said, sounding convinced. I'd kept my temper up to that point, listening to him call her cold and calculating, emotionless. Every adjective out of his mouth made me want to reach through my phone and punch him in the face. "Just listen to me, I'm trying to help you."

"I'm never going to thank you for this, Leo. And if you knew your sister—*at all*—you'd know that she is none of those things."

"Abram, man, don't tell me about my own sister." He sounded irritated. "I've known Mona her entire life. She's *my sister*. She doesn't even like people touching her."

I snapped. "And why the fuck do you think that is, Leo? You think people are just fucking born that way? You think that's normal? Did it ever occur to you to ask her why that is?"

"Would you listen?" Now he was yelling. "I've asked her, okay? I asked her why. I asked if anyone hurt her. She said no, flat out."

She said no? That was a surprise. Had she been lying? No. She wouldn't lie. She wasn't a liar, I believed that now. Mona didn't lie unless it was to protect someone she loved, unless she felt like she had no choice. *So maybe—like she said in Chicago years ago—it really is just as simple as: Mona doesn't like unexpected touch.*

That didn't seem right either. I'd touched her unexpectedly without her flinching away.

Before I could think through this revelation, Leo exhaled loudly. "You're being a fucking psycho about this. Stop. Just fucking stop. My answer is final. I'm not giving you her number so you can make an idiot of yourself. And yeah, she's my sister, so I don't want guys harassing her, okay? That includes you."

I rubbed my forehead, shutting my eyes, working to get my temper under control. "Then why don't you call her and ask her permission? Can you do that? Please?"

"No!" he shouted. Then he continued, quieter, "I know you're mad now, but you'll see I'm right."

I laughed, my chest, throat, and mouth full of broken glass, because what else could I do? "You're an idiot."

He also huffed a bitter-sounding laugh. "Yeah, well, maybe I am, because I'll still be here, I'll still be your friend when you come to your fucking senses." Leo sounded tired, spent. "I'm just trying to save you from yourself, man. It's not worth the pain, okay? Call me when you see reason."

Not worth the pain.

Fuck it. The next time I saw Leo, I would punch him in the face. All those years, listening to him talk about Mona as though she had no feelings, feeding into this narrative about her being completely callous and inhuman-levels of resilient.

Before Aspen, I'd believed him. It was easy and convenient to think of her that way.

But now, I hated it. I hated how they and everyone else talked about her like she was this invulnerable, dispassionate alien thing, too perfect, untouchable, unknowable. At some point, Mona and I would have to discuss it, because I wasn't going to be able to watch their continued abuse without seriously losing my shit.

Something has to give.

Mona opened the door and my head snapped up. Before she could close it, I was on her again, reaching for her hand to draw her through the opening, shutting the door, and pushing her back against it.

Unthinkingly, acting on pure instinct, I fit my hands under her T-shirt, seeking her skin. Smoothing my palms up, down, and then around her sides to her back, I touched my lips to hers. My heart suddenly in my throat, my irate internal rantings about her shitty siblings faded to background noise. Suddenly, I didn't want to talk or think about them at all. I didn't want to give them another second of this precious time.

Later. We would talk about it later. *Much later.*

"Hey," she whispered, pressing her mouth to mine, catching my bottom lip with a quick nip, and then moving her inebriating kisses to my cheek, jaw, neck. "Are you okay?" she whispered against my ear. She'd also moved her hands under my shirt, pausing for a split second, and then pulling me closer.

I laughed, incredulous. "Are you kidding? I'm fantastic. Are *you* okay?"

She tucked her head under my chin, her ear over my heart. "I can't think of a time I've ever been better."

I laughed again, tightening my arms. Thank God she wasn't pissed at me. Thank. God. I'd almost convinced myself she would be. This? Her reaction to my sudden appearance? It felt miraculous. Exhaling a long, quiet breath, I gave myself this miraculous moment, holding her, her holding me, and worked to memorize every touch, sight, smell—

"You shaved your beard," she blurted, yanking me out of my reflections. The statement sounded accusatory.

For some reason it made me smile. "No, I didn't. We just cut it closer."

"A lot closer. It's basically gone."

"I can grow it back, if you want me to. It won't take long. Just say the word."

Mona wavered before saying, "I can't decide. I love your wizard beard, but I've missed your dimples."

My smile widened. "My dimples, huh?" If she wanted my dimples, they were all hers.

"Oh yes." She turned her face and placed a kiss on my shirt in the center of my chest. "I can't believe you're here."

"I can't believe I'm here either." I allowed her to lean back just far enough for our eyes to meet. Again, I noticed how puffy hers were, how red, and was assailed with a forceful and frustrated sense of helplessness. "Mona, please believe me, I did everything I could to find your number or Lisa's number. I had Marie use her contacts—a security firm here in Chicago—and they found nothing under your name, no driver's license, no utility bills. Only a passport with your mother's PA's phone number and the Chicago house address, nothing else."

She gave me a wry smile. "Yeah. Sorry. That's because—"

"You don't have to apologize. I get it, you don't want crazies tracking you down. My number and details are similarly obscured. But Leo wouldn't give me Allyn's last name, so I couldn't call her either. I just need you to know, I did everything I could to reach you as soon as I could."

"I could have called Leo for your number. I should have. I'm sorry too."

"No, no. It was on me. I asked you to trust me."

"I do trust you." She beamed up at me, but I didn't like the unsteadiness in her voice. It betrayed her words, made them ring false.

"Hey." Cradling her cheek, I traced the line of her cheekbone with my thumb, and whispered, "I promise, I will never give you a reason to cry."

Mona's lips pressed together into a wobbly smile, her eyes glassy.

I groaned. "What's this? Tears?" I kissed her eyelids.

She laughed and rolled her eyes at herself. "Sorry. I don't know what's wrong with me."

I had my suspicions. My guess was that these tears were about many things, not just me, not just us. Of course, part of her upheaval over the last few days was about us. A lack of trust. She didn't trust me, not yet, but it was clear she wanted to.

Mona swiped at her cheeks, her smile now brittle. "I can't seem to stop crying and I've never been a crier. It's like I came back from Aspen broken."

Broken?

I shook my head vehemently. "No. God, no. You aren't broken. Mona, crying, *feeling* doesn't make you broken. Stoicism does. Burying your emotions—from everyone, all the time—does." I kissed her quickly again. "Don't fight the tears. Maybe you're crying so much because it's the first time you've let yourself. Maybe they'll stop, maybe they won't. But you're safe with me. Let them come."

She sniffled, her eyebrows pulling together. "You don't think all this weeping makes me weak?"

"No. I think it makes you brave, because it also makes you soft, and sweet, and honest. And those might not be parts of yourself that you value—or other people see as valuable—but those are the real, raw, essential pieces of *you*. You deserve to share them with someone, and if that's me, I'm honored to be that person. I will always, *always* treasure this side of you."

Her wide eyes moved between mine, breathtakingly, exquisitely vulnerable. I knew it was selfish but seeing her exposed and defenseless mollified a primal desire I didn't quite understand. It made me feel stronger, essential, necessary in a new way. Maybe because I was now necessary to her?

Whatever the reason, it also made my protective instincts swell. No one—and I mean *No. One.*—was going to fuck with her. Ever. No one would hurt her. No one would make her cry.

Uh, she's crying right now.

Searching her face, I could see she was overwhelmed.

So, I made my voice mock-stern, saying, "Crying is allowed—cry all day, every day—but no more apologies," guessing she both needed and wanted a reason to smile.

She did. And seeing her true smile made me smile in return.

Sniffling, she lifted an eyebrow. "Okay. Crying is fine, but no apologies. What else is allowed?"

My grin grew, my eyelids drooping, and I slid my hand from her cheek to the neck of her shirt, pulling it to one side, baring her shoulder. "I can think of some things. But first, we need to talk."

Her smile faded somewhat, became dazed, her attention lowering to my lips. She licked hers. "How long do we have?"

I'd promised myself we wouldn't do anything until plans and commitments were made, but I couldn't help myself. Bending, I took my time biting, licking, and kissing the top of her shoulder. She shivered. She also tasted like heaven, and each swirl of my tongue increased the hunger.

"Two hours." My voice was low, rough against the wet spot. Trailing my lips closer to her neck, I took another soft bite. Now that her skin was exposed, I couldn't stop.

She started to moan. She stifled it, her fingers fisting in the front of my shirt as she offered more of her neck. "Only two hours?"

"I have to catch a plane. We have a concert tonight." Reluctantly, I lifted my head, capturing her eyes again so she could see my regret. In that moment, my responsibilities to my bandmates, to my record label and my fans, they felt like handcuffs and a jail cell.

Her gaze—a mixture of disappointment and worry—turned scrutinizing. "Abram, you're exhausted. Have you slept?"

"I slept a little on the plane from LA."

She flattened her hand over my heart. "You have to take better care of yourself. Tours are stressful and exhausting. Please promise me you'll get sleep tonight after the concert."

"I will try." *Try* being the operative word. Performing in front of thousands of people was an indescribable high. But four nights in, and the tour had only made the longing, my craving for her, worse. My attention and patience had narrowed, leaving room for nothing but filling my hands and mind and memory with Mona.

"You'll try?" She narrowed her eyes, one side of her mouth tugging upward.

"I will. But after a concert, all the energy, and I'm thinking about you, wishing you were there, knowing it's not possible. It's . . ." I slid my teeth to the side, unable to stop my self-conscious grin.

"What?"

"Hard." The word slipped out before I could stop it.

Her head tilted slightly to one side. "What's hard? Going to sleep?"

She has no idea what she does to me.

My grin became rueful and I swallowed, my eyes moving between hers. "Please don't make me say it."

Mona's eyebrows slowly pulled together. I could almost see the gears turning, and the hand still loosely fisted in my shirt slid down to the front of my pants, as though she were unthinkingly confirming a hunch. Her curious fingers gave me an investigatory stroke, but it was more than enough. I sucked in a breath through my teeth as my cock swelled, lengthened, hardened, greedy for her.

"You—you shouldn't do that." Not trusting myself to hold her and not tear her clothes off, I braced my palms and forehead on the door behind her, again willing my heart to slow.

"Ah! Sorry. Sorry!" Mona completely removed her hands from my body, yanking them away. "Sorry. I should've asked permission."

Lifting my head, I peered down at her. She'd covered her face with her hands and was peeking at me from between her fingers.

"No." The single word came out gruff, raspy. I cleared my throat, reaching for her wrist and pulling it away from her face. "No, Mona. Not permission. But, if we're going to talk at all, you shouldn't—do *that*—today."

She was nodding before I'd finished speaking. "Yes. Sorry."

"Please don't apologize."

"Okay, sorry—ah! I mean, okay. Okay." Mona rolled her lips between her teeth, still nodding, her eyes wide and remorseful, but also bright, like she found my situation a little funny.

A pretty, pink blush was creeping up her neck, and it was fantastically distracting. I wanted to pull the neck of her shirt to the side again, peek inside, find out where the blush started.

Instead, I stepped away—one step, and then another—clearing my throat again and forcing firmness into my voice. "We need to talk." It was as much a reminder to me as it was to her.

"Of course." Her voice was also firm, but her attention flickered quickly to the front of my pants, her cheeks now pink, as were her ears.

I shook my head at her, increasing the distance between us out of necessity. "Do you want to talk?"

Shit. Where had that question come from? There was no choice. We had to talk.

Mona, staring at me, her eyes slowly narrowing as she chewed on her bottom lip, didn't answer.

"Mona?"

"What are my options?"

My mouth dropped open and I exhaled a laugh. "What are your *options*?"

"Yeah." She took tiny steps forward, her eyes once more dropping to my fly, and then back up. "I mean, we only have two hours, probably less now. Other than talking, what are the options?"

I stared at her, struggling, standing between the steady voice of reason and a raging hard-on. My eyes lowered to her baggy shirt, simultaneously both wishing it were see-through and hugely grateful it was so shapeless.

"First, we need to be—we need to be on the same page here." I choked out, my leg and foot conspiring to take a half step forward.

"About what?"

"About us."

This had been phase two of Kaitlyn's plan, and I'd been kicking myself all week for not being more explicit about what I wanted before leaving Aspen.

"Okay. What page are you on?"

Crossing my arms, I gathered a deep breath. If Mona could be brave, vulnerable with me, then I could be the same with her. "If it wasn't obvious, I want to make sure I'm clear now: I am not interested in anyone else. I want a commitment from you that we'll be completely exclusive."

She grinned, her eyes brightening. "Fine. Done. We're exclusive."

EXCELLENT!

"Okay." I nodded, having a hard time not grinning like a fool. "Good."

"Good." She edged closer, and her goofy grin made me feel better about mine. "Anything else?"

What else?

"Um."

Her beauty was distracting, and I fought to regather the ends of my wits.

Just as she took another half step, I remembered. "Wait. Yes! We need to make plans, so we know when we'll see each other again."

But it was more than just making plans. If we did anything now, I really would drag her out of here, take her with me to the West Coast, keep her in my hotel room, hide her clothes, and eat her out for breakfast, lunch, and dinner. And snacks.

We have plenty of time, plenty.

The hard-on was winning.

"Yes. Plans. Of course." Mona twisted her fingers in the hem of her T-shirt, showing me a sliver of smooth olive-toned skin at her stomach.

I'm sure it wasn't purposeful or meant to make me crazy, but it was like waving a red flag in front of a bull. My body lurched forward, already consumed, while I stood perfectly still, besieged, so close to giving in.

"But—and hear me out—we could make plans over the phone, or via email. However, it's much, *much* harder to do other things over the phone." She paused for a beat, staring at me as though hoping I would read her mind, and then added, "And basically impossible via email."

I swallowed around the scorching, thick knot in my throat, unable to do anything about the one low in my stomach. *Yet.*

"Mona," I started, stopped, winced, closed my eyes, then began again. "Mona, I want you. The things I want to do to you, to your body, they require more than two hours and a ten-by-ten room. As much as I missed you, as much as I crave you, as much as I've fantasized about being close" —*bare and touching and fucking your brains out*— "we need to take things slow. Two hours in the cramped guest room of your sister's apartment? No. That will only frustrate the hell out of me."

I opened my eyes, stared at her pants, waited a beat, and then lifted my gaze. Her lips were parted, her eyes hazy, reminding me of that insane, primal moment between us in Aspen, in the pool.

The memory haunted me. I'd imagined so many different endings more than a thousand times. Fantastically filthy, wonderfully selfish endings. But I had zero regrets.

Gathering my self-control and a deep, calming breath, I shook my head. "And these things I want to do, they also require trust."

Her eyes sharpened, sobered, and she frowned. "I trust you."

"Do you?"

"Of course."

"Then why have you been crying?"

Her mouth snapped shut.

"No, Mona. You don't trust me. And you were right, in Aspen. We don't know each other."

She blinked once, hard, and took two stumbling steps forward. "I thought you said I should cry."

"Yes. Absolutely. Cry if you need to, but don't ignore what the tears are about."

"What? Abram—"

I held a hand out to stop her advance. "I've been thinking, and I know you have too. A little less than two weeks, twelve days. You can't trust someone you don't know, and trust takes time."

Mona's frown deepened, her lips pinching together. "We don't have time."

I laughed lightly, because her words were a direct echo of my desperate thoughts. But we were both wrong.

The one thing we finally, *finally* had was time.

"We have all the time. We have the rest of our lives."

"I'm confused. You want to be exclusive. Now you say you don't know me? Are you saying—are you saying you don't lo—that you don't feel the same as—as—" She crossed her arms, her chin jutting out, a flash of vulnerability and hurt behind her eyes.

It was the vulnerability that had me heedlessly crossing the short distance, as though yanked, compelled and panicky to touch her before she could build any walls between us.

"No. No. Absolutely not." I held her face in my hands, ignoring how the gentle touch made her flinch, and stifled the urge to take back my words. Instead, I committed to honesty, no matter how much the thought of losing her now scared the hell out of me. "I love you. I'm crazy about you. I want you, only you. But, Mona—" I touched my forehead to hers, "—God, I don't want to rush a single moment. I want a first date, and a second date, and a third, and a twenty-third, and an eighty-seventh. I want phone calls and text messages. I want to hear about a day in the life of Mona DaVinci, every day."

I leaned away, needing to see her eyes, my heart giving a sluggish, painful beat at the conflicting emotions there.

Despite my pledge not to rush, I hurried to add, "I want to get mad at you, and fight, and make up—I can't wait to make up with you. It's going to be *so great.*"

That pulled a hesitant little smile from her and she swallowed, her gaze less stormy. "That does sound nice."

I grinned at her reluctant reassurance and didn't miss how her attention shifted to the left side of my face, the deeper of my two dimples.

While she was distracted, I pressed my mouth to hers, stealing a tender kiss and whispered solemnly, "I want to take care of you, when you want me to, when you need it. I want to trust you'll be there, that I can count on you to take care of me too."

She sniffed, nodding, her fingers gripping my forearms. "That also sounds nice."

"Good." Cautiously relieved, I let go of her cheeks. Smoothing my hands down her shoulders to her sides, I pulled her against me. She came willingly, going soft, lax, just as she'd done before, and my body hummed happily in response.

Well, happily and hornily.

I felt myself calm. "No. My feelings haven't changed. I'm still insane about you. But . . ." I stroked her hair, kissing her temple, inhaling her sweet scent. "I want to be sane about you too."

[4]
ATOMIC PHYSICS

Mona

"That takes us through September," he said, the bed depressing as he claimed his spot on the edge.

I nodded distractedly, *again* scrolling through the calendar app on Abram's phone for August and July, hunting for a possible span of time where we might be able to arrange a quick meet-up. We'd both set timers on our phones, a countdown to the moment I'd have to drive him back to the airport using Lisa's car.

I felt good-ish about February through June, but July and August were still a problem. We hadn't been able to find even one rendezvous over those two months. Abram would be in New Zealand and Australia and I would still be in Europe. No face-to-face time for over two months felt like a rendezvous dearth of ginormous proportions.

Of note, I did rather like the word *rendezvous* and planned to overuse it in the future.

"How long is the flight from London to Dubai again?" I gazed longingly at the seven-day period of free time he had between Brisbane and Perth in mid-August. Unfortunately, it just so happened to be the same week as my Spectroscopy Symposium in London, where I'd be presenting at three sessions and moderating two graduate-level panels. Dipping into my parents' travel fund to visit my boyfriend—especially when international tickets were so pricey—didn't sit right with me. However, if I skipped avocado toast for the rest of my life, I'd be able to afford the plane ticket.

Abram covered my hand, drawing my eyes back to his. "We've spent a half hour on just those two months. Let's move on to September through November."

We were situated adjacent to each other on the twin daybed in Lisa's guestroom. It doubled as a small couch, but I'd left all the throw pillows piled up behind the headboard. I was sitting against the wall, my legs crossed, with just my regular sleep pillow behind my back. Abram sat on the edge, one foot propped on the floor. He stood at intervals to pace while studying the calendar app on my phone.

Keeping it real, Abram's pacing was a problem, because I loved, loved, *loved* watching his body move. Which meant that I was staring at him when I should've been studying his calendar. He didn't seem to notice my staring. Or, if he did, he didn't say anything about it.

"We have to move on." His brown eyes flickered between mine, and—just like all the other times we gazed at each other for any length of time—I had to remind myself not to tackle him to the ground, rip his clothes off, and kiss and lick and bite every square centimeter of his rock-hard physique.

Especially his bottom.

That's right. I wanted to sample his bottom. Every time he paced away, little pheromone pixies danced on my pelvis, gleefully, wickedly smashing my concentration into a million pieces of agitated yearning. I wanted to touch it, stroke it, massage it, *bite it.*

Whew.

Clearing my throat, swallowing, I sucked in a breath and tore my eyes away from his, fanning my T-shirt. "Is it—" I had to clear my throat again because my voice cracked. "Is it hot in here?"

The thing is, I wasn't this person. No one, not even me, would ever describe me as physically focused, or fixated on touching an attractive or alluring exterior. Ever. I actively rejected external beauty as a contributing factor to how or if or when I interacted with people. I'd never been tactile. I observed. I calculated. I analyzed. I didn't even like playdough as a child.

But with Abram, I couldn't stop noticing. I couldn't stop thinking. I couldn't stop *wanting*.

"Mona."

Think of the Queen! Isn't that what the British always said? What was the US equivalent? Think of the first lady?

I worried my bottom lip, breathing in through my nose, endeavoring to get my brain out of his pants. "Okay. Okay. Where are you going after Perth?"

"Mona." He leaned close, using his hold on me to pull both my hand and his phone toward his chest.

My gaze darted up and then away, cheeks heating, because if I looked at him again, I'd be—again—fighting the impulse to tackle him and we still had three months to—

"Mona, look at me."

I did. I gave him my eyes. I also held my breath.

His gorgeous amber irises seemed to glow as they moved over my face, dropped to my mouth, lingered there. They felt hot yet controlled, self-possessed, and for some reason the self-possession took my heat level straight to plasma.

"I think " He licked his lips, taking his phone from my grip and placing it on top of the throw pillows piled by the headboard. "I think we need to do something."

"Something?" I asked, still not breathing so the words came out more like a hitching whisper. I didn't know if it was the lack of oxygen or Abram that had me feeling so dizzy.

Abram. Definitely Abram.

On my sixteenth birthday, I'd had an IUD implanted, a gift from my sex-positive parents. Lisa had received one too. Leo had received a reversable vasectomy for his.

Even with the IUD, I'd always used a condom for sexual intercourse as well as spermicide I would procure after triple-checking the lot numbers and packaging date. Anything older than three months, I would throw away.

I'd administered two blow jobs, again always with a condom, and the second one only because I was convinced I'd missed something the first time. Once, a guy attempted to conduct cunalingus using a female condom. I'd insisted after discovering he hadn't been vaccinated against HPV. It wasn't enjoyable. I'd stopped him after the timer denoted the agreed upon two minutes was over, not liking how messy and wet on my thighs it had become.

I mean, saliva. Do you know how filthy the human mouth is? Disgusting.

I'd done many, many things with my seven sexual partners—working my way through a checklist of positions and techniques, toys and gadgets—and everything I was open to exploring had been attempted at least once. Notes had been made. Items had been crossed off. Second and third attempts at pleasant activities had yielded varied results, leading me to the conclusion that masturbation utilizing a LELO vibrator was the only consistent—and therefore worthy—method of satisfaction.

But with Abram . . .

I wanted to do it all again, try it all again, even the items I'd crossed off my lists.

"We have twenty minutes left, before I have to leave," he said, the words rough. His palm came to my knee and my body jolted at the benign touch. A small smile tugged his mouth to one side, his delicious dimple making an appearance, and his voice was low and rumbly as he asked, "Do you want me to touch you?"

"Touch me?" I squeaked, clearly incapable of brain function higher than a parrot. Forced to exhale because my chest felt like it might burst, not a half second later I was gulping air again.

"Yeah." His hand slid higher on my leg, sending hot spikes of twisting tension straight to my center, and he leaned closer, rising slightly above me, filling my vision, his warm palm shifting to the inside of my upper thigh.

My feet did something weird, arching and pointing uncontrollably, almost like they'd been tickled, the muscles of my legs and stomach flexing. I sucked in an involuntary breath just as his large hand stopped at my hip, his thumb drawing a firm line over my thin cotton pajama pants from my lower abdomen straight to my clitoris.

Well, that escalated quickly.

I gasped, my eyes closing, my head hitting the wall at my back, my hands fisting in the comforter on either side of me while my body dichotomously froze and melted. I couldn't breathe.

I can't breathe.

"I can feel you," he said, his voice still a growl as the pad of his thumb circled me through the two layers of fabric, pressing, searching. "You're so wet. Is that for me?"

"As the, uh." *As the prophesy foretold.* "And thus, I die," I choked out instead and tried to shrug, making a joke of it, because—OMFG—I was ten seconds from orgasming. Honestly and truly. My lungs were on fire, my body clenching around emptiness, my skin stretched too thin.

And I was mortified.

He'd barely touched me. There'd been no buildup. One small stroke followed by two barely there circles, and my body had gone zero to the speed of light.

I can't breathe.

Some abrupt instinct had me clawing at his wrist, my hand fisting around his thumb to stop the efficient circles. I was wound too tight, it —everything—felt overwhelming.

"I—I'm—"

"Shh. Let me." His lips were on my neck, making me shiver, and he pried my fumbling hands away, threading our fingers together.

And then he was guiding me to my back.

And then I was lying down.

And then he was there, over me.

I experienced a split second of pure terror, of fear, my mind telling me that *someone* was above me, covering me, holding me down, and I couldn't move. Then Abram came into focus, settling himself between my open legs. Abram's scent filled my lungs. Abram's hips spread me wider. Abram's mouth sucked at my neck, eliciting more shivers, and my terror was nearly eclipsed by the surfacing wonder of seduction.

Abram rolled his pelvis, and the hard length his erection pressed *right* where I needed. Fear diminished, waned, but didn't completely extinguish. It became a quiet whisper instead of a clamorous shriek, inexplicably amplifying my senses without overwhelming them.

I can't breathe.

But I did breathe. I inhaled him, the Abram fragrance that both calmed and excited me. It spread like a velvety cloud, invading and liquifying each clandestine corner and hidden space and secret desire. It communicated a history without words: security and safety, longing and need.

I gasped again, my back arching sharply, my hips wanting to move. "What—what—oh God."

He made a noise, it sounded frustrated, his breathing now labored, his body heavy—so heavy—above me. Holding my hands on either side of my head, he rocked, sliding up and down, stroking me through our layers of clothes. I couldn't move. I was wholly trapped, inexorably tangled up and in and by Abram.

I should've been feeling panic. I wasn't. I was no longer the Mona who didn't like to be touched or crowded. I was a cluster of nerves and dark wants, *wanting* this man to cover me, hold me down, take over. I enjoyed the loss of control, how my fear mingled with pleasure, heightening every sense and sensation.

This, what we were doing, definitely hadn't been on any of my lists. We were fully clothed. Our bodies were touching through layers, but my hands were confined. His mouth was still on my neck, his breath falling on my skin, causing goose bumps, tingles, shivers, and *heat.* So much heat.

The only time I'd done anything close to what Abram and I were doing now had been last week, in the pool, when we'd mindlessly attacked each other. Nothing about this should have been sexy. But it was. I shouldn't have wanted to be possessed and overpowered in this way. But I did.

It was *the most* spectacularly sensual event of my life. Yet, even as it happened, I knew this conclusion made no sense. It felt incomprehensible, indecent, scandalous, and the indecency quenched some hidden, unacknowledged thirst.

"I think I'm going to—"

Abram kissed me, stopping my words, his tongue coaxing, a

complete contradiction to the hard press of his body. Releasing my hand closest to the wall, he leaned to the opposite side, still caging me in, stroking his fingers from my breast to my stomach and replacing his erection with his palm.

I groaned at the loss of him, of the heaviness and friction, until his hand slid inside my underwear and he parted me with his fingers.

I was sweating. My heart was racing. My mind was swimming. I still couldn't breathe, but his scent was everywhere. He was everywhere. He was inside me, his hand in my pants, moving rhythmically in a way that—in the moment—felt wholly illicit, forbidden. He captured my cries and moans with his mouth, keeping me quiet like my pleasure was a secret, just for him.

I came, a shock of fire searing my nerves, to my fingers and toes, bursting behind my eyes. His composure, power, and precision made me crazed, made me feel as though I was his toy, or his instrument, and he was in total control. Bafflingly, I loved it.

His fingers thrust more forcefully, deeper, rubbing and stroking, prolonging my climax until I was boneless, exhausted, spent, sore low in my belly, and left with a cavernous ache in my chest. His amazing body, big and powerful, hard and mercenary next to mine, petting me, telling me wonderful and wicked things.

You are so fucking sexy.

I love watching you come. I love the way you feel. I love watching you lose control.

Do you want me here? Do you want me inside you?

Next time, I want the taste of you on my tongue.

Or, were those my thoughts? Did he say them? Or did I wish for them?

As the last of the spasms shook me and before I could disentangle myself, I turned toward him. He was gone. He'd left the bed. Rolling off and immediately pacing away.

Discombobulated and disheveled, I watched him, his hands braced on the far wall, his shoulders rising and falling. I felt the lack of him, a cold shock. I surfaced by degrees—Mona, me, the thinking, reasoned part of myself—and a sharp spike of alarm abruptly snuffed out any lingering residual exhilaration.

Why would you let him do that to you?

Wait. Do what? Touch me?

He held you down. You couldn't move, and you liked it.

I blinked at the internal accusation, remembering the last several minutes as though watching them happen to someone else.

I'd liked that? I'd like him over me? Holding me down? I'd liked not being able to move? Being touched, possessed, controlled like that? He didn't ask. However, I didn't say no. I didn't ask him to stop. Asking him to stop had never even entered my mind.

A flood of disbelief was followed by a rising tide of reason, during which I attempted to explain and describe my own desires to myself as something healthy and normal.

But is it? Is it healthy and normal?

Yes.

No.

Maybe?

No. You were afraid.

Was I?

Yes. And you wanted to be overpowered, you liked it. He could've done anything to you, and you would've been helpless to stop him. Even now—thinking about the possibility of handing over control again—You. Want. It.

I did. Just the thought of Abram over me again, his weight covering me—but this time naked, entering me, taking his pleasure from my body—I was completely and wholly arrested by the mere notion. It made me breathless, achy with a new dazzling, blinding thirst.

Yes. I want it.

And yet, I shouldn't want to feel helpless, right? I shouldn't want to feel overpowered physically. I'd felt that way once, against my will, and it revolted me, it kept me up at night, it gave me nightmares.

On the other hand.

With Abram it felt different—the loss of control, the lack of explicit consent, the being conquered sexually, emotionally—and what did that say about me? Was I turning a difficult moment in my life into a fantasy? Just the thought made me sick.

My internal arguments were becoming circular. Disbelief and reason were pushed aside by a creeping sense of shame and guilt.

Is there something wrong with me? I shouldn't want this, should I? I shouldn't—

"Mona."

My name in Abram's voice pulled me out of my shadowy reflections, and I looked at him, comprehending my own position at the same time. I'd rolled to my side, my knees bent and pulled to my chest, my arms locked around my legs. He was kneeling at the side of the bed, his hand hovering over my temple.

"Are you okay?" he asked, his gaze searching. "Did I—I didn't hurt you, did I?"

The trepidation in his voice was a sobering bucket of ice water and I immediately shook my head, pushing myself up. "No. No, not at all."

He didn't look convinced. "What did I do wrong?"

"Nothing." I shook my head more resolutely. "You did everything right, you are great."

I'm the one who is wrong. I didn't tell you to stop.

Abram seemed to be watching me closely, but he still wasn't touching me. "I had to leave the bed, I was too—uh—worked up, and I only have this one pair of pants." His mouth curved in a self-depre-cating smile, one that didn't quite reach his eyes and quickly waned. "Do you want me to hold you?"

Swallowing against a lump in my throat, not trusting myself to speak, I nodded. His hand covered mine in the bed, and—*damn it!*—I flinched, not meaning to and immediately rebuking myself for the involuntary response.

Abram's eyes widened and he moved as though he was going to withdraw, so I caught him, grabbing his arm and using it to pull him forward. Wrapping my arms around his neck, I slid to the floor, to my knees, and held on.

He hesitated only a fraction of a second, and then closed me in an embrace. But it felt careful, hesitant, as though to communicate I was free to come or go, and that frustrated me.

*There's something wrong with me, I shouldn't want—*I shook my head. I would have to think about this later. We had no time, and I'd

43

just come apart under his skillful hands. Which meant our relationship was operating under a climax disparity. My confused turmoil would have to wait until the scorecard was even, and he was on a plane back to the West Coast.

"Hold me tighter," I demanded. "I need you to hold me tighter."

"Are you sure?" His strong arms flexed, but he didn't draw me any closer.

"Yes." I crushed him to me. "Please."

It must've been the please that did it, *thank goodness*, and I liquefied in his powerful embrace, loving the constricting feel of the hug, snuggling closer, smelling him, and admitting unthinkingly, "I already miss you."

I felt him smile against my shoulder, placing a kiss there. "I already miss you too."

"How much time do we have?"

Abram sighed. "Not enough."

Moving my hands down his shoulders, I worked my arms inside his embrace, placing a kiss on the underside of his scruffy jaw, and slid my fingers to the front of his pants.

"Whoa—" He released my body to capture my hand before I could reach for his fly. "Wait—Mona—what are you doing?"

I stroked him over his pants with my free hand and a wild thrill raced down my spine at the feel of him, so hard, so ready. I'd never been a big fan of male sex organs, but—in this moment—I wanted to take out an ad in all the newspapers announcing my everlasting devotion to his.

"I'm going to give you a blow job."

"Whoa, okay, stop." He caught my roaming fingers, his breath a gasp. "First of all, we don't have time."

"I can be fast."

"Hold on. I don't want you to be fast. Like I said before, that would only frustrate me."

I kissed his jaw again. "But—"

"No."

I grunted, my hands going slack in his grip, and I leaned away to capture his eyes. "It's not fair to you."

"I'm not worried about fairness," Abram said on a laugh, his gaze wary, like I was tricky, or had magical powers and couldn't be trusted.

"But I—*you know*—and you didn't. You didn't get anything out of it."

"Believe me." His stare softened, warmed, and he released me, sliding his fingers into my hair. "I *definitely* got something out of it. I will be writing poetry about that moment for the rest of my life."

I grunted again. "You should let me reciprocate."

"I don't want you to reciprocate."

"I feel like . . ." *Like I haven't earned it.*

Once more, he seemed to be watching me very carefully, and when I didn't continue, he prompted, "Like?"

"It feels like an injustice, that only I should have this experience. Alone. And the next time we'll see each other isn't for three weeks."

Abram's eyes narrowed. "Is that what it's really about? Because you don't owe me anything."

"I know that," I said automatically.

"Do you? Do you know, do you understand, that I'm always going to want to pamper and please you? That making you come, seeing you blissed out and hearing you panting is like a drug for me?"

My stomach twisted delightfully at the picture he painted even as my spine straightened at the use of the word *drug*. "I don't want to be your drug."

"Too late." He grinned, his glorious left dimple completely adorable, almost distracting me from my concern.

"Can't I just be your person?" I asked, my eyes flickering between his and the thought-derailing dimple on his left cheek.

"Can't you be both?" Abram slid his nose against mine, giving my lips a tender kiss. "Can't I be both for you?"

"No. I don't think so," I said honestly, tilting my head such that I had his eyes again. "Drugs are altering. Addictive."

"That seems just about right." Another grin, a chuckle, and his arms came around me.

"But, Abram, I don't want to alter you. I want you—who you fundamentally are—to stay intact. And being someone's addiction automatically implies an unhealthy dependence. And—"

He stopped me with another coaxing, seductive kiss, his hands sliding into the back of my underwear and massaging my bottom, muddling my brain. *God, that feels good.*

Wait. *What were we talking about?*

I had no idea.

Must not be important.

Relative to his mouth moving against mine, his hands in my pants, the press of his erection against my belly, and the building "bliss" (as he called it), whatever I'd wanted to say didn't seem terribly important.

I kissed him back. I floated on the high that was Abram's mouth and hands, taste and smell. And when we were interrupted, it was the alarms we'd set on our phones.

He had to go.

Our time was up.

[5]

KEPLER'S LAWS DERIVED

Mona

I spent the entire drive back from the airport and the climb up Lisa's four flights of stairs calculating and recalculating the number of hours, minutes, and seconds until I would see Abram again. Was I doing this to avoid dwelling on my earlier shame-confusion? Perhaps.

Pushing aside cloudy uncertainty had been easy while Abram was here. Our time was short. Therefore, reason told me I shouldn't waste a single second on self-assessments and second-guessing a *fantastic* orgasm.

I mean, fantastic orgasms don't grow on trees. And if they did, they'd be avocado trees, where the flowers bloom only once a season as female, and then forever after as male. They're a fruit miracle.

But now, now that he was gone, now that I'd walked him as far as I could, wrapped him in my arms and kissed him one more time, and waited until he waved at me from the other side of security, now I had no excuse. Except, I really needed to double-check my numbers with a calculator, just to be sure. Or maybe I'd make a countdown on my phone.

Yes. That was the right answer.

I was going to *hard core* make a countdown until Abram-time on my phone, or maybe using one of those countdown apps. Perhaps I'd even order a scrolling style marquee for my temporary housing in Geneva.

Nope. You need to save your pennies for plane tickets.

On that note, I decided sorting through my simmering shame-confusion would have to wait for a while longer as I had discount travel alerts to set up. Perhaps I would poke around a bit, see if I could fly out now for a visit. Where was he this week? Portland? San Francisco? Las Vegas? So close to LA.

After checking on tickets, I should probably check my emails, take a peek at the backend data processing requests I'd put in before leaving for Aspen, finish my lit search of two of my upcoming papers, and then —*whoa, look at the time!*—I should go to bed early. A good night's sleep was the key to being well-rested, and being well-rested was the key to Satan's liquor cabinet—

Wait. No. That's not right.

I frowned at the exterior to Lisa's apartment door, twisting the key in the lock, pushing it open while I considered what being well-rested might be the key to, and came face-to-face with Gabby.

AH! "Ah!"

"There you are!"

I flinched, retreating one step into the hallway, but she was fast. Before I knew what was happening, she'd pulled me through the door, shut it, and tugged me into the living room.

"You startled me. How did you—"

"I could hear you coming up the stairs. You have the gait of an elephant." Gabby waved one hand in the air while steering me with the other. "Come. Sit. Tell us everything that happened." Before I'd thought to extract myself from her grabby hands, she'd deposited me onto the couch, picked up a glass of wine, and pushed it at me. "Take it and spill."

"Don't spill the wine, spill the story," Lisa clarified, juggling three bowls as she walked out of the kitchen, a big, anxious-looking smile pasted on her face and aimed at me.

The last time I'd seen Lisa was this morning, when I'd asked

Abram to give us a minute to talk. She'd been visibly flustered and rushed to offer the use of her car before leaving the apartment in a hurry to give us some space.

I was a little surprised to see her now.

"I put out the sundae stuff already." Lisa placed the first of the three bowls next to me on the couch. "Therefore, you have your choice of a banana split or whatever you want."

"Ta-da!" Gabby stepped to the side, revealing a coffee table covered in ice cream sundae toppings.

I had to swallow because my mouth was abruptly watering. *What time is it? Is it lunchtime?*

As though reading my thoughts, Lisa said, "It's ice cream and storytime," shoving a bowl at Gabby. "Don't forget to take your Lactaid."

"Thanks, mom." Gabby accepted the bowl and turned to kneel next to the table. "Okay, Mona, let's hear it. What's going on with the Redburn front man? Yesterday you were crying at a bus stop over his band's poster, and today—according to Lisa—he's kicking in the door and giving you movie kisses. Consider me *shook*. Last time I heard, he was still a manwhore. Fill in the blanks, please."

Manwhore?

My gaze drifted to my sister where she was perched on the other side of the sofa, her eyes wide and watchful, biting her lip as though trying her best to hold her tongue.

"Abram isn't a manwhore."

Gabby shrugged. "Okay, a goodtime guy."

"He's not that either." I cleared my throat, and then took a sip of the wine. It was nice. Not too dry. Good balance. "And I'm not really sure where to start."

"I'm sorry!" Lisa's sudden exclamation drew my attention. "I'm so sorry. I was—I was a complete asshole when he showed up here with Tyler. Tyler makes me so angry! But I—he—I mean, Abram was right. I shouldn't have talked to you that way. And I'm sorry. So sorry. So, so sorry."

I stared at my sister, surprised, perplexed, and yet also warmed by her unexpected apology. For Lisa, it was practically gushing.

Gabby cut in, "Assuage your guilt later, Lisa. Let Mona talk." She then turned to me. "Start with what happened in Aspen. Lisa already told me about your phone call, where you asked her permission to tell him the truth. Did you? What did he do? What did he say? Tell us everything."

I took a deep breath, and then I took another sip of wine. Well, it had started out like a sip, but it ended up being a gulp.

Licking my lips, I sorted through all the details of our latest week together, the hurt, the misunderstandings, *the burned letters,* our first kiss, and I blurted, "Do you like to be dominated during sex?"

Both Gabby and Lisa reared back, their eyes wide as they shared a look and I glanced between them, wondering what on earth and the Sagittarius Arm of the Milky Way I had been thinking. *Why would you ask them that?*

Before I could dial back the random, Gabby said, "Is Abram into that kind of stuff? Does he, I mean, is he, like, a dom?"

Her voice was free of judgment. Even so, I was shaking my head before she'd finished her first question.

"No. That's not what I mean. I mean, do you like—or I guess, do you think it's healthy—to like it when a guy holds you down? Or if he's over you when you do stuff? Even if he's heavy and physically stronger than you? Do you like that? Or is it wrong to like it?"

Gabby and Lisa shared another look, with Lisa speaking this time, "I don't have a ton of experience with lots of guys—as you know, there was and has been no one before, during, or after the T-bag—but . . ." Her eyes moved up and to the right, like she was searching her memory. "Are you talking about missionary? I liked that position okay. I thought other positions were better, though. Is that what you're asking?"

I gathered another deep inhale, trying to figure out what I was asking, when Gabby beat me to it. "Are you worried that liking something you've done with Abram—while *intimate*—makes you somehow screwed up?"

I nodded, because that was a decent approximation of my question.

"Hmm." Lisa seemed to be considering. "I don't think sex works like that. I mean, I don't know for sure. But sex is like, I mean, aren't we tapping into a different part of ourselves? It's like, not something you can apply logic to, you know? You like what you like, and as long as it doesn't hurt someone, or it's not illegal, then I'm pretty sure anything goes. Don't you think?"

Gabby didn't wait for me to respond, instead asking, "First, did he do anything to hurt you?"

Now I shook my head vehemently. "No. Not at all."

Gabby's gaze flickered over me, and I got the sense a suspicion was forming in her mind. My heart quickened as a result and I finished the rest of the wine in three large gulps.

"Mona."

"Gabby," I rasped, my throat tight, experiencing one of those odd moments where you know what's going to happen, what another person is going to say, but you're powerless to stop it.

"Is this about that thing that happened when you were fifteen?"

Our gazes locked, her green eyes intense. Mine were probably cagey.

"Is there any more wine?" I asked. Now my heart was hammering.

"You should slow down." Gabby motioned to the bowl beside me, her tone firm. "Eat your ice cream and answer the question."

"What am I missing?" Lisa sat forward on the couch, reaching for a spoon and dusting her chocolate ice cream with peanuts. "What happened when Mona was fifteen?"

Gabby made a choking sound. "You never told Lisa?"

I had to clear my throat. "I told you, nothing—"

"Holy shit, you still believe nothing happened? I swear to God, Mona. Get a fucking grip. You were assaulted!"

"What?" Lisa whisper-shrieked, dropping the peanut spoon with a clatter.

I stood up, setting my bowl on the table, turning toward the kitchen first, then the front door, and then the bathroom. "I have to—"

"No, you don't." Gabby also stood, placing herself in my path and grabbing my shoulders. "Tell your sister. Tell her. Or don't but tell someone! Why do you insist on carrying this trauma around? As my therapist always says, you have to confront trauma or else you'll never be able to move past it."

51

"Okay." I nodded, not really hearing her, my mind in disorder, my hands trembling, but my voice was perfectly calm as I said, "But first I need to pee."

Gabby released me, shaking her head and lifting her arm toward the bathroom. "Go, then."

I sprinted toward the bathroom, catching the first part of Lisa's whispered, "You need to tell me what the hell happened before I . . ."

Once I was safely closed within the small rectangular space, I leaned my back against the door, gulping in wine-flavored air, and fought a fresh wave of tears. My hands were still trembling. I was sweating. My heart was still racing.

And this time, inexplicably, for whatever reason, when I repeated to myself that nothing actually happened, the words felt like a lie.

* * *

"Mona?"

I stirred, my back straightening at the sound of Lisa's voice. I had no idea what time it was, just that I'd been sitting on the closed toilet lid for such an extended period, I'd passed the excuse "needs to pee" a long while ago and firmly entered "may require serious medical attention."

"Open up," she said.

Staring at the closed door, I debated my options. I'd heard Lisa and Gabby's murmuring voices, and then I'd heard the front door open and close. And now, some minutes later, Lisa was standing outside, and I was extremely reluctant to let her in.

"Mona." Her voice was gentle, and I thought I heard her place something on the door between us, maybe her hand. "Gabby told me what happened at school, when—when you were fifteen. Open the door."

Those tears I'd fought so hard to dispel threatened another appearance. I swallowed convulsively, blinking, fighting the stinging behind my eyes, and stood. I didn't want to cry. With Abram I would. But with Lisa? She'd said they made me weak. Therefore, no. I didn't want to

52

cry with her. I needed to get a handle on these zany feelings before I could face her.

Then she said, "You know that you're not to blame, right?"

I covered my mouth with my hand, breathing in through my nose, waiting for the wave of emotion entropy to pass.

"You're allowed to be mad," she continued, her voice quiet yet firm. "You're allowed to call it an assault, you're allowed to say you were terrified, and you're allowed to admit that it—what he did—had an impact on you. Admitting the truth doesn't give him power over you." She sounded like she was quoting someone, which made me wonder if Gabby had coached her.

Lisa made a soft sound. "Mona, open the door."

Letting my hand drop, I shook my head. "I don't want to talk about it."

"Come on, Mona. Why not?"

Try being honest. Abram's voice, the ghost of Aspen past, filled my ears, spurring me to confess. "Because I don't want to cry."

She paused, as though considering this, and then said, "I won't make you talk. But how about, if you open the door, I will teach you a trick that will help you not cry."

That had my attention.

Eying the doorknob, I quickly unlocked it, hesitated, and then twisted it to open the door a centimeter. I then stepped back and crossed my arms. My sister peeked inside, her gaze wary, and she gave me a little smile.

"Hey."

I was busy pressing my lips together—because I was now a crier—and said nothing.

Stepping completely inside, Lisa's stare moved over me, as though I were somehow different, or she was searching for visible bruises. She then bent down to open the cabinet beneath the sink and extracted a black rectangular bag.

"Sit down," she said, motioning to the closed toilet lid and unfastening the gold-toned zipper of the bag.

"Where's Gabby?" I asked once I was seated.

"She left."

I nodded faintly, watching as she pulled a brush from the black case. "What are you doing?"

"I'm going to do your makeup."

"Why?"

"Because you don't want to cry."

I lifted an eyebrow. "And makeup will stop me from crying?"

"It's a great deterrent. If you have makeup on, crying will ruin it. It's helped me keep my shit together." She lowered her eyes, took a deep breath, and finally finished, "It's helped me a few times."

I stared at my typically prickly sister, sensing that she considered this statement a secret, a valuable weapon that might be used against her. It was a window—albeit, a closed window—into a softer, gentler core than she showed the world.

Nodding, I uncrossed my arms and said, "Okay."

Lisa's gaze cut back to mine, her eyebrows jumping. "Really?"

"Yes."

"Are you serious right now?"

"Yes."

"You're actually okay with me doing your makeup?"

"Sure." I shrugged, admitting the truth, "It actually sounds fun." Compared to talking about *the incident,* everything sounded fun. Even a colonoscopy. Even a mammogram. Even a root canal. Even all three occurring at the same time.

"Who are you and what did you do with my sister?" Lisa gave me a smile I suspected was supposed to be teasing.

"I wear makeup."

"But you don't wear it often." She shifted her attention to the contents of the bag. "And you don't wear much."

"True. But that's only because it's not high on my list of priorities. Like, eating zucchini isn't high on my priority list, but that doesn't mean I don't enjoy a good stuffed zucchini every once in a while."

"Are you pulling my leg?" She scrunched one of her eyes, making a face. "I thought you hated makeup."

"No. I didn't—okay, I don't. I never hated it, but—admittedly—I used to judge people who wore a lot of it all the time as being superfluous. Now I don't."

"Why not? Here, close your eyes." She approached me holding a brush she'd dabbed in eyeshadow. "What changed?"

"I guess." I did as instructed and closed my eyes, feeling the gentle swiping over my closed lid. "I guess it happened when I was pretending to be you. I had to wear eye makeup, and then I began looking up tutorials because I wanted to make sure I was doing it right. And then I found I actually liked it."

"And yet you still don't wear makeup."

"It's an expensive habit."

She snorted. "Yes. Very."

"Plus," I debated whether or not to continue. Ultimately, I decided on honesty. It had served me well recently and I fully committed to it. "If you want to know the truth, there have been a few times where I get one eye done and then I get distracted, forget, and show up to work with makeup on just one eye."

"No, you don't." I heard the smile in Lisa's voice as she switched to my other lid.

"I do. At least four times that I know about."

"Oh my God, Mona! You crack me up!" The eyeshadow brush stopped moving, so I opened my eyes, watching my sister hold her stomach as she laughed. "You are so cute sometimes, I can't stand it."

I felt a smile tug at my lips. "And the worst part is, no one says anything to me except my friend Poe. Everyone just lets me walk around with one eye done. It's infuriating."

"Maybe they think you're making a fashion statement?" She dabbed at the corners of her eyes with the back of her hand, sniffling.

"No. They're just cowards."

"Ha! Cowards. I love it."

"Think about it. If you see someone with spinach in their teeth, you tell them. If you see someone with yogurt on their face, you tell them. If you see a person with eye makeup just on one eye, you tell them."

"See, now, I would tell someone if they had yogurt or spinach, but not the eye makeup. I would assume it was purposeful and move on."

"Coward."

"No." She grinned at me. "Not a coward. Shut your eyes again so I can finish the other side."

I did, and she continued thoughtfully, "I'm giving people the space to be themselves. When is the last time you asked someone about their makeup? I mean, if you noticed something strange."

"I've never noticed something strange, but if I did, I would tell them."

Lisa was quiet for a few seconds, and then asked, "Don't you think that's because you never notice people?"

"What? That's not true."

"It is true. You never recognize people, even if you've met them a hundred times."

"You suffer from gross exaggeration syndrome."

She chuckled. "Fine. Maybe not a hundred times. But I've introduced you to people more than once and you never recognize them the next time you meet them."

"Like who?"

"Like my friend from boarding school who helped me play that prank on you during your graduation."

A stunned jolt had me reaching out blindly, my fingers connecting with her wrist and moving her hand away so I could open my eyes. "Wait, what?"

"Yeah. Evelyn? From the newspaper? You'd met her three times before she called you to confirm the "details" of the interview. She was so worried you'd recognize her voice and figure it out, but you didn't."

I stared at Lisa, incredulous. "So, you knew her? And she was in on it? The whole time?"

"Of course. What did you think? That I actually pretended to be you and gave an interview to your university paper saying those crazy things?" Lisa smirked, dabbing her brush in the eyeshadow palette again.

But when I said nothing, she glanced at me. She blinked, flinching back, comprehension sharpening her stare. "Oh my God, you did. That's what you thought."

"It's not important." I twisted my lips to the side.

"Like hell it's not." Lisa snapped shut the eyeshadow palette, tossed it to the black case, and placed her hands on her hips, her gaze darting over me. "How could you think I would do that? That would've been hugely damaging to your reputation, made you look like a fool."

I swallowed, but said nothing, sorting through all the assumptions I'd made about my sister.

"Mona, you—" She huffed, glanced over my head, then shook hers.

"What?"

"You are intensely frustrating sometimes."

"Thank you."

Lisa made a short growling sound. "Why are you thanking me?"

"I don't know. I feel like I need to say something and I can't say, *in this economy?* It doesn't make enough sense in this context."

A reluctant laugh tumbled from her lips and she sat on the edge of the bathtub, her gaze moving over me. "What can I do to make this happen?"

"Make what happen?"

"Prove to you that I love you?"

I bit my bottom lip, reminding myself that I couldn't cry because I was wearing eye makeup. Surprisingly, it worked, and one of Abram's statements from earlier floated into my brain.

Cry if you need to, but don't ignore what the tears are about.

Gathering a deep breath, I cleared my throat, and said, "I don't want you to prove that you love me."

"Then what do you want?"

"I want—"

"What can I do?"

"I—I want—why didn't you ever tell me what happened with Abram? In Chicago? That morning after I left." *Whoa. Where had that come from?*

"What do you mean?" She gave her had a subtle shake.

"He told you that he loved me." I didn't mean for the words to sound like an accusation, but they did.

Lisa met my stare for a protracted moment. "Mona, if you remember, you didn't want to talk about it. Every time I brought him up, you said you didn't want to discuss it and would sing "Bohemian Rhapsody" until I changed the subject."

"But I didn't know that he told you he loved me!"

Her eyes clouded with remorse. "For what it's worth, I did try to tell you, a few times. But, you're right, I should've made you listen. I'm sorry. I didn't know what to do. I was such a mess back then. And I honestly didn't believe him at the time. I truly, truly didn't. And when he seemed to move on so quickly, I took it as proof that I was right not to believe him."

My stomach sank, remembering the pictures of Abram and other women I'd found during my initial online searches after Chicago. I rubbed the ache at my sternum. He'd already explained, but still. I was never going to be able to think about Abram with someone else and feel "okay" about it. I wasn't like my parents that way. I never would be.

"Anyway," Lisa continued, "Now, it's clear to me that I was wrong. And I'm sorry I didn't push you on this, make you listen."

Frowning, I grunted at my wayward contemplations and silliness. "No. You're right. I didn't let you tell me."

"I could've emailed you, then you would've read it before you realized what it said."

"No. I was being a stubborn moron." I needed to let this go.

Universe, take note: this is me letting this go.

Her gaze moved over me, assessing. "I am sorry."

"I know. I am too."

"I'm also sorry I always seem to be making mistakes and doing the wrong thing with you."

"You're not."

She gave me a look, like *come on.* "Mona. Be honest. I irritate you."

"No! What? It's not like that. It's—"

"What?"

"I want you to—to treat me like—like—"

"Like?"

"Like you like me." Gah! That sounded trite. Unfortunately, it was also the truth.

She blinked at me, her gaze clouding with confusion. "You don't think I like you?"

"Do you?"

Lisa opened her mouth, hesitated, and blinked, as though surprised by her own thoughts. Closing her mouth, she frowned at me, swallowing and shaking her head. "Don't be ridiculous," she said, but she looked ashamed, her gaze shifty, her posture stiff.

Her outward display of guilt helped my own thoughts crystalize. "I think, you and I, we've spent a long time not knowing each other. I think we've made assumptions about each other that might not be true."

She considered this for a moment, then asked, "Like what? What do you assume about me?"

"You're bossy. And stubborn."

"But I am. And so what? I know for a fact you deal with bossy, stubborn, *arrogant* people all the time."

"Those people aren't my sister."

"So what? What difference does that—"

"Because I don't care about what *they* think. I'm not scared of losing *them*."

Lisa snapped her mouth shut, flinching back, her eyes growing large at the vehemence in my voice.

But for me, the floodgates had opened. "You push your experiences on me, like I'm responsible for them, like I should be able to read your mind, or like I shared those same experiences, and completely disregard that my life was—is—different than yours. That doesn't mean my life is better, or harder, or easier. It's just different. You think that I'm emotionless, or that I should be. But I'm not. I don't *want* to be emotionless."

Lisa blinked, her eyes watery, and shifted them to some point over my head.

"I want to believe you love me, and part of me does," I admitted quietly, the words sticking in my throat. "But another part of me is constantly worried that you don't, not enough. I wonder, if I do something or say something you don't like, will you ignore me again?"

Her face crumpled and she closed her eyes. My heart gave an aching lurch. A rush of heat flooded my neck and cheeks. Now I felt like a big jerk, and I wondered if I'd said too much.

"Lisa." I struggled with the impulse to take it all back.

She swallowed, sniffling, shaking her head, her eyes still closed. "I don't know what to say."

I couldn't think of what to say either.

Were things so broken between us? These last few years, we'd made progress, hadn't we? We spoke. I knew her daily, weekly, and monthly routines. I knew how she liked her coffee. I knew who her least favorite teachers and subjects were. But how much did I know—really, really know—about my own sister?

In a way, it was ironic. I'd spent twelve days total with Abram, but felt like I knew him better, felt more confident with him, trusted him more than I did Lisa. If I were honest with myself, I had similar feelings toward Leo, and my parents. Similar concerns.

Do they love me enough for me to be myself with them?

My heart gave another painful twist, one that nearly robbed me of my breath. I hoped they did, but looking back, looking at their actions, or lack of actions, I faced the facts I'd been ignoring for maybe my whole life.

I couldn't be certain. I didn't trust it. I didn't trust them.

Watching my sister's struggle with her wobbly chin, none of my words felt right.

At a loss, I decided to repeat something Abram had said to me at a critical time between us, something that, in retrospect, had made all the difference to me.

"Lisa, will you be brave with me?" I reached forward, covered her hand with mine, and waited until she met my eyes. "Will you let me know you?"

[6]

RADIO ASTRONOMY

Abram

S he picked up on the second ring. "Hello?"

My leg stopped bouncing. *Finally.* "Mona."

"Abram! How are you? How was the flight? Did you sleep? And the concert? Did you make it back in time? Did it go well? Are you all done?"

I closed my eyes and lay down on the bench of the stretch limo, covering my forehead with my arm. Her intoxicating voice washed over me, covering, surrounding, lifting. Relief. Sweet, sweet relief.

"It is so good to hear your voice." *Finally.*

I spoke into the darkness, holding the phone to my ear. This moment was the very first moment since I'd left her ten hours ago that I felt like I could breathe.

She didn't say anything for a moment, but I could almost see her smiling. I could certainly feel it, and an answering slow, spreading smile claimed my mouth. This was how it should have been for the last six days.

"Thank you," she said, definitely smiling. "It's good to hear your voice too." I heard her move, or something rustle in the background. "Do you feel like talking? Or are you too tired?"

"Not too tired. Tell me . . ." I began, not quite sure how to ask my next question. I didn't want to put her on the spot, but I was worried. "How were things after I left? With your sister?"

A moment of near silence followed, during which I could make out the faint sound of her breathing. My jaw working, I struggled to keep a lid on my temper, but her silence led me to assume the worst.

No one fucks with Mona. No. One.

"Mona—"

"It was good."

A short, surprised breath fled my lungs. "Good?"

"Yes. Good. We spoke. We talked things through, I think. It wasn't an easy conversation, and tears were shed. I know how you're a fan of tears."

I chuckled, stunned. Actually, I wasn't stunned. I was disbelieving.

"She was nice to you?" I asked.

Now she laughed. "Yes. She was nice to me."

Huh.

For some reason, I couldn't let it go. "Are you sure? You know, you could come out here, meet me in San Francisco. I'll be *very* nice to you."

"Yes." I heard the shy smile in her voice, and I imagined her face wearing it. "I could, and I thought about doing that."

My heart swelled, ballooning with hope.

"But I think, after my conversation with Lisa today, it's important for me to stay here."

I tried not to be jealous or resentful of Lisa. I tried and tried and tried and would likely have to try again tomorrow.

"Okay. Well, the offer is an open one." I stretched my arm over my head, bringing my hand back to scratch my beard. "Any time you want to join me on tour, please do it."

"You sound tired. Your voice is scratchy."

"That's because we did four encores." I yawned, relaxing a little. *Finally.* "I'm not tired."

"You, Abram Harris, are telling me a falsehood."

"I would never." I yawned again around my grin. "Are you always going to call me Abram Harris?"

"Probably. Is that a problem?"

"No. I'm not complaining either. I'm Mr. Fletcher to everyone these days, he feels more like a role I'm playing rather than really me."

"I get that." Her voice was low and soft in my ear, and the constant ache of our separation became something else, something warm, less painful. "People have been calling me Ms. DaVinci since I was little. Can I tell you something? I don't even like my name."

"Mona DaVinci? I can't imagine why."

She chuckled, and then exhaled. "I've always thought about changing it."

I settled more firmly against the bench, shutting my eyes, grateful we'd spent so much of our time together in Chicago sorting out when we would see each other over the next few months.

As convoluted as it was—twenty-four hours in New York, three days in London, forty-eight hours in Miami, another thirty-six hours in London— we were making it work.

Now that things were settled, now that we had plans and had made promises, now that I knew when and where and for how long I would see her until June, conversations like this one were possible.

"What would you change your name to?"

"You have to promise not to laugh."

Still grinning, I shook my head. "Nuh-uh. I'll laugh if it's funny."

"Then I shan't tell you."

"Shan't?"

"Affirmative."

That made me laugh. "Is it Wolf?"

"Is what *wolf*?"

"You want to change your name to Wolf?"

"Wolf? Where did you get that idea?"

"Because then we could talk about *the Wolf* coming, and it would take on a completely different meaning."

She busted out laughing, and so I laughed, and then we were laughing together. *God,* this was so great. So great.

"You are—" She couldn't speak, she was laughing too hard.

"What? What am I?"

"Never mind. I shan't tell you that either."

I loved her voice. I couldn't wait until the end of the month and our first scheduled meet-up in New York.

"By the way." She'd stopped laughing but the happiness in her voice remained. "Where are you? Still at the venue?"

"No. In the car, on the way back to the hotel."

"Oh. Is anyone with you?"

"No. Everyone else is still at the stadium. I left right after the last encore."

"Because you're tired."

"Because I wanted to talk to you." I stifled another yawn, clearing my throat. "Tell me about your day. What did you do after you took me to the airport? Thanks for driving me, by the way."

"You're welcome. And, let the record show, you got there on time."

"That's because you weren't driving like my Uncle Harry. For once."

She laughed again, and the seductive sound relaxed every muscle in my body . . . but one.

"You've only driven with me twice. That's not enough datapoints to make any meaningful extrapolations."

"I love it when you talk data to me. Say extrapolations again."

Her laugh was harder this time, and I imagined her blushing. "Tell me about the concert."

"Well." I yawned again, irritated because I didn't want to yawn at all. "It was fine. Vicious Pixies opened for us, do you know who they are?"

"No." She sounded regretful. "I'm not up on the music scene."

"That's fine. You don't need to know who they are for the story. Their bass guitarist showed up to the stadium around the same time I did, except he was totally shit-faced. High out of his mind."

"Oh no!"

"Oh yes. I filled in."

"Oh no!"

"Oh yes. It worked out though. No one realized it was me. I stood in the back, where the light was bad, and wore a beanie."

That made her giggle and I heard her typing on a keyboard. "I think it'll take more than a beanie and bad lighting to hide yourself."

I loved talking to her. Was this what it would be like all the time between us? So easy. Effortless.

"You'd be surprised. When I checked into my flight today, I walked right by two posters of me in my boxers. No one batted an eye."

"Oh, hey." A new edge entered her voice. "I'm glad you brought up those posters." Mona was quiet for a moment, giving me the impression she was gathering her thoughts.

"Are you?" I prompted, a little worried.

"Can I have one?"

I choked, my eyes flying open. "What?"

"Can I have one of the posters?"

I sat up on the bench and immediately regretted it, my vision swimming, and had to lay back down again. "Uh, I guess?"

"Thank you! That's excellent. Oh, and can it be one of the big ones? The life-sized ones?"

I laughed and I had no idea why I was laughing, maybe because this conversation felt hugely absurd. Maybe because I was insanely tired. Or maybe because she was so fricken cute.

"Mona, if you want a picture of me, I'll send you one. You don't need one from an advertising campaign."

"You'll send me a photo?"

"Yes."

Another contemplative pause before she asked, "Will you be in your underwear?"

I barked a startled laugh, and then I was laughing so hard, I couldn't breathe. She was also laughing, but it had an edge of self-consciousness, shyness.

"Fine, fine. You can wear clothes," she conceded, sounding embarrassed.

"Now, wait a minute." I wiped at the tears of hilarity, sobering slightly as an interesting proposition took shape. "Wait a minute. Of course, if you want sexy photos of me, I'll send them."

"Thank you, I do." Now she sounded prim, official, like we'd just agreed I'd send her a contract, or I'd confirmed a conference call.

Even exhausted and fighting another yawn, I was grinning. Yes. Absolutely I would send her photos. I couldn't wait to see her again in person. But if our prolonged separation meant that she'd be willing to send me pictures of herself? Well. That would definitely make the waiting more bearable.

"Here's the deal. I'll send you sexy photos, and then you'll send me some photos too."

Silence.

Dead silence.

I waited, pressing the phone more firmly to my ear. "Mona? Are you still there?"

"Yep."

"Is there something wrong?"

"No." Her answer was higher pitched than normal and sounded like a lie.

"You don't want to send me photos?"

"I'll send you photos."

Hmm. That was easy. *Too easy.*

I felt like I was missing something, so I said, "Okay. Then it's settled?"

"Yep. All settled. Where are you staying? What hotel?"

"Um." I thought about that, my brain full of static, and then shook my head. "Honestly, I don't even know. I'm so tired, I didn't ask."

She made a soft sound of sympathy. "I wish I were there."

"Why?"

She said nothing.

I rephrased the question. "Tell me why. Tell me what you would do if you were here." My words were a little slurred.

"I would have you rest your head on my lap as we drove," she answered immediately, and I learned something I didn't know about Mona. She didn't do well with vague questions. The more precise, the better. "And I would stroke your hair, give your head a massage, and watch over you until you fell asleep."

My scalp tingled at the idea. "Then what would you do?"

"Then, when we got to the hotel." I heard the springs of a mattress compress. "I would take a bath with you."

66

I stifled a groan.

Pain. Ache. Longing. I couldn't breathe. I could only stare at the ceiling of the limo, streetlights strobing through the windows, but otherwise I was enclosed in darkness. If I concentrated, it was almost like she was here, next to me, whispering in my ear.

"And I would sit behind you, with you between my legs," she continued, making me glad I hadn't interrupted. She sounded distracted by her own imagination and the last thing I wanted her to do was stop. "I would wash your hair, and your body, and give you a massage."

"What kind of massage?" My voice had gone from sleepy and slurred to strained, and I was suddenly very much awake, hanging on her every word.

She was silent for a beat, and I worried she might not answer, but then she asked in a less dreamy, very Mona voice, "Are we going to have phone sex?"

Hopefully. "We don't have to."

"I've never had phone sex."

I thought for a minute, realizing and saying at the same time, "Neither have I."

"Oh! That's exciting."

My grin widened and I closed my eyes again. "It is."

"Wait! I know a joke about it, though. Why should you always use protection when having phone sex?"

I pressed my lips into a flat line so I wouldn't laugh before she got to the punchline. "I don't know. Why?"

"Otherwise you might get hearing *aids*."

A beat of silence.

I rolled my eyes. "That's a terrible joke."

"Yeah. It's pretty bad. I was on a call once with the CDC and an immunologist told it. I think medical doctors have the most inappropriate jokes." She laughed. "But you know, they still crack me up. Does that make me a bad person?"

"What? No. No, you are not a bad person."

"I often worry."

"Why would you worry about that? You're one of the best people I know."

"I think it's good to worry about being a bad person. It's good to question yourself, you know?" She asked this question like she was confessing something about herself, a secret, and I wished *again* that my brain didn't feel so slow.

"You don't need to question whether you're a good person. Take my word for it, okay?"

"Have you ever read Bertrand Russell?"

"No. Who is that?"

"He was a mathematician. Anyway, he said, 'Those who feel certainty are stupid, and those with any imagination and understanding are filled with doubt and indecision.' I think that's especially true with knowing oneself. As soon as you grow certain of something, you've closed your mind to other possibilities."

I was too tired to give the words the consideration they deserved, so I said without thinking, "Then I guess I'm stupid for you."

A short beat, and then she replied quietly, "That's a relief."

"Oh yeah?"

"Yes. Because I didn't want to be the only one of us who was stupid." The tenderness in her voice had me imagining her face, her smile, her eyes.

My heart constricted painfully, I lost my breath for a moment, overwhelmed by how much I wanted . . . I just wanted . . .

I want her to be here.

Before I could catch myself, I said, "I miss you. So much."

Her laugh tapered, and I heard her release a soft breath before responding earnestly, "I miss you too."

[7]

STELLAR PARALLAX

Abram

"Here you go, Mr. Fletcher." A PA hired by our manager, this one also happened to be his niece, placed a cup of tea in front of me, giving me a nervous smile. "I put honey and lemon in it, just how you like."

"Thank you," I whispered, distractedly picking up the cup while I flipped through the list of interview questions for later in the day.

Seconds later, the sound of items clattering to the ground had me glancing up. The items were photos of the band and black markers for signing them. She must've bumped into the stool where they sat, but she also must've done something else, like push the stack at an odd angle, because they were now everywhere.

"Oh God. Sorry." She squatted, flushing red, and worked to gather the fallen items. "Sorry about that."

I stood, sending a look to Charlie.

Charlie stepped up. "Don't worry. Abram and I will pick it up."

"It's fine." Her voice was high. Clearly, she was embarrassed. "I'm almost done."

She wasn't almost done. The photos had gone flying in all directions, falling like confetti. Thankfully, Charlie had already moved to her and helped gather the photographs. I crossed to where the markers had rolled—just under the couch—and bent to retrieve them.

As I straightened and turned, I caught her staring at me, her gaze in the vicinity of my stomach, her eyes dazed. Combatting a spike of frustration, I cleared my throat. Her gaze lifted. She seemed to smirk, her eyes heating suggestively.

What the hell? I grit my teeth.

"Hey. What happened?" Ruthie's greeting pulled everyone's attention to the door of our shared suite. We all had our own suites, but this one was larger. It was where the band gathered over these last few days —to meet, to give interviews, to take photos and whatnot—leading up to the LA concert.

Our guitarist, standing just inside the suite door, frowned at the mess, bending to pick up one of the photos near her feet. "Are we signing these or what?"

"Yes, yes. It was my fault," the PA said, pushing her hand through her hair. "I'm so clumsy."

"Don't worry about it." Charlie took the photos from her, added them to his stack, and brought them to the table. "I don't know why they were on the stool anyway. Could've happened to anyone."

Walking past the woman to the square kitchen table, I felt her eyes on me. Just as I reclaimed my seat and Ruthie took the spot next to mine, the PA tripped over her own feet as she walked backward. And then, instead of clearing the door, she bumped into the wall.

Finally, she turned, tucking her hair behind her ears and walked from the suite.

"She's got it bad for you, Abram." Ruthie kicked me under the square table. I shifted my gaze to her, and she lifted her chin toward the tea. "Did she make you that tea? I wouldn't drink that if I were you."

Charlie snorted, taking the chair next to Ruthie, which placed him across from me. "Why? You think she's going to drug him?"

Our guitarist lifted both her hands, palms out. "Hey, man. I'm just saying, the women lose their fucking minds over him. I've never seen so many bras on so many stages before, and bras are expensive. It's raining lingerie *every night*. That's not you, and that's not me."

Charlie shrugged good-naturedly, but mumbled, "I think it's a little bit you and me." His quiet words held an unmistakable edge of defiance.

Ruthie continued like she hadn't heard him. "If someone has lost their mind, there's no telling what they'll do. Alls I'm saying is, if I were Abram, I'd be careful. I wouldn't accept tea from any of the PAs." Turning to me, she poked at the teacup. "Wait for Melena to get back. Have her make your tea, just to be safe."

Melena was our chef, had a master's degree in nutrition, and was a registered nurse. Other than the three of us, she was the highest paid member of the crew, which made complete sense. She kept us healthy and well-fed. It was her tea blend that the PA had made. I was supposed to drink it three times a day.

"Am I missing something? Isn't Melena also a woman?" Charlie glanced between the two of us.

"Yes. But she's not one of the ones coming in here, tripping over her own feet, staring at him like he's cotton candy. I don't get boiled bunny vibes from Melena. Some of the other ones, however." Ruthie gave a little shiver of revulsion. "They give me the creeps."

I frowned at my bandmate. None of the PAs revolted me, but some of them worried me. Yeah, I was uncomfortable around a few, but not enough to complain. I didn't want them to lose their jobs, that didn't seem fair. So what if they had a crush? They were harmless.

Although, even though I was convinced they were harmless, I'd taken steps to ensure I was never alone with any of them. Hearing Ruthie's take on the situation did nothing to put me at ease.

Glancing at the tea longingly—because it helped, and my throat hurt, but what else was new—I removed it from the table and set the cup on the countertop behind us.

"Let's get these signed," I said, more of a rasp than a voice at this point. "We have that interview later this afternoon."

Charlie made a face. "Man, Abram, you sound like shit. Come on, you're being crazy. Just drink it."

"We don't—" I held up a finger, sneezed into a napkin, and then continued, "We don't have the show until tomorrow. I'll be fine by then, if you two do all the talking at the interview."

"Are you sure you're not getting sick?"

"I'm not getting sick." I blinked, my eyes scratchy.

"You know, Leo will be there. Tomorrow," Ruthie said conversationally. "He asked if you would be at the VIP thing after, cause' he's bringing all his Hollywood friends and they want to meet you."

Scowling, I reached across the table for a pen. "I won't be there."

Leo and I still weren't speaking. I didn't know if he was aware of my relationship with Mona, and I didn't care.

"Why're you so pissed at him?" Ruthie asked.

I opened my mouth to answer, but instead sneezed again. When I was sure no other sneeze was on the way, I responded, "I'm not pissed." *Damn.* My eyes hurt.

"I think you're getting sick." Charlie squirmed in his seat.

"I told you, it's fine." My phone buzzed in my pocket and I reached for it.

"It's not fine. I'll make your stupid tea," Charlie grumbled, standing, grabbing the cup. "Where does Melena keep this shit?"

I was only partially listening, the notification on my screen capturing most of my attention.

Mona: Finished early. Let me know if you have time to talk, would love to hear about your week. Miss you.

Staring, standing, smiling, and turning from the table, I unlocked my phone to read the message again. My heart thrummed with happy nerves. This was an extremely nice surprise.

Mona and I had spoken to each other every night until she'd left for Geneva. Since, we'd texted a lot, but talking over the phone had been spotty, now down to a weekly thing mostly because of the time difference and our schedules. But that was okay. We were making it work and we were set to see each other in less than two days. I planned to leave LAX via a chartered plane directly after the concert.

The promise of uninterrupted time with Mona, in New York, for twenty-four hours felt like a luxury life raft in this pitching sea of adrenaline highs and lows. The concerts were an intense high. Which made after the concerts—with no Mona—a huge source of frustration for no one but me.

"I'll show you where to get it," Ruthie said behind me, probably speaking to Charlie. "We'll be back with new *non-creepy* tea. And save your voice. Don't talk to anyone while we're gone."

Glancing over my shoulder to watch my bandmates leave, I navigated to Mona's number as soon as I estimated they were out of earshot. I dialed.

Two rings later, she picked up. "Hey. You're free? How are you? How long can you talk? Did I interrupt?"

I closed my eyes, smiling to myself. She did this. Every time we spoke, she answered with a *hey,* and then a barrage of questions. I loved it.

"I'm free. I'm better now. I can't talk long. You didn't interrupt me. But, Mona—"

"Abram. Your voice sounds bad, and you sound stuffy." She said this around a yawn. "Are you sure you're okay? Are you sick?"

"No." I cleared my throat, trying to deepen and firm it. "I'm not sick, I just need to rest my voice. What's going on with you? You sound tired."

"Should we be talking if you need to rest your voice? We can text instead. Have you seen a doctor? What does Melena say? Are you drinking your tea?"

"Stop. Listen to me. I want to ask you something. Actually, two things."

"Oh. Okay."

I could almost see her face. Her eyes were probably wide, a wrinkle between her eyebrows. Maybe she was biting her lip.

Her lips.

"First, have you been sleeping?"

She replied, "Yes."

That's right. I needed to ask specific questions. "Let's try this a different way. When was the last time you slept?"

"Uhhh, yesterday. I think. Wait. What day is it?"

She needed to take better care of herself. "Here it's Friday midmorning."

"So that makes it—"

"Friday night in Geneva."

"Then, yes. I slept Wednesday."

"Yesterday was Thursday."

"Then I slept the day before yesterday."

I shook my head, a frustrated grin on my face. "Mona. You have to take better care of yourself."

"I can't help it. I only get so many hours with the LHC, and then I have to go through the data. It's too much to backup, and my project isn't priority. And then there's the inevitable white whale hunt, which only seems to yield anything of value when I'm exhausted and my brain stops overcomplicating everything."

White whale hunt was what she called her process of choosing which hunch to follow, how to prioritize her time and energy searching for answers to the unknown, something about understanding or explaining quantum mechanics within the frame of Einstein's general theory of relativity.

Although, maybe that wasn't it? Most of the time, when she spoke of her research, it sounded like a different language.

Over the last several weeks, I'd come to the conclusion that Mona didn't sleep enough. She worked herself until she was exhausted or manic with exhaustion, and this was because Mona DaVinci both was and was not her genius.

Her genius was a paradox, terrifying in its complexity and beauty, but also severe, punishing, rigid in its demands of her. It didn't care about the frailty of the body. It didn't care about her relationships, even with herself. It explored, relentlessly, dragging her along—sometimes willingly, sometimes not—often at the expense of her health and wellbeing-.

"I understand the urge to work through the night and into the next day. I get it." I paced to the window, staring at the blue sky. "I'm not going to tell you what to do—obviously—I'm just going to say, as someone who cares deeply about *you*, I hope you get a chance to take a night off the whale hunt."

"I will. I'll be sleeping in tomorrow. I already packed, so I'll wake up, catch my flight, arrive in New York Saturday evening, and then I'll see you early Sunday." The unmistakable smile in her sleepy voice encouraged me to smile.

"Sunday."

"Yes. Sunday." She yawned again. I didn't take it personally. "I can't wait. But—uh—was there something else? You said two things?"

"Oh yeah." I nodded, almost forgetting. "I asked you to send me a picture of yourself, and you sent your faculty headshot from Caltech." I couldn't stop my smile from growing. When she'd sent it, I'd laughed on and off for an hour. I wasn't even mad. It was such a Mona thing to do.

It did, however, leave me unsatisfied. I'd sent her a few shots of me lying in bed, wearing nothing but my boxers, and she sends me a picture of her in a lab coat, smiling with no teeth. I wasn't looking for reciprocation, but, *man*, a candid maybe? A genuine smile?

She was quiet for a beat. Then she cleared her throat. "You didn't like the picture?"

"You are sneaky. You know what I mean."

"Are you saying it's a bad picture?"

Sometimes she was too fucking smart, especially when we debated. I loved it. I also hated it.

"It's a great picture, as you know. I've seen it in magazines, next to interviews of you. But I was hoping for something a little more candid."

"Candid? I can do that." The offer was made too quickly, which made me suspicious.

"Let me be clear. No pictures of you in a lab coat or at work. Or at school. Or doing anything for your charities."

She made a sound between a huff and a growl. "Those are the only pictures I have of myself."

I bit back a laugh, covering my eyes with my free hand. "God, Mona. I mean candid like, send me a photo of you, taken right that minute."

"Right that minute?"

"Yes. What are you doing now?"

"Uh, about to take a shower."

My smile vanished. I opened my eyes, my brain stuttered, and the hoarseness of my words had nothing to do with needing to rest my voice. "That'll do."

"Abram." She made another growling sound. "I can't send you those kinds of photos."

"What kind?"

"You know, me in just a towel."

"I don't need you to be in just a towel. If you don't feel comfortable sending a particular photo, definitely don't send it. I'm not trying to get you to do something you don't want to do. I want to see your smile, your real smile, not something your graduate program uses for promotional purposes."

"Fine. Then candid pictures of me. I can't send those." Her tone had me straightening, she sounded almost hostile.

"Why?" I asked softly, wanting her to know that I wasn't trying to push her, I just honestly wanted to know. "What am I missing?"

Mona sucked in an audible breath. "I've worked hard for my reputation. I've been so careful. I've never done anything that might jeopardize me being taken seriously."

She was solemn, severe. She sounded like a different person. Her voice was deeper, held a hint of dry antagonism, like she *dared* me to challenge her. I wasn't put off, but I was confused. It was a side of Mona I'd never seen in person, but one I'd witnessed last year when she'd given her testimony to congress. Basically, she sounded superior and aloof.

I waited for her to continue. When she didn't, I asked, "Am I asking you to do something that might jeopardize you being taken seriously?"

"Yes." Now sadness entered her voice, unmistakable melancholy, and my throat tightened in response. "Abram, this world I live in, it is an intellectual world, but it is not enlightened. Women are not seen as equals, young women in particular. And if you're at all attractive, it's an impediment. I've been called a distraction. Do you know what that's like? I've been called emotional when I raised my voice to match that of my male colleagues, I've been called bitchy and conceited and judgmental for recognizing my own intelligence, and not just by men."

As she spoke, she started to sound more like herself, but the despondency only increased.

"I have to demonstrate the appropriate amount of gratitude daily for being included on projects and grants that are full of my original ideas. I can't take for granted that I've earned anything, because I never will, because everyone—even other women—are just waiting for me to prove everyone right, that I'm too young, too sensitive, too female to be worthy of my place at the table. They want my ideas, my research, but not enough to change the culture or be inconvenienced. Not enough to entertain the notion that I'm just another person, just like them." Her voice lowered to a whisper. "I have to be faultless. I have to be perfect. I can't afford mistakes."

My heart in my mouth, I asked without thinking, "Am I a mistake?"

"No! God, no. Never."

"But sending me pictures of yourself, that's a mistake." I didn't know why, and I didn't understand the impulse myself, but bitterness had leached into my voice. Not even the rawness of my vocal chords could disguise it. And yet, I wasn't mad at her.

I was just . . . bitter.

"If—if your phone got hacked, and pictures of you in a bathing suit were leaked or published." Now her tone was soft, almost pleading. "Or—or the photos you already sent me, if those were leaked, would it be a big deal? Would it damage your reputation?"

"You already know the answer to that question. I'm on billboards in my underwear. No one would care."

"Oh, they'd care. But if any picture of me *not* looking uptight and professional were leaked, I'd never live it down. It would be 'Girls gone wild, rocket scientist edition.' Women—especially women in science, or politicians—aren't allowed that freedom without lasting consequences. It's not just my male colleagues who will judge me, it's everyone. And that's just the way it is."

I felt like putting my fist through a wall, growling, "The way it is sucks."

"I agree. But—" I could hear her breathing, it had quickened, like she was working herself up to say something difficult, and a spike of alarm had the hairs on the back of my neck standing up. Before I could interject, she finished her thought, "Abram, we live in two different worlds."

My bitterness morphed into anger, making me seethe. "I refuse to accept that. We live in the same world."

"Our paths are—they're very different."

"No. They're not. They're the same. We're on this road together, Mona. We're on this path together. And I want you—I want you to feel empowered, because you are powerful. You. Are. *Powerful*. Someone should be telling you that, making you believe it, every damn day. You feel like you have to hide part of yourself and it pisses me off. So, yeah, I need a minute here. Because I need to mourn the fuc—" I stopped myself, taking a deep breath, grinding my teeth, telling myself to calm down. "I need to mourn this world in which we live, where *gentlemen* and *ladies* exist who are less, so much less than you. And yet, because of how a flawed system is built, they get to decide how and when you share yourself with me."

"Abram! Are you on the phone?"

I glanced up at the sound of Ruthie's shrieking question. She stood just inside the doorway, holding a tray.

She also wore an impressive scowl. "That better be your priest, because Imma kill you now."

Suddenly tired, I gave my guitarist a quelling look and turned away, lowering my voice to a whisper. "Listen. I have to go. We have a —a thing. Stuff to sign and this interview later."

A few seconds of quiet, and then Mona said, "Okay. See you soon." She sounded distracted. I didn't like it.

"Hey. See you soon. I lov—" I'd wanted to say *I love you*, but she'd already ended the call.

Cursing under my breath, I turned to the table and sat down in front of the tray, ignoring Ruthie's death stare and navigating to my texts.

Abram: I love you. I don't need a picture, I just need you.

. . .

I didn't need a picture, not if it would be a source of anxiety for her, but she was wrong. We were in this together. If something affected her, it affected me. Reading back over the message, I decided to send one more.

Abram: What you have to deal with is ~~complete fucking bullshit~~ completely unacceptable. I wish I could do something to help and I shouldn't have ranted at you. I'm not mad at you, but I would like to punch some physicists right now.

    Abram: Not you, obviously.

    Abram: I miss you. You're incredible. I'm awed by you.

Staring at my phone, I waited for Mona to respond. Ruthie cleared her throat. Obnoxiously. I ignored her. Charlie came back in, took a seat, and began signing photos. Still, I stared, my stomach slowly sinking.

After a few minutes, I set the phone face down on the table and glanced at the tray. A mug, a teapot, cut up wedges of lemon, packets of honey, and a plate with some kind of cookie covered the surface. Ruthie must've been a butler in another life.

I poured myself tea, unable to shake a nagging sense of doom. Ruin set up residence in my chest, distracting and tight, telling me I'd fucked up.

But I'll make it right in New York. I'll—

"Do you like the *tea*?" Ruthie asked, somehow making the question sound like a threat.

"Yes. Thank you," I whispered, so as not to further provoke her ire.

"You're welcome. The cookies are sugar free and paleo," Charlie said. He reached for one of the cookies, shoving the whole thing in his mouth. "I made the tea. She assembled the rest and carried it."

"Fucking paleo asshats," Ruthie mumbled. "I hate those people."

"What? Why?" Charlie asked around another bite of a cookie.

"Their snacks are pretty good. Clever. I like that they use dates in energy bars."

Blowing steam off the surface of the tea, I checked my phone again. Nothing. Now my throat not only hurt, it was full of glass shards of regret, making it nearly impossible to swallow.

"No, Charlie." She rolled her eyes. "I'm talking about people from the paleolithic time period. I can't stand those fuckers. With their stupid pet dinosaurs."

Charlie and I shared a look, because sometimes Ruthie was odd, and we couldn't tell if she was serious or joking. This was a woman who hated the most random things—like the word *chartreuse* and all-natural history museums—so there existed a very real possibility she actually hated people from the paleolithic time period.

Rubbing my sternum, I took a sip of the tea, set it down, and picked up a marker. "Pass me a photo."

"No talking, Abram," Ruthie chided, giving me a whole stack of photographs. "When you finish these, Charlie and I will take turns giving you more."

I nodded, grimacing, because the ache in my chest hadn't eased. *Was this our first argument?*

No. Our first argument had been in Aspen. This definitely wasn't that. I wasn't upset with her. I was upset with a system that rewarded hypocrisy.

My phone buzzed. Immediately, I snatched it up, almost knocking over the tea. A text.

Mona: I was saving this for New York, but I thought you'd like a sneak peek.

I frowned, reading the message again, searching for a hidden meaning. Then a picture came through and I almost dropped my phone.

It was Mona.

Standing in front of a full-length mirror.

Wearing a white string bikini.

It didn't matter that I had no voice, because I was now speechless, with profound lust.

"What's wrong with you? You watching porn or something?" Ruthie leaned toward me. "Who is that?"

I yanked the phone back, pressing it to my chest, glaring at her.

She immediately reared back, her eyes wide with surprise. "Sorry, sorry. Don't mind me, I'll just be over here hating paleos and signing photos, as one does."

Standing, I paced away from the table and toward the window, peering at the picture of Mona again, hungry for it. God, she was so fucking beautiful. So gorgeous. Her expression, smiling, confident, but with a hint of challenge, like she dared someone, anyone to make this picture of her something shameful. And her expression erased any worry I might've had that she'd felt pressured into sending it.

I loved it. I needed hours with this photo.

You'll have hours with her, and the bikini, in less than two days.

Two days.

Just two days.

Two days that stretched in front of me like an eternity.

[8]

THE MAGNITUDE SCALE

Mona

U sually, if I'm booked on a flight and the airline offers a voucher to take a later flight, I am the first person to give up my seat. Discounts on air travel excites me more than well-timed puns and cookies combined.

Vouchers. *Vouchers*. Even the word sounds seductive.

But not this time. Nothing would induce me to give up my seat on the overbooked flight from Frankfurt to New York for a later flight, not even $800 in travel vouchers. Such was my commitment to arriving in New York as soon as the laws of thermodynamics would allow.

My plane was set to arrive around 9 PM. The plan was for me to check into our hotel, reserved under the names Abram and Mona Harris, and wait for his flight to land at approximately 6:00AM the following morning. Using the aliases had been his idea and made sense given how nuts the paparazzi had been over him in the last several months. Our hotel, called Inn New York City, wasn't one with which I was familiar, but he'd insisted on the location. I honestly didn't care, just as long as we were together.

The flight itself was uneventful, albeit slow, further buoying my theory that feelings influence perception of motion and the space-time continuum. Perhaps feelings were the key to unraveling the mystery of quantum gravity. *Hmm.*

Eventually, we landed at JFK safe and sound, and I immediately switched off the airplane mode of my phone, wanting to text Abram as soon as possible. I'd just opened my messaging app when a series of texts came through, the first one sent just after my flight had taken off, but the second one was from less than a half hour ago.

Abram: Can't wait to see you.

Abram: Call Marie at this number when you land.

Marie?

Frowning at the last text, my heart fluttering anxiously, I called Abram's number as instructed and turned toward the window at my right in order to achieve maximum privacy despite being packed into the very back of coach like osmium.

Three rings later, a female voice answered, "Mona?"

"Uh, yes?"

"Hi. It's Marie Harris, Abram's sister."

MARIE! How could I have forgotten awesome Marie?

Oh jeez. I quickly tested my breath, and then abruptly stopped myself when—obviously—I realized it didn't matter if my breath smelled bad. Unless they'd invested in olfaction-phonics and updated my phone without telling me, the status of my breath didn't matter.

"Hi, hi! Hi, Marie. It's nice to, uh—" SCHRÖDINGER! And all his cats, dead or alive. I couldn't say, *It's nice to talk to you again,* because when we'd first met, I'd been Lisa. Damn lies. Clearing my throat, I said the first thing that popped in my mind, "How may I be of service?"

"Uh, yes. Well, Abram asked that I call. He's here."

"In Michigan?" my mouth asked, just as my brain thought it.

"No. In LA. We're at the hospital—"

Hospital. Hospital. *Hospital.* Why did that word feel like being hit on the back of the head with a large, heavy, blunt object? All concerns about my previous lies vanished.

"—found him this morning. His fever was quite high, and an ambulance was called. Leo called me as soon as he found out and I arrived just an hour ago. They've been able to bring down his fever, and he's tested positive for the flu. The doctors were worried about a secondary infection, but the CT scan and blood work came back okay. The doctors say he looks good to be discharged tomorrow, but they want to keep him overnight for observation."

Hospital. Oh God.

My throat was choking me. "Is he okay? I mean, I know he has the flu, but is he—I mean—will he—is he—"

"They think he's going to be fine." Marie's voice was infinitely patient and reassuring and was exactly what I needed to hear. "Just to be safe, they're keeping him overnight and plan to get another blood draw in the morning. But, yes, he seems to be okay. Cranky, obstinate, and giving me dirty looks from across the room, but okay."

"He's there? Can I—is it okay for him to talk?"

"Yes. Absolutely. I just wanted to explain the situation first, answer any questions, to save him from having to speak unnecessarily, since he is *very sick*."

I swallowed around a lump of guilt. I wanted to talk to him—desperately—but not if it would endanger his recovery. "If he's too sick to talk, I completely understand. It's obviously more important that he recover than—"

"No, no. It should be fine if you two talk. I just wanted to remind my brother that he is *very sick* and—under no circumstances—will he be performing tonight or flying to New York this evening. Here, let me put him on."

I heard a grumbly, angry voice in the background, and it mollified the sharpest edges of my anxiety. Being well enough to feel and express anger was far better than the worst-case scenarios I hadn't even realized I'd been imagining.

A brief silence on the other side was followed by the muffled sound of Marie saying, "Yes, I will keep it on speaker. And no, you can't hold the phone. Fight me."

And then Abram said, "Mona."

Suddenly, my eyes stung with a heated rush of disarrayed emotion. "Oh, Abram. You sound so sick. Don't speak, okay?" I closed my eyes, resting my forehead against the frame of the plane window. "Please don't worry about New York, don't worry about anything. Like you said, we have the rest of our lives. Concentrate on getting better and being well. I love you."

"I love you too."

I winced as he spoke. His rattled breathing and the sound of machines beeping in the background made my chest feel heavy and tight. Very little about his voice sounded like him, but it did make obvious how sick he was.

"We can text. I'll—I'll send you pictures, okay? Lots of candid shots."

Abram made a sound that I assumed was one of agreement or amusement. "No pressure, but that sounds great."

I winced again, because he'd said a lot of words, and speaking at all seemed to cost him. I wanted him to get better. Overextending himself on the phone—just so I could hear his voice—was not helping.

"Okay. No more talking. Put Marie back on. Go to sleep. Rest. I love you."

"I love you," he said, the last word sounding fainter.

A second later, the sound of the machines also faded, and Marie said, "Mona? Hey. Thanks for calling. You've definitely improved his mood."

"No problem, I—" I shook my head, opening my eyes and staring at the tarmac beyond my oval window. "I want to be there," I confessed, not caring how miserable I sounded, not caring that she was basically a stranger. "We were only going to have twenty-four hours in New York, but now I'm thinking about abandoning all my responsibilities for the next week and flying out to LA."

"I'm not advocating it, but can you do that? I mean, how big of a deal would it be?"

"I'd have to start my project from almost scratch, which means I might lose my spot in the program, which means I might lose my graduate funding." I would probably lose at least part of my funding. One of my grants was contingent on presentation of findings at the August conference. The math part was easy, getting time with the LHC was not. If I started from scratch, nothing would be ready for August.

But, strangely, uncovering the mysteries of the known and unknown universe didn't seem important relative to the reality of Abram being horribly sick.

"He's in good hands, Mona. I'll be here in LA until he's fully recovered. Our parents are coming later today. I promise, I won't let him do anything that will jeopardize his recovery and we'll keep you updated."

"I just—I need to—" I heaved a watery sigh. "I'm sorry. I need to be there. I think we're almost to the gate. I'll get a flight to LA as soon as I can."

"Mona—"

"You're not going to change my mind." I'd already been traveling for fourteen hours—Geneva to Frankfurt, Frankfurt to New York—what was another six or seven in comparison? No big deal.

"Take a step back and think about this, be rational. He'll be fine. You being here isn't going to—"

"I can't—I physically *cannot*—fly back to Geneva. I know myself, and I would regret it so much, the gravity of my feelings might cause the formation of a black hole somewhere over the Atlantic Ocean, and then we're all dead. As such, I'll text you as soon as I know my new flight data."

After a brief pause, she asked, "You're in New York?"

"Yes."

"Which airport?"

"Uh, JFK."

"I'll make a deal with you. If you promise to stay just for the original twenty-four hours, I can get you on a private plane leaving New York in—uh—forty-ish minutes, *and* a flight back directly to Geneva on the same plane. You'll have to make a short stop in Chicago to pick up my parents, but you'll definitely get here faster than a commercial flight."

I wrinkled my nose, pulling my bottom lip through my teeth as I considered her offer. "Whose private plane?"

"A friend's."

I shook my head quickly. "No. I can't promise that. What if Abram isn't better in twenty-four hours? What if he takes a turn for the worse? I wouldn't be able to leave then."

"Okay, if he's better, then you have to leave, go back to Europe as planned, and get back to work so you don't lose your funding. If he's sicker, you can stay."

A few sounds emerged from the back of my throat, all of which were disbelieving. "I'm sorry, but this doesn't sound like a deal. This sounds too good to be true."

"Do we have a deal?"

I didn't hesitate. "Yes."

Usually, I didn't accept gifts. And I never accepted anything without knowing the source, definitely not anything as luxurious as a flight on a private plane. But desperate times call for a relaxation of rigid ethical codes. I would have to sort through my overthinking on this subject later. *Much later.*

"Is that a promise?" Marie pushed, as though she sensed a statement of explicit promise was necessary.

"Absolutely."

"Good. I'll text you the details once I work things out with my friend. I'll also—hold on, Abram is trying to get my attention. Just a sec."

The phone went quiet for a minute, maybe two, during which I calculated the precise moment I would have to leave LA to make it back to Geneva on time. To my delight, we'd actually end up with more time together than if we'd met in New York. This realization was tempered by the reminder that Abram was extremely sick. I'd prefer less time and him well, not because I felt like I was missing out on quality time with him, but because I just wanted him to be better.

"Okay, Mona. Are you still there?"

"Yes. I'm here."

"Abram has a few stipulations for your visit, which I'm going to communicate. Item one: you can only come if you've had your flu shot. Have you?"

"Yes! I had it. I had it in November. Ha!" I did a little triumphant fist pump and accidentally hit my knuckles against the overhead reading light. I stifled an *ow*, also earning an irritated side-eye from the woman next to me in the center seat. Doing my best to ignore her glare, I cleared my throat and asked, "What else?"

"Item two: you will sleep while you are here whenever you are tired, and you will not spend all your time taking care of him."

"That sounds like two things, but sure. I'm fine with item two." I would definitely shower when we arrived.

"Item three: you will allow him to pay for a car to pick you up, your hotel room, and anything else you need while you're here."

"That seems gratuitous." I crossed my arms. We hadn't talked much about the money thing, but I felt like it was a conversation looming on the horizon. He had *a lot* more than me, and that was fine. But I wasn't penniless, I had pride, and I liked paying my own way. I liked knowing I'd earned what was mine, and that included experiences.

"He said you would have a problem with this one, so he said it was nonnegotiable."

"Define nonnegotiable? If he covers this visit, can I cover the car, hotel, and meals of our next rendezvous?"

"Hold on, let me ask. She wants to know—" Marie must've covered the phone because I didn't hear the remainder of her question. Less than a minute later, she was back. "He agrees. Also, nice use of the word rendezvous. I approve."

"Thank you." Her praise flustered me a little and I had to give myself a slight shake to refocus.

"Next item: you are not to sleep at the hospital. When you sleep, you have to sleep in the hotel. Basically, he wants you to get good sleep."

I made a sound of displeasure, but eventually said, "Fine. Anything else? Any other terms?"

"Nope. That's it. I'll be in touch with the details for the flight. Let me call my friend and get that ball rolling. See you soon."

"See you soon. Bye."

The call clicked off. I lowered my phone, releasing an expansive sigh. It did nothing to ease the knots in my chest and throat. I wanted to help. I wanted to help but was stuck on the other side of the USA, waiting to deplane. I was helpless.

I thought back over my last few conversations with Abram, searching for some clue, something I could do to help from afar. Perhaps picking up something from the gift shop? Personally, I liked snow globes. I wondered how he felt about the Statue of Liberty.

"Is your hand okay?"

Glancing at the woman next to me, the one who'd just given me the side-eye, I asked, "Pardon?"

"Your hand. You hit it on the reading light."

"Oh. Yeah. It's fine. I just, uh, got excited about something."

She gave me a small smile. "I once broke two fingers in my right hand closing them in a car door. It was awful, being one handed for weeks. But you know what? It made me realize how many selfies I took, because I just can't take them with my left hand." She laughed, shaking her head at herself.

Grinning, I found myself curious. "How many selfies did you take?"

"Oh, like, a few every day. But my boyfriend at the time—husband now—was always asking for them, so I think it just became a habit."

Ah!

AH HA!

Of course!

"Thank you," I said, already unlocking my phone and switching the camera around to face me. "You just gave me an exceedingly excellent and exploitable idea."

* * *

Abram was asleep when his parents and I arrived at the hospital.

Wait. Let me back up for a second, because I'm sure you're wondering. Seeing Mr. and Mrs. Harris for the first time in over two years was significantly less awkward than I'd feared it would be.

Pamela stepped onto the jet, saw me, walked over, and gave me a hug. "I'm so glad you're coming, but I worry for you, Mona. Abram says you're not sleeping enough."

Perplexed by her (shouldn't she be mad at me for lying to her about who I was years ago?), her words (like we knew each other extremely well and often discussed such things), and my body's reaction to both (which was to immediately return her embrace without nary a flinch), the profuse apology I'd planned stuck in my throat.

What is happening? What has just happened?

Stepping back, she held my shoulders and regarded me. "I also want to tell you how proud we were when we saw you on TV over the summer, giving those corrupt Washington jerks—excuse my French—a piece of your mind. But, honey, you look tired, and I don't mean that to be insulting, I mean that because I'm concerned. Here—" she let me go and reached into her bag "I brought muffins. This one is lemon poppyseed. Or, if you like, you can have blueberry."

"I like the blueberry," Mr. Harris said, standing a little bit behind his wife, giving me a matter-of-fact look. "She uses the fresh ones."

"It's because this one—" she pointed her thumb at Mr. Harris and chuckled merrily "—built me that greenhouse in the back. I can get blueberries in the winter. Isn't that something? Oh, I also brought you a de-stress mix of jojoba oil, lavender, and rose." Looping her arm through mine, she steered me toward the back of the plane and to a built-in couch. "They just added this couch last year, it's much nicer than sitting in the other seats."

She took a breath, so I took my chance.

"Mr. Harris, Mrs. Harris, I wanted to apologize for lying to your family when I attended your birthday party several years ago. I have no excuse, and I—"

"Oh, don't worry about that. You do have an excuse, a good one too, and Abram explained everything. It's like roses. You're still you. No matter what we call you, you're still just as sweet. Now, I've been doing some steam distillation, and you know it takes thousands of roses to make just a bit of essential oil, but I got so many blooms the last two years, I managed a few drops."

And so it went.

Slightly shell-shocked, I spoke of essential oil extraction techniques with Pamela—as well as various other topics of interest to us both—while Mr. Harris ate his blueberry muffin and read the newspaper. All the while I fretted.

Their forgiveness felt too easy. Who forgives this easily? No one I knew. Definitely not the world. People don't just *forgive* anymore. Forgiveness, like everything else, needed to be earned, hard fought, won after proving oneself with huge, unwavering acts of self-punishment and atonement.

But for now, so as not to make the flight awkward, I decided to—as Gabby would say—*just go with it*.

Oh! Also, Pamela and I took a candid selfie and sent it to Abram just before takeoff. Sending Abram that photo yesterday had been a big deal for me, not because the picture was risqué, but that was definitely part of it. It was a big deal because I truly wanted to send my boyfriend a risqué photo. And so I did.

As I deplaned my Frankfurt to New York flight, I'd sent a text message of warning to Marie via Abram's cellphone, informing her that she should expect several candid selfies over the next few hours. It was the only action of potential value my brain could conjure to reach beyond geography and maybe, possibly help Abram.

Perhaps it would cheer him up?

I hoped so.

Anyway. Back to the hospital and a sleeping Abram.

His room was in the VIP wing—a very real thing in LA—and Marie had come out to gather us from security. We'd arrived late evening, therefore the paparazzi were minimal, really just one guy with a big lens, taking shots of us while wearing a perplexed expression.

Marie had also greeted me warmly, with a big hug, a sweet smile, and no mention of my prior offenses. For the record, she was just as lovely as she'd been years prior. A very weird voice in my head mentioned that it would be pretty cool if Abram and I got married, partially because Marie would then be my sister-in-law and Pamela would be my mother-in-law.

Not that I'm advocating marriage based on the groom's family. I'm just sayin'. You know. Throwing the facts out there, he had a stellar family.

IT WAS A VARIABLE! OKAY?

Moving on.

Upon entering his room, I held back with Marie, allowing Pamela and Mr. Harris the first approach, though my heart ached to see him in the hospital bed. It was too small for his big frame, and he looked pale. He never looked pale, so this was definitely distressing.

Neither of his parents woke him, they just took a peek and hovered for several minutes. Pamela made a sad sound. Mr. Harris put an arm around his wife's shoulders and whispered something in her ear. She nodded. Then Mr. Harris sniffled, and she bent her head toward his, giving him a kiss on the cheek.

It was so damn sweet. My eyes were misty. *They really love him.*

"Of course they do," Marie whispered, turning to look at me like I was strange.

"Yes. Right. Of course." *Yikes.* I must've spoken my thoughts aloud.

She continued her survey of me for a few seconds, then said, "How are you doing with all this?"

"Me?" I frowned at the obvious worry for me in her voice. "Forget about me, how are you doing? You must be exhausted."

Marie gave me a closed mouth smile, her eyebrows high on her forehead. "I'm not the one who spent the last twenty-four hours traveling. Mona, really, how are you? Are you hungry?"

I shook my head, her genuine concern disconcerting. "Marie, I—" I snapped my mouth shut, shaking my head harder, turning to face her fully, and whispering, "Why is your family being so wonderful to me? I lied to you, all of you. I want to earn your forgiveness, prove to you that I can be trusted, prove myself. I need to be the one—"

"Oh my goodness, stop." Once again, Marie was looking at me like I was strange, a little bubble of quiet laughter escaping her lips. "Abram said you were like this. But, honey, we don't want you to prove anything."

I eyed her suspiciously. "Then what do you want?"

She shrugged, her gaze flickering over my face. "I don't know. Kindness, I guess. Just be kind."

Swallowing around some unidentified thickness, I nodded. "Okay. I can do that."

"Good." Marie's smile grew, as did the warmth in her eyes. She slipped her arm around my back and held me next to her, hip to hip, turning us to face Abram again. "He wanted me to wake him up when you arrived."

I worked to keep my chin from wobbling, my mind in disarray. "No, no. Don't do that. He needs rest."

"That's what I decided too. I thought, instead, you could write him a note? Something for next to his bed? And then come back in the morning before he's discharged."

"Or, I could stay here."

Marie squinted at me. "You promised not to sleep at the hospital."

The potential for a debate helped clear my chaotic mind and rein in my emotions. "Correct. But I've been on Geneva time, so it's morning there. Plus, someone should stay. Plus, you've been here all day. Plus, your parents must be exhausted. Plus—"

"Okay, okay. You had me at Geneva time." Marie released me and covered her mouth to yawn. "You stay, we'll go, and we'll be back early in the morning." She stepped closer and embraced me again, giving me a full body hug, like she meant it. "Thank you for coming. He's been in a much better mood, been a *much* better patient, since you called from New York."

"No problem. I'm just—" I couldn't continue, choking back some emotion I couldn't identify. It was the strangest thing.

Obviously, I was worried for Abram. I hated that he was so sick, in pain, frustrated and disappointed. But I was also bizarrely happy, to be here, with this loving family who supported each other, who forgave so easily. It made me feel like, during this anxious time of crisis, everything was going to work out just fine.

Abram was an essential part of something real, meaningful, stable, safe. Which meant, by extension, so was I.

Taking a deep breath, I finished roughly, "I'm happy, so happy, to be here."

I felt Marie's cheek smile against mine and she held me tighter. "We're happy, so happy, that you're here too."

[9]

THE QUANTIZATION OF ENERGY

Mona

Not going to lie, I spent a considerable portion of the night staring at him, unable to fully comprehend that, after so much time spent waiting and wishing and longing, we were together. But let the record show, I didn't smell him, though the temptation was a strong force.

I also took a shower, changed into fresh clothes, and got a good amount of work done, chasing a random hunch that ended up leading to a different hunch that ultimately yielded an extremely promising preliminary result. I ended up sending my calculations to Poe, asking him to double-check my math and assumptions. This was not unusual for us—sending notes, data, and calculations back and forth for comment—and he was the only one I'd trust with inception work like this.

After sending the email, I stretched my arms over my head, giving into a yawn, and glanced up to find Abram's eyes open and watching me. My body jolted, him being awake startled me. His mouth hitched higher on the left side.

"Hey, brown eyes," he said, sounding just as sick as the day prior. But his voice was soft, sleepy, and full of affection. Part of me melted, part of me tensed.

"Do you need anything?" I set my computer aside, closing it, standing, and stepped next to his bed. My hand sought his. Our fingers entwined. My other hand gently sifted through his hair, testing his forehead. "What can I do? Are you uncomfortable?"

He shook his head in a subtle movement, his gaze lowering to my lips. "I'm great."

I grinned. "You have the flu, you're not great."

"I'm so great."

That made me laugh, and I indulged myself by caressing his cheek, his stubbly jaw, trying not to frown when I noticed the slight green tinge to his skin, how his eyes lacked vibrancy. He turned his head toward my touch, his lips brushing against my knuckles.

"Thank you for coming," he whispered against my fingers.

"I'm not sure I had a choice," I admitted thoughtfully to his profile. "I think I might've gone crazy if I didn't see you for myself, make sure you're okay. Are you sure I can't get you anything? Some water?"

"Just you." He lifted his hand to mine and opened my fingers. He then pressed his cheek against my palm, closing his eyes. "Just you."

We stayed like that for a moment, holding still, *being* together. He took a deep breath and I heard the rattling in his chest, the crackle and wheeze as he exhaled. He winced, and then so did I.

Yes, I knew, reasonably, rationally, that thousands of people had the flu every year. It was rarely fatal. Most recovered with no lasting effects. And yet, Abram was in pain, now, in this moment. I wanted to alleviate it with a desperation I rarely felt. Emotion was the enemy of physicists—especially theoretical physicists, who spent more time chasing shadows than answers—and desperation had no place in my life.

But I felt desperate now, desperate to *do something*.

Therefore, hoping to distract him from whatever was making him wince, I asked, "How long have you been up?"

"Not long." He shook his head lightly, opening his eyes and giving them back to me. "You're very sexy when you're concentrating."

"Oh, well, thank you." I wagged my eyebrows. "Is it the cargo pants? Or the baggy T-shirt that caught your eye? Or perhaps the glasses?" I only wore glasses to read.

His lips twitched, like it took too much effort to smile again. "Hey, by the way. Thank you for the photo, but—"

"You're welcome. I hope you liked it."

"I do. But, uh, Mona. I don't want you to feel pressured to send me that kind of stuff. I've been thinking. I'm going to delete it, and you should too. I honestly just wanted to see your smile, I wanted—" he had to stop himself, covering his mouth as he coughed.

Gah. It sounded painful and it made me anxious for him. I passed him a cup of water. He took a sip. I placed it back on the adjustable tray table.

Needing to touch him, I placed my hand on his forearm. "Okay, first. Please don't delete it. I honestly wanted to send it."

His eyes narrowed slightly, the subtle curve of his lips telling me he didn't believe me.

"It's true. When you called me powerful, it struck a nerve. You were right. But you were also wrong."

Abram's eyebrows lowered over his eyes, making him look like that news eagle from The Muppets.

I didn't want him to waste his energy arguing with me about this, so I rushed to add, "I'm not powerful, not like I want to be. Think about it, how powerful can I possibly be if I'm constantly acquiescing to the very people who want to keep me powerless?"

His brow cleared, his eyes were hazy with fever, but I saw I'd said something that resonated.

"Therefore, I sent the photo. I could've sent you one of me smiling, just my face, but I didn't. I wanted to send you *that* one. And so I did." The picture made me feel sexy, and it reminded me of that moment between us in the pool, in Chicago, after he'd forfeited the race. The way he'd looked at me, I loved it. Just thinking about his eyes at that moment made my heart race. It was a memory I cherished.

"But." He tried to clear his throat, wincing slightly. "But if it ever gets out there—"

"I know the risks." I gave him a resigned smile. "I'm an adult. I'm aware of the possible damage it might do to my credibility, should the photo ever be shared. But if our phones are hacked and it goes public, I'm prepared to weather the storm. In fact, I've begun to think of it as an opportunity."

"Opportunity?"

"Yes. Someone has to be the woman who stands up and proudly says, 'Yes. I send my rock star boyfriend sexy photos of me. Why is that relevant to my work?'"

He made a weak sound that almost resembled a laugh. "Mona, if you change your mind—"

"I won't." I knew myself. For better or worse, when I committed to an idea or a cause, I was married to it in the old testament biblical sense.

Abram stared at me quietly, as though searching for some sign of uncertainty or regret. "Tell me something."

"What would you like to know?"

"What were you doing over there? What are you working on?"

Obviously, he was trying to change the subject. Which made me wonder whether he believed me about wanting to send the photo.

But since he was sick, I let the issue drop. "I was just sending off some preliminary work to a colleague of mine. Poe is a planetary astrophysicist, and my thesis is moving more in the theoretical physics direction and less planetary. Even so, Poe should be able to give it a glance and help me focus my energy in the right direction or tell me who I can trust to take a look."

"Good," Abram croaked, giving me another miniscule smile, his gaze moving over me with a sluggish, foggy quality betraying how awful he felt. "You seem energized."

"I think I made some good headway last night. It's like, so much of what I do is wandering around in a pitch-black room of indeterminate size, not knowing if I'm going in circles or a straight line or approaching a cliff."

"Searching the ocean for your white whale."

"That's right. I only have so much time, you know? I realize time is a faulty construct, which some argue doesn't even exist, but yet we've made it central to everything. I postulated at one point that time was not a single thing—a thread, if you will—but multiple threads, infinite threads *and yet* also beads, and feathers, etc., all woven together into a thick tapestry. Pulling one thread wouldn't change the overall structure of the tapestry as we know it, but it would change the reality for the feathers and beads that rely on that thread. Yes, it might allow us to bend space, but lose reality in the process. Generally, we see time as the past, present, and future, but what if it's both more and less?"

"How can something be both more and less?"

"Everything is both more and less. Everything is balance. My chromosomal arrangement is more XX, less XY. You are more musician, less airplane pilot."

His lips curved weakly, but a spark lit behind his eye. "I could listen to you talk about this forever."

"Then you're the only one." I grinned wryly. Seeing the light in his gaze did something wonderful to my stomach, making me feel both full and warm.

"I doubt that." Abram brought my hand to his lap, cradling it in both of his.

Considering, I sat on the scant sliver at the edge of his bed and amended, "Okay, yes. I do have a few colleagues who also enjoy theorizing with me."

"You mean philosophizing with you." He cleared his throat, his head seeming to sink deeper into his pillow.

"Of course, yes. Theoretical physics is married to philosophy. The nature of things, of reality. Perception."

"And art is the product of how humans interpret their reality."

That made me smile. "Look at you, smarty-pants. So, what you're saying is, physics and philosophy are married, and their child is art?"

"Or, the marriage of physics and philosophy *is* art."

I loved that. My smile deepened, my attention lowering to where he held my hand. He'd moved it to his chest, pressing my palm against his heart.

"Being with you . . ." he began, drawing my eyes back to his face. His were dazed, unfocused, like he was looking within and without.

"Being with me?" I prompted after almost a minute, curious, a bubble of something reluctantly hopeful expanding in my chest. So of course, a joke slipped out. "Is as the prophesy foretold?"

Abram's gaze sharpened on mine. He smiled, a real smile. His left dimple making its first appearance, stealing my breath before his words could.

"It's living artistry, Mona." Abram's gaze turned cherishing, earnest. "Being with you is like living in a song."

* * *

As the sun came up, I read the latest Lisa Kleypas novel to Abram. I'd already read it, but he hadn't, and I didn't mind at all. Eventually, he drifted back to sleep. A nurse came in to unobtrusively check his vitals. A doctor stopped by and asked if I was family. I explained that his sister and parents would be arriving soon. The nurse then returned with a food tray—for me—and then left again, informing me that I should call for his breakfast when he awoke.

Peeking at the food on the tray, I was surprised—but not really—to discover the fancy nature of my meal. Two poached eggs on avocado toast, a kale and rocket salad, a berry compote, freshly made yogurt, and cinnamon granola. The coffee came in a French press and the orange juice was pulpy, freshly squeezed.

Ah, Los Angeles VIP treatment. It was truly another world.

Marie and Abram's parents arrived just as I finished breakfast and was setting the tray outside the room. To my surprise, Leo was with them. My brother didn't seem at all surprised to see me. Confused, but not surprised.

We didn't hug. He made no move to do so and neither did I, a fact that hadn't struck me as strange in Aspen or at any point in the past prior to right this minute. But now, after being embraced by the Harris family, and seeing how they greeted each other, how genuinely they seemed to look forward to and enjoy each other's presence, I felt the lack of greeting between my own brother and me.

Almost immediately—as soon as we exchanged our tepid, polite hellos, and the Harris family was no longer within ear shot—he steered me a little further down the hall, away from Abram's room, and pulled out his phone.

"I thought you should know, you were photographed last night, coming in with Abram's parents. But they assumed you were Lisa. Let me show you the pictures."

Studying my brother's profile as he stared at the phone, and despite the unresolved tension between us since our conversation in Aspen, I had the sudden urge to hug him. Therefore, I did.

I gently pushed his phone out of the way, slipped my arms around his torso, and tried to mimic Marie's hug from last night. I wanted to hug Leo like I meant it. He didn't respond at first, and his body tensed like this might be an assault rather than an embrace. But as I continued to hold on, my big brother's arms encircled me, held me with an equivalent tightness ratio, and he pressed a kiss to my temple.

"Hey," he said against my hair. "Are you okay?"

"Yes." I tried to relax, turning my head against his shoulder and resting it there. "How are you?"

"I'm good." The tension left him by degrees until his big arms held me comfortably. "What's going on, Mona? Do you want to talk?"

"We should hug, I think. When we see each other, and just sometimes for no reason, because I love you, Leo. And I think I haven't been so great at knowing how to show you in a way that you understand."

I felt his cheek curve with a small smile. "I'm sorry."

"For what?"

"For being a dick."

Leaning my head back, I expected to find him smiling—since his voice held a smile—but he wasn't. He looked remorseful, serious.

"In Aspen?"

"Yeah. In Aspen. But also, I guess, for a long time. Lisa and I, we —uh—talked last week." He readjusted his hands at my back, I felt him lock them more completely together, and his eyes grew dark, heated with anger. "And she told me about what happened to you at school."

Oh.

Oh God.

Lisa told Leo?

Yes. Of course she did. She's worried about you.

I forgave my sister immediately, but wished she'd warned me. I wasn't prepared to discuss this with my brother.

Therefore, I tried to say, *Nothing happened,* but the words wouldn't form. I tried to draw a complete breath but couldn't. I stared at Leo, helpless to the rising anxiety. However, when it came, when the cold sweat broke out over my skin and panic reached eyeball level, it rose no further.

"I haven't been a good brother to you," he continued, sounding angry, solemn. "I've been pretty fucking blind about you, not taking the time to think about what you might need. I've replaced you, and Mom and Dad, and Lisa to an extent, with friendships, building my family elsewhere. Because Mona, I need family." Leo lifted a hand to my head and gently returned my cheek to his shoulder.

"I need people. I need a network, a community. I thought maybe you didn't. I thought you weren't built that way. But what I think now is that it doesn't fucking matter how you're built. You're my *sister.*" His voice now a harsh whisper, I could feel the restlessness in his body, the frustration. "You should've come to me, you should've told me when it happened. But that means I should've been—before that, way before that—someone you trusted. Someone you never doubted would help. Someone who put you above his friends. I should've been checking on you, letting you know I was interested, making it clear you mattered. That's all on me."

The panic slowly receded, with each breath I exhaled bits and pieces of the memory, of the strangling fear, until it simmered in my stomach instead of suffocating my lungs.

And my brother continued to hold me, petting my hair and making a suspiciously watery clearing-of-the-throat sound that—for some reason—made me smile.

"Mona baby," he said suddenly, breaking the moment, and I couldn't stop my laugh, because that's what he used to call me when we were little. "You need to see someone, to help you work through this."

Now I tensed. A second later, I removed myself from his grip. He let me go, but I could feel his eyes on me as I paced away.

"Uh, I don't think that's necessary." The last thing I wanted to do was talk about it. To anyone.

"Mona, I'm not letting this go. I have a list of good psychologists who you can do phone sessions with from Geneva."

I glanced at him. He'd withdrawn a piece of paper from his jacket pocket. Abruptly, the expansive hallway felt too small.

"I don't think I need—"

"Yes. You do. You're doing this." He reached for my hand and placed the paper in my palm. I didn't flinch. "I already made you an appointment with the first person on the list."

"But how will I pay for it?" I asked, using the easiest, most obvious excuse, and crumpling the list. "Insurance only covers so much. I can't afford—"

"You can." Leo reclaimed my hand and, using both of his, straightened the paper out. "You have your monthly allowance account—from Mom and Dad—and the money is all in your name. I bet it's just sitting there. I bet you've never touched it."

I scowled, because he was right. In addition to the travel account, our parents had set up accounts for each of us when we hit eighteen, depositing the maximum tax-free gift amount yearly as a fun money fund. It was one of their ways of demonstrating how much they supported us, in addition to all the other bank accounts.

Because *money* was how they supported us. Money. Just money.

"It must have over a hundred thousand dollars in it by now. Use that."

"I don't want their money," I whispered between clenched teeth, not knowing I was going to hurl the words at my brother until they were already out. The fervor in my whisper surprised both of us. I swallowed, trying to figure out why my heart was beating so fast, and why my mouth tasted like persimmons.

Meanwhile, Leo's eyes had widened, concern replacing the self-recrimination from moments prior. "Mona—"

"No. No. I don't want it. I don't want money from them." I stuffed the list of psychologists in my pocket, next to the poem Abram had written me in Aspen, mostly to get it out of my sight.

My brother's gaze softened, and he stepped closer, commiseration etched into his features. "I get it, okay? I mean, I really do. It feels like a payoff, right? Like, to them, the money replaces all the things they didn't give us, or couldn't."

Staring at him, I admitted nothing, working to tuck away these untidy emotions.

Abram inspired emotions? Yes. I was ready for those, I wanted them all, even the untidy ones.

My parents? No. I didn't want any of the untidy emotions or second-guessing they inspired. I loved them. They did their best. I understood that. No one was perfect. I wasn't perfect. They had responsibilities beyond their children. I understood that too. See? Look how reasonable I was. See how tidy and rational?

And yet, just the thought of taking money from "Mona's fun fund" made me want to throw a chair through a window just to hear the glass break.

Leo frowned, clearly frustrated. "Then let me pay for it."

"Leo, I don't need—"

"You do." He advanced, stopping abruptly when he seemed to realize that he'd backed me up until I was against the wall. Taking two steps away, he cursed under his breath. the line of his jaw was stern, but his gaze appeared apologetic. "You do. I wish this never happened to you. I wish it didn't take hearing about it to wake me up to how I've been a shitty brother. So, yeah, I'm going to hound you about this until you do it. And Lisa will, and Gabby too. Good luck avoiding this. Good luck dodging Gabby. You know she'll fly out to Geneva, and so will I. We're not letting this go. And if you don't do it, I'll tell Abram. I know him a lot better than you do, and he'll—"

Unthinkingly, I covered Leo's mouth with my hand, rocks in my throat. "You wouldn't."

He turned his head slightly to the side, lifting an eyebrow as though to say, *You wanna bet?*

I gritted my teeth, because I was angry. So angry.

He gently encircled my wrist, pulling it from his mouth and holding it. "Your hands are shaking."

"Because I'm angry," I seethed.

"Why?"

"You're bullying me into this."

Leo's mouth curved into a sad smile. "I love you, Mona baby. So, yeah. Whatever it takes. Because that's what family does. Because that's what love looks like."

[10]

THE THEORY OF SPECIAL RELATIVITY

Abram

"What are you thinking about?"

I blinked, struggling to focus, looking for Marie and finding her leaning against the doorframe. "What was that?"

Marie's smile was soft. "I asked, what are you thinking about?"

My answering smile was flat. "Missed opportunities."

She chuckled, walking further into the hotel bedroom and taking the armchair next to the bed. "So, Mona?"

I grinned and glanced at my hands. "Yeah."

Mona had left eight days ago, keeping her promise to stay just twenty-four hours. Mona called every day since to check in, even if it was just for five minutes while she hid in a bathroom, stealing the time from her projects and work.

"You look better. Do you feel up to talking?"

"I do feel better. Yeah, sure, I could talk." My label cancelled the rest of my commitments for the week—interviews, appearances—so I could recover, and my fever finally broke last night. I still had a little cough. My throat wasn't bothering me much, thanks to Melena and her tea.

"So, let's talk. Abram."

"Marie."

"You look better, but you also look frustrated."

Inhaling deeply, because I finally could without coughing, I nodded. "I guess I am."

I was better, but I was unsettled. Restless. Dissatisfied. I knew Mona couldn't and shouldn't stay. But that didn't stop me from wishing things were different.

"What is this?" Marie pointed at my face, waving her index finger around. "Is this melancholy? Or ennui? Please tell me it's not ennui. Ennui is for dissolute dukes, not dissolute rock stars."

That made me smirk. "Maybe it's melancholy. Maybe it's *Maybelline.*"

She laughed, which had been my goal, and rested her elbow on the arm of the chair, tucking her hand beneath her chin. "I'm glad you told me the whole story—with you and Mona—when you got back from Aspen last month. I was pretty confused over the summer, after seeing her on C-SPAN and CNN, thinking I was going nuts."

"Yeah." *I know how you feel.* "Thanks for your help trying to track down her number when Leo wouldn't give it to me. I appreciate your secrecy about everything, crazy as it is." I hadn't told her the *whole* story. Just enough to make sense of my desperate request.

"It is crazy," my sister agreed readily. "Thanks for trusting me with it, but how you and Mona met might be the craziest love story I've ever heard. And you know how wacky my friends are."

We shared a look and I grinned, thinking about her wacky friends.

"Anyway, sorry I couldn't help you uncover the number. Quinn and Alex were very impressed with Exotica and DJ Tang's security measures. They went to great lengths to hide their children's contact information. If we'd had more time, Alex might've been able to narrow down some potential options."

"But it makes sense, right?" I readjusted the pillow behind me. "They're just trying to keep their kids safe."

Marie made a face. "Eh, I don't think that's it. From what I know of Exotica and DJ Tang, I think it's more that they want to be able to text and call their kids without fearing their own privacy will be violated. They're extremely fastidious about public image. Speaking of which." She gave me a pointed look.

"What?"

"You should let Alex do the same for you. The last thing you need is your phone getting hacked."

Oh shit.

Staring at my sister, I was gripped with a sudden suspicion. "You looked at my photos."

Immediately, she shook her head. "I did not look through your photos. If you recall, I texted Mona from your phone that morning in the hospital, asking her to call me at your number. You gave me the phone, you unlocked it, you asked me to send the message. And that means the last photo she sent to you before I texted her—the one of her looking stellar in a bikini—was already in the chat window when you gave it to me."

Sometimes I forgot how great of a reporter my sister was. She had the most detailed memory of anyone I knew.

I shook my head, pushing my fingers through my hair. "Fuck."

"Abram, it's no big deal. I'm your sister. My job is to keep your secrets and love you unconditionally, and your job is to do the same for me. I don't care what you and Mona send each other. You should see the stuff Matt and I send back and for—"

"STOP." I buried my face in my hands. "Please, stop. I do *not* want to know about you and Matt."

My sister chuckled. It sounded sinister.

I wasn't laughing, because now I was concerned. Photos of Mona with my parents, coming to visit me in the LA hospital had surfaced, but the photographer had mistakenly assumed she was Lisa. Since we hadn't been photographed together—because there'd been no opportunity—rumors of my involvement with Mona's twin sister had already faded.

My family knew about us. According to Mona, Leo knew, but I hadn't talked to him since our disagreement. Obviously, Lisa knew, and if you didn't count Tyler or Gabby, which I didn't, that was about it.

It's not that our relationship was a secret. It wasn't. We just weren't advertising it. Keeping things quiet, being private, especially when everything was so new and we saw each other so rarely, seemed to be an unspoken desire we had in common.

But if my phone was hacked, and the photos we'd been sending each other were leaked, it would make national news *for sure.*

Lifting my head, I frowned at Marie. "Okay, do you mind? Can you ask Alex to help?"

"I already did." She picked an invisible piece of lint off her jeans. "It's being taken care of as we speak. The invoice will come from Cypher Systems, just make sure it gets paid. He's very expensive."

"Thank you. Whatever it takes. I don't want any pictures of her out there. It would be, uh, not good."

Marie's eyebrows flickered up a half inch. "You mean, it would be terrible. For her. And her career."

"Yeah. Exactly." I scratched my beard, which was now thick and bushy. I should have thought of this. *Crap.*

"Are you two keeping things secret for a reason? I get the sense that no one here knows about your relationship."

My sister's tone, like she was choosing her words carefully, had me inspecting her. "It's not a secret, but I don't think the crew knows. They might suspect." I thought back to the argument Mona and I had in front of everyone in Aspen, and how we'd missed dinner the last two nights. "Honestly, I have no idea. Charlie and Ruthie were in Aspen with us, but I don't think either of them were paying much attention. And, I mean, from the outside looking in, it's not like we make much sense. Plus, according to Leo, Mona has this reputation with his friends of being completely disinterested in musicians."

"Do you think dating you will impact Mona's career?" Again, her tone seemed suspiciously careful.

"What do you mean? In what way?"

"I'm not certain, because I'm not a stunningly gorgeous and brilliant twenty-one-year-old PhD student in astrophysics, who is also the daughter of two hugely famous—but also slightly ridiculous—pillars of the global music community."

"Are you asking if, by dating me, she'll have even more difficulty being taken seriously?"

Marie's gaze moved up and to the left. "I don't know. It's not like she's inconspicuous, no matter who she dates. But I do know, just from watching famous couples trying to navigate the media, how one of you acts or behaves will definitely make an impact on how the other is perceived."

"I guess that makes sense." I shared a glance with my sister.

She'd given me a lot to think about, issues I might've already been aware of subconsciously, but hadn't consciously considered. If how I behaved, the choices I made, had consequences for Mona, well, then I was determined that my choices would be stellar from now on.

"Hey." I gave Marie a grateful smile. "Thank you for your help getting my phone secured."

"No problem." She smiled sweetly. But Marie was sweet. "What are older sisters for? Oh! And before I forget, I asked Mona to be a bridesmaid."

I flinched, my head rearing back, not sure I'd heard her correctly. "You—you what?"

Marie cupped her hands around her mouth and mock-shouted, "I asked Mona to be a bridesmaid."

I rolled my eyes. "I can hear just fine, Hufflepuff. I'm just surprised."

"Why? She's great."

"Yeah. But you barely know her."

"Well, you're in love with her, which means so am I." My sister shrugged, her blue eyes twinkling. "And, may I say, you have exceptional taste in women. She is a friggin' *delight*."

"She is, right?" Unable to stop my grin, I dropped my eyes to my hands again, thinking about her goodbye kiss before she left. Obviously, she couldn't kiss my mouth. So she'd kissed the tips of my fingers—all ten—and my forehead, cheeks, chin, nose, and temples.

"You know who she reminds me of?"

"Janie?" I guessed, only because Marie's friend Janie was also brilliant.

She tilted her head back and forth, her eyes narrowing as she considered. "Um, yes, her too. But I was actually going to say Matt."

"Matt?" Again, I reared back, but this time I frowned. "Don't get

111

me wrong, you love Matt, therefore so do I, but what about Mona reminds you of Matt?"

Matt Simmons was Marie's fiancé, a super good guy, and a nerd. Matt was great, really great, but he didn't make me want to write poetry until sunrise.

Marie chuckled. "Think about it, doofus. They're both in science, at the top of their field, in high demand. They both love to tell science jokes and puns, they both—"

"Wait a minute, wait a minute. When did you hear Mona tell a science joke?"

Marie gave me a smirk, it looked self-satisfied. "We talk."

My eyebrows jumped. "Who?"

"Me and Mona."

My eyebrows pulled low. "When?"

She glanced at her nails, saying loftily, "All the time."

I choked. Because—with the time difference and her schedule and my schedule—I could barely get Mona on the phone.

Marie laughed. "Okay, okay. Not all the time. But Mom, Mona, and me are in a three-way."

Wincing, horrified, I closed my eyes. "Please. Please never use the phrase *three-way* while referencing you or Mom ever, ever again. In fact, you're not allowed to use the phrase at all."

My sister laughed, good and loud, and a second later a pillow hit me in the face. "Get over yourself! A three-way text message conversation, you ass."

Now I was laughing, and I opened my eyes to locate the pillow she'd thrown, tucking it behind my back with the others. "Thank you. I needed another pillow." God, it felt good to laugh.

Mona makes you laugh.

My smile waned and I swallowed, breathing through the tight pain in my chest. *I miss her.*

"But back to what I was saying." She rested her cheek against her palm. "Mona and Matt, very similar."

"Other than being brilliant, into science and nerdy puns, I don't see the similarities."

"What about their parents?"

Lifting an eyebrow, I settled more completely against my pillows. "What about their parents?" I didn't know much about Matt's parents.

And, now that I considered things, other than what could be read in the newspaper, in magazines, etc. I didn't know much about Mona's parents—as parents—either. Leo didn't talk about them, but I always thought that was understandable. As Marie had said, they were hugely famous. I figured he wanted to protect them, like I would want to do with my parents.

"They both grew up with neglectful parents," Marie said, as though this was common knowledge.

Crossing my arms, I shook my head. "What are you talking about?"

Now Marie lifted an eyebrow. "Matt was raised by a series of nannies, housekeepers, and cooks. So was Mona."

"Just because a family has a nanny doesn't mean the kids aren't raised by their parents."

"Oh, I definitely agree! Just like, if a kid goes to daycare, it doesn't mean the parents don't raise the child. But in their cases— Matt and Mona—they were. They were neglected."

"How do you know this? I mean, about Mona. How do you know this about Mona?"

Marie seemed confused. "Uh, it's obvious."

Staring at my sister, I struggled to complete a thought, my brain was going in too many directions.

Taking pity on me, she leaned forward. "Look, tell me if any of this sounds familiar, okay? And this probably applies to Leo too. Mona feels like she needs to prove herself to people in order for them to be her friend or love her. True? You know how Leo is always doing people favors? Worrying about the status of his friendships? That's what it's about."

I scowled, but I didn't know why I scowled.

Marie continued, "But back to Mona. She doesn't open up easily, at all, and trust is super hard for her. In fact, she can count the number of people she trusts on one hand. Maybe three fingers. But once she trusts, she *trusts*. She bends over backward to make those people happy, worries she'll lose them if she does something wrong. So, she tries to put people in boxes, assigns labels to relationships, so she can lower her expectations, so she's never hurt."

My body ached. It had nothing to do with recovering from the flu. I had to clear my throat before I could speak. "That's, uh, that's pretty accurate."

My sister gave me a sympathetic smile. "That's Matt."

"So, what do you do?"

"What do you mean?"

"How do you, you know, make sure he's happy?"

She frowned, her mouth forming a subtle sneer. "Uh, I don't. Making sure Matt is happy is not my job. It's his job, and only if he wants to be happy."

I blew out a breath, frustrated. "How do you keep him from worrying?"

Marie shrugged again. "I can't. If he wants to worry, that's on him."

"Marie," I growled, gritting my teeth. "Come on. You know what I mean."

"Actually, I don't. It almost sounds like you think you're responsible for Mona's feelings. That's one hundred percent wrong. You're only responsible for your own feelings, just like she's only responsible for hers. If she wants to worry, that's her decision."

"But what can I do to help her worry less?"

"You're not hearing me, Abram. You do nothing. You love her—which you're going to do anyway—and that's it."

I didn't like that answer, and my sister must've realized it, because she chuckled, shaking her head as she stood and walked to the door. "The horse is going to do what it wants. You can't make the horse drink the water, even if it needs the water, even if it's miserable without it." She turned and walked backward out of the room. "Once you figure that out, and if you need to commiserate with someone about stupid, brilliant thirsty horses, give me a call."

* * *

Mona picked up on the first ring. "Abram! How are you? How was the concert? How many encores? You didn't push yourself, did you? Please be careful not to push yourself. Did you get the package I sent?"

A slow grin spread over my features and I fell back on the bed, covering my eyes with my forearm. "God, it's so good to hear your voice."

One beat of silence, then, "Uh, I think you called the wrong number. This is Mona, not God. Related, do you have His number? If so, please ask Him to reconcile quantum gravity with the theory of relativity. I'll wait."

I laughed. "You are a nut."

"As long as it's a do-*nut*, I'm fine with that. Hey, did you know, donut-shaped planets are theoretically possible? Great. Now I want a donut." Her voice and her cute facts relaxed my muscles and nerves and bones. My smile deepened.

This was perfection, almost. *Almost* exactly what I needed. Her being here or me being there was actual perfection, but this was pretty darn close. And yet, even as I relaxed, the shadowy thought, *I miss her,* made drawing a full breath impossible.

"What time is it there?" she asked.

I thought about looking at the clock on the side table, or at the screen of my phone, but laziness had me shaking my head. "I don't know. Almost two?"

"Yeesh. You sound so tired." In a quieter voice she added, "Please take care of yourself. Don't get sick again."

"I won't, I promise."

"You can't promise that. Germs have a mind of their own. And if it's a virus, well, let's just say it has a hive mind of their own." She chuckled at her joke and so did I.

"How about, I'll do my best. I can't wait to see you." I'd promised myself I wasn't going to say it until later in the conversation.

"I can't wait either! London in March. Have you ever been to London?"

"No. Have you?"

"Oh yes. My parents have a house there. We would go around Christmastime, if we went. The cook made yule logs, which were my favorite."

I frowned, removing my forearm from my eyes to rub at my sternum. *Our cook.* I'd wanted to ask Mona about her family, her upbringing, since Marie had raised the topic two weeks ago, but I didn't know how to start. Our phone conversations hadn't been exactly satisfying recently. One of us was either extremely tired or in a rush.

Before I could make up my mind whether or not to ask her about her family, she said, "So, speaking of London, I actually have a question about something related to the trip."

"Uh, okay. Shoot." After she asked her question, I decided I would ask how her conversation with Leo had gone at the hospital in LA. We hadn't discussed it yet, and it would be a good segue into asking about her parents.

"Great. So. About sex."

My eyes flew open.

"Tell me what you like."

I stared at the white ceiling of the hotel bedroom, thoughts and concerns and planned questions fleeing my mind as all blood rushed south. "You mean, phone sex?"

Were we doing this? Now? We still hadn't done it yet. I was tired, but I'd get untired real fast if phone sex was on the table.

"No, no, no. I mean sex-sex. Tell me what you like so that, when we see each other, I'll be able to do precisely what you like. Here, you can't see me, but I have a notebook for taking notes, to make sure I get it all down."

Most of my blood had abandoned my brain for my pants, so I think I can be forgiven for the slowness of my response. "You want to interview me and take notes? About what I like during sex?"

"Exactly. And then I'll tell you my preferences the next time we talk, because you sound really tired now and probably don't have pen and paper ready."

What the hell?

I made a face, speaking without thinking, "That's cheating."

"Cheating?"

"Yes, cheating." I sat up, mildly irritated. "No. I'm not telling you what I like. I want you to figure it out."

She made a noise, it sounded indignant. "But if you don't tell me what you like, then I might do something you don't like as much, and the sex will be mediocre."

"Yeah, I doubt it. I'm pretty sure I'll love it all." I bit my bottom lip, thinking about her face when we were in Chicago as she came, the feel of her silky heat on my fingers.

Now I was awake.

"Abram. I'm serious."

"So am I."

Another sound of indignation. "I need some direction. I want this to be good for you."

"Oh, I have no doubts it will be. But I'm not giving you instructions to follow. I'm not a recipe."

She laughed, it sounded surprised. "Okay. That was funny. But, look, like I said, I'll tell you what I like, and—"

"No. No way. Don't you dare. Come on, Mona. Give us a chance to be good at this. I don't want you to tell me."

"But—"

"That's the same as telling me what you got me for my birthday before I get a chance to open my presents."

"No, it's not. It's being communicative," she said through renewed laughter.

"Nope. You are *not allowed* to tell me a thing. I don't want short-cuts. I want to discover you. Giving me a grocery list takes all the fun out of it."

"It absolutely does not." She huffed, but her voice held a smile.

"No, Mona. I'm not a menu. You don't get to order what you want." Jeez. All these food references. *I wonder if room service is still open.*

"That's not—"

"It is. It absolutely is."

Mona made a strangled sound. "How can you be so laissez-faire about this? If we tell each other what we like now, and how we like it, we can skip over all the awkwardness and just get straight to the great parts. It would be very efficient!"

I bit back a laugh because she reminded me of Mary Poppins when she said, *very efficient!* Like efficiency was superior to seduction.

"Have things been awkward?" I asked. "You don't like what we've done so far?"

"You know what I mean." Her voice was quieter.

"I don't, honestly. And if we skip over all the awkwardness, we'll never discover anything new—about you, about me—and the discovery *is* the fun. Yes, maybe we'll have some bad sex, but nothing —*nothing*—is ever perfect, and that should be okay. I don't want you to be perfect, to get things right all the time. How boring would that be?"

She didn't respond, but I could almost hear her thinking, debating with herself.

So I added, "Think of it this way, if I only did what you *think* you like, then you'd never be pushed out of your comfort zone."

"Why do I need to be pushed out my comfort zone?"

"Because it's exciting."

She grunted. "It sounds unnerving."

"It might be. But it might blow your mind. Give us a chance to find out. Give us a chance to win big, and also fail spectacularly. And if we fail, know and trust that it's no big deal. We can always try again, and again. And again."

Mona was quiet for a moment, and when she spoke next her voice was more serious. "You know what? Fine. Okay. I see your point and it's valid. The idea of trying new things with each other, discovering each other sounds really, *really* good. But, two things."

"Okay."

"You should know, I have an IUD to prevent pregnancy, but I've never had sex without a condom. Even so, I've been tested for STDs and I'm negative, for all of them. How about you?"

Her candor, honestly, turned me on. I loved this about her, how direct she was about things that mattered. *So fucking sexy.*

But being turned on and tired meant I had to really concentrate on what I wanted to say. "Uh, so me: I've had sex without a condom, once, and regretted it. She didn't get pregnant and she didn't have any STDs, but I never did it again."

"Did you get tested after?"

"For STDs? Yes. I have none."

"But were you tested for HPV?"

"I was vaccinated when I was a teenager, so I don't think they tested me for that." All this clinical talk of STDs and HPV actually did help with my concentration.

"Okay. Good. Next question. When we have sex, will we use a condom?"

And, just like that, all the blood rushed south again. I'd never thought of myself as someone with an active imagination until Mona and Aspen. But every time she brought up sex between us, as though it was a forgone conclusion, I saw it. Vivid flashes of imagery, sights, smells, sounds. It was like describing a ten-course meal to a starving man. I could almost taste it, taste her.

I had to clear my throat before speaking. "Mona, if you want to use a condom, then we shou—"

"I don't. I don't want to."

Shit. Shit, shit, shit.

A spike of unadulterated longing shot down my spine. I had to press my hand against my dick. I hurt. Now I needed a cold shower. All this talking about it with her on the other side of the world was hugely, *hugely* frustrating.

She continued, "But if you want to, then you have veto rights. I guess what I'm saying is, we both have veto rights."

"Yes. Makes sense. Can I think? I'll let you know later?" A subject change was desperately needed if I was going to sleep at all tonight.

"Yes, yes. Absolutely. One more thing, before we move on from our planned sexual activities."

Fuck, fuck, fuck! I bit back a groan. She was killing me. Killing me dead.

But then she said, "I have hard rules, lines you can't cross. And I think, when you're not so tired, we should definitely talk about those."

Coming out of the lust fog, I said, "Yes. Perfect." This was definitely a sobering topic. "Tell me those. We can talk about it now if you want."

"We can talk later, but I just want to be really clear." I heard her take a few deep breaths, like she was working up to something. "Abram, pushing me about these lines will not be appreciated."

She couldn't see me, but I was shaking my head. "I absolutely do not want you to do anything that crosses your lines. I will never, ever push you on your lines. I consider them sacred. I respect you, deeply, and agree that discussion of boundaries is unquestionably important. And I'll tell you mine."

She released a relieved-sounding breath. "Good."

"*But*! Keep your favorites a secret, until I discover them. Then and only then, order from me like I'm a menu."

"Okay," she said softly, sounding a little shy. "I will. It'll be like a sexy scavenger hunt." I sensed she was pleased, excited, but maybe also a little uncertain.

The uncertainty concerned me, and I didn't want us to hang up until she felt certain. "I hope you know, you can always, *always* tell me, when we're together, or at any time, if anything I'm doing isn't your jam. My hope is that I'll be able to read you by your reactions. But if I don't, or can't, tell me. I will immediately stop, completely if you want, or move on to something else if you prefer. If things aren't spectacular for *you*, Mona, then—I guarantee—they'll be shit for me."

She laughed. "Spectacular, huh? I like the sound of that."

"Yes. Spectacular." I swallowed, closing my eyes against the imagery assault of everything that conjured, and my voice gravel, I added, "Let me discover you. Slowly. Over time."

[11]

FAILURE OF GALILEAN TRANSFORMATIONS

Abram

Z ero months.
  Zero weeks.
Zero days.
Fourteen Hours.
And then, *finally.*
"Why're you always in such a bad mood?"

I moved my eyes to Charlie, watching him slip inside the green room. Beyond the open door, I spotted Stan. He lifted his chin in greeting, I lifted mine.

Stan was the security guard who'd been assigned to stand outside my door and was part of the team for the stadium. On our first day here, he and I had bonded over pinochle. We both played it. His landlady had taught him, my mother had taught me.

Last night, he'd brought his landlady to the stadium, I invited my mom, and we made a game of it over pizza from Giordano's. Best night I'd had in a long time.

Charlie closed the door, cutting off my view of Stan and reducing the noise emanating from both the stage and backstage. Lifting two bottles of champagne deftly in one hand, he grinned.

Drummers.

"Come on. Celebrate. We're in our hometown." He set one of the bottles down in front of me, right next to my feet propped on the glass coffee table and began removing the foil of the other bottle. "I brought the good stuff to get you started."

One and a half months. The last time I saw Mona in person. I'd been sick with the flu. She'd come to LA for twenty-four hours. I'd been delirious when she arrived, but only half-delirious when she left. Her visit had made all the difference, but the missed opportunities—to spend actual quality time together—haunted me.

"Nah, man. I'm good." I strummed three chords on my Dread-nought, the opening to "Hold a Grudge," but in D minor.

One week. The last time we'd spoken on the phone. Thirteen minutes, a quick call in the middle of the night, her time. She'd been so tired, I hadn't wanted to keep her up when she needed her sleep.

"No. Man. You are not good. You're depressing as shit. Ever since Las Vegas, you've been a real wet blanket. When are you going to get over that shit? Everyone thought it was funny but you. Come on, that woman was *gorgeous.*"

Keeping my face carefully impassive, I shrugged, because by now I'd realized Charlie wasn't ever going to share my ire about the situation in Las Vegas.

It was our first show after I'd recovered from the flu. After the concert, we were all backstage with the VIP ticket group, and this woman who I'd never met grabbed my dick and offered to give me a blow job. Since most people were drunk at this point, her offer spurred others to make similar offers until they started to sound more like requests, and then demands.

And that was the last VIP session I attended. My label was pissed. I told them to eat shit. Attending VIP sessions wasn't in my contract. Getting groped and propositioned by drunk fans, no matter how attractive they were, wasn't either. It didn't fucking matter if she was gorgeous. But everyone—Charlie and the crew who'd been present—

made it clear that I was the strange one. I was the one who couldn't take a harmless joke. So, I kept my mouth shut.

Charlie popped the cork, sending bubbles cascading over his hand and onto the carpet. Shaking his fingers of the excess, he licked the back of his knuckles. "This one is for you. Here." Charlie held out the bottle.

I leaned forward. I took it. I set it on the floor under my legs. "Thanks."

Two days. The last time Mona sent me a candid picture. I kept opening it. A shot of her with one of my CDs at a music store in Geneva sent while I was asleep, giving me a huge smile and a thumbs-up along with the words, *I'm so proud of you!!*

And then I would scroll through all the pictures she'd sent, taking my time with each. My favorite was still her in the white bikini. But a close second was her in a lab coat, the front of it slightly open, just enough to show me she had nothing on underneath. The night after receiving that photo had been a long, frustrating one.

He grumbled, saying, "You know, I'm supposed to be the dark, broody member of Redburn."

"Oh yeah? What am I supposed to be?"

"The sexy one."

I cracked a smile though I felt no humor. "Maybe we've switched places."

Ten hours. The last time she'd sent me a text message.

Mona: We see each other in just twenty-four hours!! AHHHH!!!! If I get out of here on time, I'll text you to see if we can talk before my flight. I miss you.

I thought about the nature of those words, *I miss you.* Three words that fell colossally short of conveying the truth of their sentiment.

I miss her. I miss her. I miss her.

Charlie was right. I was depressing as shit and it was just getting worse.

It was the tour.

Every concert, the rush, the adrenaline, the energy of thousands of people singing my songs, chanting my name. And then afterward, nothing. The emptiness of praise that sounded like white noise, an ocean of bodies, people I didn't want, standing where she should've been.

In a way, I was glad Mona wasn't touring with me. I wasn't quite myself after a concert, after the last encore. A high like no drug I'd ever tried. I wanted . . . *things,* from her, only her.

But all would be better soon. I would be leaving tonight right after the concert, taking a direct flight to London. We would have three days. *Three days.* Just us, together for three days.

Thank God.

Since our phone call about sex and likes and dislikes, the conversations and texts weren't helping anymore. They left me unsatisfied and surly. I wanted to *touch* her. I wanted it so badly, my mouth went dry every time I thought about it, which was all the fucking time.

But I still wanted to talk to her on the phone when she called. Even if I was frustrated, and even if it felt more and more like a punishment, I needed to hear her voice.

I miss her. I miss her. I miss her.

"Nope." Charlie patted his lean stomach, making a show of sticking it out. "You know how I like that ice cream. I've never met a flavor I wouldn't eat a carton of. Besides, you're already on all those billboards in your designer tighty-whities. Too late for me to take that crown."

"Hmm." I nodded distractedly, glancing again at my phone where it rested next to me on the couch.

Recently, if Mona was able to talk, it happened about an hour before our central time concerts, 5 AM her time, 10 PM mine. But sometimes she was stuck at CERN, pulling an all-night shift, and she wasn't reachable. Even during the day her availability was spotty. Too many meetings, conferences, time with the instruments and resources and people she needed was difficult to secure. Too many *variables* as she called them. If she could make the call, she'd let me know with a text. *Any minute now.*

Charlie huffed, sitting down hard in the chair directly across from me. Leaning forward, his elbows on his knees, his eyes large and expectant, he shrugged.

"Well?"

I mimicked his shrug. "Well, what?"

"What the fuck is going on?"

"Nothing."

"Nothing? Nothing? Come on. We're on a world fucking tour. We're about to play Chi-fucking-cago. Do you know how many celebrities, Hollywood *actresses* are out there, dying to meet you before the show? We missed out on LA, so they all came here."

"We didn't miss out on LA. We tacked it on at the end of the tour. We're still doing LA."

"You know what I mean. Come meet some beautiful people."

I shrugged again, my eyes flickering to the phone. *No messages.*

"But you won't, because you're in here, waiting for a phone call." He didn't sound disgusted or exasperated. He sounded perplexed.

"That's right."

"Fine." He tossed his hands in the air, leaned back, and crossed his arms. "I'll bite. Who is she?" "Come on, Abram. Who is it?"

I smirked. "You know I'm going to say your mom."

Charlie squinted at me, his grin more like a baring of teeth. "You're fucking hilarious."

"Fine. It's your sister."

This joke was only funny to us, and only because Charlie has no siblings.

"Fuck you."

"No thanks. She already did."

"You know. . ." Charlie shook his head, looking reluctantly amused, but a second later, his stare turned thoughtful.

I said nothing, opting to instead quietly strum my guitar.

"It's not Leo's sister is it? I mean, the genius. Not Lisa."

I stopped playing, moving just my eyes to his.

He made a face. "Am I crazy? I only ask because you guys had that argument in Aspen, and then both of you skipped out on dinner the last two nights. It seemed like, uh, something was going on there."

Taking a deep breath through my nose, I considered my friend. We'd known each other for a long time. Yeah, he could be a real dick sometimes, but he'd always had my back. The truth about me and Mona was going to come out eventually. Maybe it was better if I preemptively told him.

Before I could figure out how to start, he said, "You should know, in Aspen, she told me she was hung up on some guy."

"Some guy?"

"Some guy she'd been with in college, I think."

"In college?"

"Or, uh, maybe in high school? I don't know, man. Honesty, I don't remember anything she said other than she was hung up on someone from her past. That trip is kind of a blur now." He laughed, presumably at himself. "Plus, after she shot me down, I kinda zoned out because it was fucking freezing outside and she was talking too fast. I didn't understand half of what she said. Something about dark matter and the space between planets? I couldn't follow."

That sounded like Mona. "Was this when we all went sledding?"

"Yeah. I asked her if she wanted to hang out and she just, like, started telling me all this physics shit."

"Huh." Thinking back on that afternoon, I remembered that I'd suggested she try to let Charlie down by being honest. In her very Mona-like way, she must've taken my advice.

"Anyway, what I'm trying to say is, if it is her, if you two hooked up in Aspen and are trying to keep it on the downlow now, then you should know, as of January, she was still hung up on someone else."

Clearing my throat, I lifted an eyebrow, working *really hard* not to smile at that. "Thanks for the information."

"So, is it her?"

"If it was her, would it bother you?"

"No." He shook his head, shrugged. "Why would it bother me?"

"You seemed interested in her."

"Uh, *yeah.*" His eyes rounded. "I mean, she's fucking gorgeous, right?"

I smirked but didn't answer.

"But Abram, there's a million gorgeous women. And that's my

126

point, man. The last thing you want on your first world tour is to be in a relationship with DJ Tang and Exotica's daughter, unless you want to be under a microscope all the time. We might be famous, but that's a whole different ball park. They're level one billion famous, like in the stratosphere famous. People would go *nuts*."

"I think it'll be okay. People might be interested at first. But then it'll die down."

"Holy shit, man." He reared back, gaping. "It's true?"

"We're—" I began, but was cut off by the swelling sounds in the hall mixing with the Vicious Pixies in the middle of their set.

Ruthie stood just inside, frowning at us both. "What are you doing?" She shouted over the ruckus. "Do you even know who is out here? Nico-fucking-Moretti! I swear!" She stepped inside, shutting the door, and made a beeline for the coffee table.

"I know," I said. "I invited him."

"You invited him?" Ruthie frowned at me, picking up the closed bottle of champagne and began working to remove the foil. "How do you know Nico Moretti? You two in the same underwear ad or something?"

I felt myself grimace at her joke, just a small one. *That stupid ad.* "His wife is friends with my sister." I'd had lunch with Nico and Elizabeth earlier in the day. In fact, we'd driven to the venue together after. They already knew I planned to leave right after the concert.

"Huh. Well, you should go say hi. He brought his hot actor friends and has everyone laughing. We go on in less than an hour and you two losers are in here doing what?"

Charlie lifted his hand toward me. "Abram is waiting for a call from—" he paused, studying me for a moment before deciding on, "His mystery lover."

"You mean your sister?" She twisted the wire holding down the cork.

"That joke isn't even funny. Fuck you."

"No thanks, your sister already did." Ruthie grinned at me, wagging her eyebrows. "He falls for it every time."

I smirked, shaking my head, glancing at my phone again. Any minute now.

"I'll tell you what, Nico is *hot*. If I weren't so into lady parts, I'd definitely be confused." Ruthie braced the bottle against her hip, twisting the cork and indicating to me with her chin. "You know his wife? She is also hot. Some kind of doctor, right?"

Nodding, I set aside the acoustic guitar and picked up the phone, touching the screen just to make sure Mona hadn't texted while I'd been distracted by my bandmates.

"See? See what I mean?" Charlie gestured to me again, and then let his hand fall to his knee with a slap. "He keeps checking his phone. Every night, it's the same. Fucking hell, Abram."

Glaring at Charlie, I gave my head a subtle shake. "Why do you care?"

"Because." Now he gestured to Ruthie. "Ruthie broke up with her girlfriend after Aspen." He pointed to himself. "I made sure to stay single. Even the roadies are unattached. Why would you do this to us?"

Examining my friend, I couldn't tell if he was serious or joking. "What am I doing to you?"

"You're raining on our parade." Charlie said this like it was obvious.

"How so?" I rubbed my face, scratching my beard.

"Listen, fine, be in a relationship. Okay. But people want to meet you. They come here for *you*. Your lyrics. Your music—"

"Kaitlyn's music."

"—and night after night, you're in your dressing room, hiding from everyone, waiting for a phone call. You've wasted the first two months of the North American tour. If your girl cared about you, she'd want you to have a good time. It's sad, man."

"It is kind of sad." Ruthie pressed her lips together, looking me over. "We're only young once. We only get this experience—of our first tour—once. You're missing out."

"See?" Charlie, again, made a big show of lifting his hand toward our guitarist.

"I don't feel like I'm missing out," I mumbled to no one, and it was only half true. I didn't feel like I was missing out on the drugs, and the sex with strangers, and the hangover sex with strangers. But I did feel like I was missing out on Mona by being *here*. If there were some way to do the practices and the shows without the rest of it.

Checking the time on my phone, I frowned. My stomach dropped. She never texted this late. *She probably can't make the call before her flight.*

"But I also think it's kind of sweet."

Ruthie's declaration had me glancing at her. "Sweet, huh?"

She gave me a small smile. "You look like a fucking porn star pirate fantasy, but you're a sweet guy, Abram."

I lifted an eyebrow at her. "Thanks?"

"It's a compliment. You should be flattered." Ruthie kicked my leg lightly with her boot. "Also, Charlie is right. You need to get laid."

Glaring at Ruthie, because she was right, I said nothing. But it wasn't just that I needed to get laid. I needed Mona.

Long-distance relationships totally sucked. Fantasies, jerking off, cold showers, vivid dreams, her pictures, more fantasies. I'd filled ten notebooks since Aspen. I had songs for decades. I'd sent a select few of the more complete poems to Kaitlyn and she'd been hugely inspired. She'd composed ten solid arrangements for the next album, we only needed four more, five tops.

Then what? Another album. Another tour? No.

No more tours.

A firm knock drew our attention to the door and had me gritting my teeth. Other than Charlie and Ruthie, who were always welcome, Stan and the crew knew not to knock. Not to enter. Not to seek me out or introduce me to some fucking VIP.

"Who is it?" Ruthie asked, glancing between us.

Our drummer shrugged, looking a tad defensive. "Don't look at me. I have no idea."

"Ohhhh." Ruthie made a wincing face, her wide eyes on me. "Someone is going to get fired, then."

Standing, I strolled to the door, fighting a spike in temper. Stan knew better. Taking a quick, deep breath before opening it, I reminded myself to stay calm. My fuse was too short these days. Everything and everyone pissed me off.

But then, upon finding Leo, his hands shoved in his pockets, a big smile on his face, my anger reluctantly diminished until I was more curious than irritated. I glanced between Stan, still at his post by the door, and Mona's brother. The security guard's face seemed carefully impassive, like both Leo and I bored him. *Hmm.*

"Leo," I said, not masking my confusion.

"Hey," Leo shouted over the noise, his grin widening. He looked like he was up to something. "Just in the neighborhood. Mind if I come in?"

I ignored the screams and voices calling my name from somewhere to my right, stepping to the side. "Please. Come in."

"Leo! Good to see you."

"It's Leo!"

Charlie was already on his feet, but Ruthie blocked the way, insisting on a hug. Giving stoic Stan one more searching look, I closed the door, reclaimed my spot on the couch, and picked up my guitar. Checking my phone again while my three friends exchanged greetings and banalities, I frowned at the screen. *No messages.*

"I'm so relieved to see you, man. If it had been anyone else, I think Abram might've lost his shit." Charlie chuckled, steering Leo to the chair where he'd been sitting earlier.

"Really?" Leo glanced at me. "What's going on, Abram? Isn't the tour going well? From everything I've seen—other than the rescheduled LA show—the reviews are awesome."

"Tour is fine." I strummed a series of chords, the beginning of a new song Kaitlyn had sent through. "What are you doing here? I thought you were in Miami."

"Uh." Leo's eyebrows jumped, and he glanced at my bandmates. "Hey, you two, do you mind giving us a minute? I have some, uh, business to discuss. Label stuff."

"Oh, sure. Yeah." Ruthie looked confused and I understood why.

The excuse of *label stuff* made no sense. Leo may have introduced us to our EP and label, but he didn't work for them.

"That's Leo's polite code for *leave us the fuck alone.*" Charlie backed away toward the door, opened it, and the building roar of backstage paired with the music of our opening act blared through. He motioned Ruthie forward. "Totally cool. We can catch up later."

"Yes. Absolutely." Leo pointed at Ruthie, then at Charlie. "See you after the concert. We'll hang out."

As soon as Charlie shut the door, the noise level returned to a faint hum, and Leo turned back to me, his smile falling away.

We stared at each other for a minute, but I didn't get the sense he was upset, nor did he seem contrite, like he was here to apologize for anything. The last time I saw him had been in Aspen, and the last time we'd talked had been when I'd called to get Mona's number. I was aware that he'd come to the hospital in LA, but he didn't stay to visit. I'd been too sick and he needed to get back to Miami. Mona had seen him, though, but she never told me what they'd discussed.

"How you doing, Abram?" He sounded honestly curious. "You look like you're recovered."

"Why are you here, Leo?" Yeah. I was definitely *in a mood.*

My dissatisfaction and frustration with life on tour was bleeding into every facet of my personality. Charlie was right. Ruthie was right. I needed to lighten up.

"The truth?" He shrugged, leaning forward to rest his elbows on his knees. "I promised Mona I would come."

I stopped strumming my guitar. "What?"

"She's worried about you."

I set the guitar aside, sitting forward. "What? She is? She said that?"

"I was supposed to go to the Cincinnati concert, but couldn't make it. So, I'm here instead." His stare turned scrutinizing. "She wanted to make sure you were happy, doing well, getting enough sleep. She said you've been kind of distant the last few weeks."

I pushed my fingers through my hair, and then brought them back to rub my forehead, eyes, and beard. "Shit."

"Don't be mad at Mona. It took me two hours of careful questioning to get it out of her, why she was so keyed up when we spoke." Leo huffed a little laugh. "It was kind of cute though. For the first time ever, she was asking *me* hypothetical questions about the opposite sex instead of the other way around."

"I'm not mad at Mona. Not at all. It's just—" I bit back a curse and said the words out loud before I could catch them. "I miss her."

Glancing up, I locked eyes with my friend. "I miss her, man. It's like, I can't breathe. I'm drowning, suffocating in how much I miss her. I just need—"

Leo lifted an eyebrow when I didn't continue. "What do you need?"

I didn't know where to start. I needed to talk to her for hours, submerge myself in her brilliance and presence, debate and discuss, tease and laugh. I needed to not talk to her, sit with her, be quiet, together.

And yes, should things progress in that way and she was up for it, I needed to fuck her brains out.

I needed to taste every inch of her body, I needed her under me, above me, next to me. Reclined, kneeling, bending, on all fours. I needed her skin and sounds and lips and legs and neck and breasts and *everything*.

But I wasn't going to say that to her brother. She was right. I had been distant.

"I need everything," I finally said, and then laughed at myself.

"Oh? Is that all?" Leo also laughed, shaking his head. But his laughter quickly tapered. "You seem unhappy. And that's a shame. I mean, this is your dream, right? Playing your own songs, music, live, for tens of thousands of people. They adore you, man. They can't get enough. I think I can speak for Mona when I say she'd want you to enjoy it, not sit around and be miserable, missing her."

"It's honestly not even about missing Mona, not really."

Leo sighed. "Then what's it about?"

"What am I doing? What is this life? I want this?" I continued shaking my head. "I don't. I thought I did, but I don't. You're right, playing my songs is my dream. But the adoration, the chanting of my name, the echo in my ears, in my heart, it's a high and I hate it. It's like living inside a theme park for months."

I closed my eyes, leaning back against the couch. "At the end of the night, there is only me and an empty hotel room. Another city. Another audience. Another set. It's always the same. Even if Mona and I weren't together, even if she wasn't mine to miss, *that* wouldn't change."

"But if you were with someone else, someone who could tour with you and didn't have so many responsibilities, someone who made you their main priority, then *that* would change."

I opened my eyes, glaring at my friend. He seemed to be glaring at me as well, not with hostility, but with suspicion.

My friend. That didn't sound right.

My former friend? Possibly.

It took me a moment, and I had to swallow a few times, but eventually I was able to ask without shouting, "What the fuck does that mean? Hmm? Why would you even say that?"

A hint of a smile, there and gone, tugged his mouth to one side. "I'm just saying—"

"Fuck you. I love God and Mona and my family and music and words and that's it."

"That's it?" Now he was smiling. A stupid grin on his stupid face.

"Yeah. That's it." I'd had enough, and distrust lanced me, sharp and strong. I stood. "Wait. Why are you really here? What do you want?"

Leo also stood, still grinning, looking like he was trying to hold in laughter. "I told you already, because Mona—"

"Cut the shit, Leo. Did Mona also tell you to encourage me to replace her with a warm body? She's not replaceable, dipshit."

"Listen, calm down. Okay? Calm down." Now Leo did laugh, and now he was shaking his head. "Mona did ask me to come and check on you, and she is worried about you being unhappy when you should be having a great time. That was true. But the other stuff, that was me. That was big brother stuff, okay?"

I lifted my chin, inspecting him. "What the hell does that mean?"

"It means Mona is crazy about you, okay? She's—" Leo's eyes drifted to the wall behind me, like he was searching it for the right word "—completely crazy about you. Obviously, my sister fell for you in Aspen, and she fell hard, and I don't want to see you mess her up. I needed to, you know, make sure your intentions were honorable before I could give this thing my blessing."

Placing my hands on my hips, I narrowed my eyes on Mona's brother, not hiding my irritation. "Your blessing? Why would I need or want your blessing?"

Leo's demeanor instantly changed. He straightened to his full height, his eyes growing cold and hot at the same time, a subtle sneering curl to his upper lip. I knew that face. That was the face Leo made when he was about to threaten someone.

"You better believe you need my blessing, because Mona is my family. My. Family. *Mine*." His voice was a rumble, and it raised the fine hairs on the back of my neck. I'd seen him angry, but I'd only seen him this angry once before, when another of our friends insulted Lisa in an extremely—uh—unsavory way. "And no one fucks with her, got it? No one. I will *ruin* you if you break her heart. You know I can, so don't doubt that I will."

Staring at my friend, I found myself fighting a smile. "Yeah. Okay. I see your point. Good talk." I was still irritated with him about how he'd treated Mona, but it was clear he was making an effort now to be a good brother.

Leo continued scowling at me, his aggression fading slowly, but doubt remained. "We clear?"

I smiled. "Mostly." Before he could get too upset, I added, "I believe you can ruin my music career, I believe that. But the truth is Leo, the only way you could ruin *me* is if you somehow convinced Mona to leave me."

The frost left his stare, and the heat diminished to warm affection.

"So, no." I turned, reached for my phone, and glanced at the screen. *No messages*. I tucked it in my back pocket. "I don't believe *you* can ruin me."

My friend's mouth curved into a pleased smile and he nodded. "Glad to hear it."

I missed having him as a friend. Leo was a good guy. Clueless sometimes, but someone who was truly trying his best. "You have anything else you want to add? Anything you want to apologize for? Now that you're here, sharing feelings."

"Nope."

"Nope?"

"Nah, man. I did what I did. I was wrong, yeah, but not about you. I was wrong about Mona, and I've already apologized to her."

"You apologized?" That surprised me.

Mona and I still hadn't talked about her family, though she always wanted to hear about mine. I had a suspicion Mona talked to my mom and sister more than she talked to me.

"I did. She deserved more and better than I was giving her."

"Huh." Inspecting Leo, I absorbed this information. When Mona and I were in London, face-to-face, I would make a point to ask her about her family, get her talking about her upbringing. I wanted to understand her, know her. Maybe I needed to do a better job of showing Mona the depths of my interest. "What changed your mind?"

"About Mona? Or about me being a shitty brother?"

"I guess both."

Leo stared at me, like he was searching for something behind my expression. Eventually, frowning, he said, "You'll have to ask her. It's not my—uh— story to tell."

"Okay. Fair enough."

"So, we good?" Leo extended his hand. "No more psycho phone calls?"

I snorted a laugh and rolled my eyes. "You know I can't promise that. You're the first number I call when I drunk dial. But I'll try to keep them to a minimum."

I accepted his handshake just as the door opened and we both turned toward the intrusion of noise. It was Charlie and he was bouncing on the balls of his feet, a bundle of nerves and energy, as per usual right before a concert.

"If you two are finished holding hands, we need Abram. Showtime."

"Right." Leo released my hand, giving me that grin again. "Well, see you after the show."

I shook my head. "I'm leaving right after the last song. I've got to catch a plane to London. But Charlie and Ruthie will be here."

Leo continued smiling but said nothing. He left with Charlie, but neither closed the door. No need. It was time for me to go to work.

And then London, Mona, three days.

I was just pushing my way through the backstage crowd, trying to find Melena to hand over my cell phone—she was the only one I trusted with it—and grab my mug of pre-show tea, when I felt my cell go off in my back pocket. I waited until I made it past the security rope where no fans were allowed before retrieving my phone and checking the screen.

My pulse stuttered. It was a message from Mona followed quickly by a candid shot.

I glanced at the photo first, but it confused me. She was standing in what looked like a darkened stadium, lights and stage behind her. She wore a dark dress, maybe blue, hair down, heavy—for her—makeup, and a giant smile. On one side was Allyn making a funny face and on the other side was Marie, grinning like she'd just done something brilliant.

Then I read the message and experienced a shock, current racing up my spine, wrapping around my heart, an electric tremor. I read it once, and then had to read it again and again to comprehend its meaning. Even then, even as I smiled widely, and my heart beat wildly, I read it again.

Mona: SURPRISE! I'M HERE!!! I'm sitting in the center section with your sister and can't wait for the show to start! LOVE YOU!

[12]

THE LORENTZ TRANSFORMATIONS

Abram

"No," I called over my shoulder, shaking my elbow out of Charlie's grasping grip, knowing he couldn't hear me. But he'd get the picture. "No more encores. We're done." I handed my bass off to Geoff, one of our roadies, and darted around a group of smiling techs for the security rope at the side of the stage.

Melena said she'd be here. She'd promised to meet me *right here*, after the concert was over.

"Abram! Hey, man!" Charlie was suddenly at my shoulder, holding my bass and yelling in my ear over the persistent chanting of the crowd. "They're not stopping. They're nowhere near stopping. We got to give them at least one more."

I shook my head as I glanced around, searching for Melena and mouthing an emphatic *no*. I pointed to my throat. We'd already played nine encores. Nine. The most we'd ever done. My voice was raw, on fire. I would be paying for these extra songs for days.

"Come on." He held my guitar out, his eyes pleading and wild, like a druggy looking for another hit. "Come on. One more. This is

Chicago. Our hometown. They love you. You owe them one more song."

Gritting my teeth, I glared at my drummer, but said nothing. I'd already given my answer. The pleading eventually morphed into frustration, and then rage. Charlie's jaw ticked in time with the chant, *Redburn, Redburn, Redburn.*

"Sometimes, you're a stingy motherfucker, Abram." He seethed, stepping back, wiping his upper lip.

Charlie's hands were shaking, his knuckles white where he held my bass in one hand. He was covered in sweat. So was I. I was hot and sweaty, and wired, full of adrenaline, just like him. And the high, the current and cadence of euphoria still held me in its grip. But I wasn't insane with it, desperate to prolong it, like he was.

I had something else, the thought of someone else making me crazy.

God, she was so close. *So close.* I'd gone off script, walking into the audience during Charlie's drum solo in the middle of our sixth song, unable to wrestle the anticipation into submission. Our security and lighting people scrambled, and I felt like an ass, but I needed to see her up close. I'd walked past the barricade, the guards, down the stairs, to her section, searching for her.

And there she was. Grinning at me. Eyes shining, looking so proud and excited. She also looked goddamn *hot*, wearing a skintight blue dress that ended mid-thigh, her hair down, red lips. My lungs on fire, it took everything, *everything*, every ounce of self-control not to grab her and kiss her gorgeous face off.

But we were surrounded by thousands of people, and that pledge I'd made to myself—that all my decisions from now on would be stellar ones, because my decisions impacted her—screamed between my ears. She deserved my circumspection and thoughtfulness, not a big, showy, dramatic, extremely public outing of our relationship. That wouldn't be romantic. It would be selfish.

So I'd taken a few photos with fans. I'd quickly signed a few shirts. And then I'd climbed back onto the stage and finished the concert, restless, eager for it to end. Yet also wanting to give Mona my best version of *our* songs.

Now the show was over.

Now it was our time.

So where the hell is Melena?

Movement behind Charlie snagged my attention and I pushed past him, Melena and one of the PAs running toward us, coming from the side hall leading to the dressing rooms and offices.

"Sorry." Melena stopped directly in front of me, holding a travel mug in one hand and a large water bottle with ice in the other, wearing a massive grin and shouting over the continuing chants.

The PA, however, bumped into me. And then brushed her body against me.

"Sorry, we thought you were going to do another song," she said, peering up at me, sounding breathless even though she was shouting.

I took a half step back. The PA swayed forward. Frustrated, I gently set her away with the palms of my hands, grinding my teeth.

"I'm glad you decided not to. Here." Melena pushed the travel mug into my hands, giving the PA an irritated look. Then to me, she said, "Drink this. It has something to numb the throat. You must be hurting."

Taking the mug, my eyes flickered to the PA who now was staring at me like I was food and she was starving. She licked her lips. *Give me a fucking break.*

Maybe it made me a dick that I didn't take the time to learn any of their names. Maybe if just one of them treated me like a person I would have. Regardless, I noticed she was holding one of my T-shirts and I frowned at it, and her, lifting my chin in question.

"Oh!" The PA shook herself, shoving it toward me "I noticed the sweat, I mean, you're all sweaty. You look great but your shirt is sticking to your body and you're, uh, all, uh, wet. So I went to your dressing room and got it for you."

I scowled, my jaw working. How many times did I have to tell these people? I didn't want any of them in my dressing room.

She flinched back, presumably at my expression. "I thought—I thought you might—"

"Did you bring me a shirt?" Charlie asked, standing at my shoulder. "Or how about Ruthie? We're just as sweaty. Stop trying to fuck

Abram, okay? Can't you see it pisses him off? Plus, he's got a girl already."

The PA blinked at me, and then at Charlie, her mouth moving without sound as a red blush climbed up her cheeks, visibly mortified.

I didn't have time for this. Ignoring both Charlie and the offered shirt, I tried to get Melena's attention. But she seemed to give her eyes a half roll, and shoved the water bottle at Charlie.

"This is for you," she shouted over the crowd. "It's my electrolytes mix. Where's Ruthie? I have one for her too. And if you have a problem with one of the PAs, talk to their boss, Charlie."

I reached for Melena's arm before she could dart off in search of our guitarist, released her when I was sure she wouldn't leave, and held my hand out.

She shook her head, her forehead wrinkling. "What?"

I made the universal symbol for phone with my thumb and pinkie finger since I couldn't risk shouting.

"Oh! Yes. I have it." She pulled out my cell from her back pocket. "I had it the whole time, never left my person."

Mouthing thank you, I snatched it and hurriedly marched past the trio, down the hall toward the dressing rooms, needing to get there before the backstage area flooded with fans and VIP ticket holders.

Stan was there, next to the door, and he turned as I approached. "Mr. Fletcher."

"Stan," I said, my voice raspy and tired. "I need a favor, man. I need you to go get someone for me. Her name is—"

"Mona DaVinci."

I drew back, surprised.

He pointed with this thumb toward the door. "She's already inside."

My brain stuttered to a stop, and I looked at the door. "She's . . ."

"Already inside."

Inside. The room. And suddenly, this steel door became a magical fucking portal to heaven.

"You going in?" Stan asked.

I nodded. "Yes." *This is it. Fuck, this is it.*

Was I ready?

No. I wasn't. I was still hopped up on adrenaline, the crowd was *still* chanting, but had switched to my name. If I went in there now, I would probably . . . *I will definitely do something selfish.*

"I just need a minute." Pushing my phone into my back pocket, I took a sip of tea, gathering my thoughts.

"Here." Stan reached in front of me, twisting the doorknob and then taking the mug out of my grip. "Let me get that for you."

Before I could stop him, he'd pushed it open. And—again—there she was.

She stood in profile, a hand on her hip, looking at something. But when the door opened, she turned, immediately smiling, her eyes huge and happy.

"Abram." She said my name breathlessly, hesitating a fraction of a second before launching herself forward.

Time skipped. She'd been across the room a minute ago, but now she was in my hands, her body pressed to my body, her mouth on mine, her fingers in my hair, and I was so, so right. I was definitely going to do something selfish.

Kicking the door shut, I turned her, pressed her against it, and feasted on her glorious mouth, demanding her tongue and drinking from her perfect lips. My hands traveled south, wanting the skin of her legs, my fingers curling into the fabric of her dress and lifting it.

She yanked her mouth away with a shocked gasp, her hands immediately gripping mine and trying to hold them still. "Wait, wait. You have to stop."

My mouth lowered to her neck and I bit it, wanting to consume her, taste every inch of her skin, rocking my hips forward urgently. "I need you."

"Abram!" she squealed. "We're not alone!"

We're not alone?

Breathing hard while my brain worked to make sense of her words, the sound of a throat clearing somewhere behind me had my back stiffening.

Mona ducked her head, whispering hurriedly against my ear, "Your—uh—sister is here with her fiancé. And so are Allyn and my brother."

Well, fuck.

Actually, no. Not fuck. No expletive existed that could adequately describe the magnitude of my frustration in that moment. Instinct told me to toss her over my shoulder. Leave. Find a room that didn't have a fucking housewarming party in it. Pick up right where we left off, with my hands up her skirt.

And when Marie said, "Don't mind us, we were just talking about the—uh—show. Not this show, the other show," and everyone laughed, I almost did it.

But we'd be photographed. Fans would have their phones ready and there'd be no escape. Everyone would know. Mona in her tiny blue dress, me looking like—what did Ruthie call it?—a porno pirate, covered in sweat, my shirt sticking to my body, my eyes a little wild. Not an image I imagined Mona wanted out there.

Mona.

My fingers tightened on the fabric of her dress. She was sifting her fingers through my hair, placing little, sweet kisses on my neck, murmuring words meant to calm and coax. "Let's visit. Just for a minute. Then we have three days, you and me. All the time in the world, right?"

Slowly, reluctantly, I gathered a deep breath and removed my hands from her, bracing them against the door and glaring down at this woman I loved, and wanted, beyond description, beyond the limitations of language.

"Ten minutes," I said, not sure if it was a threat or a promise. "Five if someone gives me a reason to kick them out."

Mona rolled her lips between her teeth and nodded, peering up at me, looking pleased and excited and a little dazed. "Ten minutes."

* * *

I wasn't much of a drinker anymore. But tonight, when offered whiskey by Leo, I downed the two-ounce pour just to take the edge off.

"Slow down," he said, grinning and taking my glass to pour me another.

Accepting the refill and looking over my shoulder at Mona, I took his words to heart. Slow down. *Slow. Down.*

Mona sat on the chair facing the sofa, talking animatedly to Marie and Matt. She seemed galvanized, like the show, the energy affected her too. And as I watched her, doing my best to slow down, I savored the sight. Her smile. Her bright eyes. Her laugh. Her voice, here, live, not carried across the planet over a phone.

I'd spent the last six weeks—hell, I'd spent the last two and a half months and the last two and a half years before that—wanting this. Just this. We were together, no secrets or lies between us, the promise of a great future on the horizon, and the reality of a great *now*.

And yet, amped-up from the concert, I was still shaky and preoccupied by selfishness.

"Great show, by the way. Nine encores." Leo poured himself a drink.

I nodded distractedly, my eyes still on Mona in her tiny dress. I wanted to take it off.

"Has Broderick been in contact about the next album? I ran into him and Kaitlyn in New York. They said you already have most of it done."

"Yep." My eyes followed the line of her toned legs to her feet. She'd taken off her shoes. She was barefoot. Her toes were painted bright blue.

"That's amazing, man. When did you find the time to write?"

"Here and there." I shrugged, watching with rapt concentration as Mona tucked one of her legs beneath her, the skirt hiking higher, showing me more thigh. My fingers tightened on the thick crystal tumbler as she leaned forward, her position highlighting the curve of her back and waist. My gaze traveled to the thin straps over her elegant bare shoulders, collarbone, the scooped neckline, the swell of her breasts.

I swallowed.

"Hey."

Reluctantly, I tore my eyes from Mona, glancing at Leo. He wore a frown, his eyes seemed to be narrowed with concern.

"Are you okay?"

Was I okay?

Was he really that dense? Had he never felt this way about

someone before? Completely consumed. Destroyed. Rebuilt. Desperate.

No. I wasn't okay. But what could I say?

Sorry. I'm distracted by thoughts of fucking your sister, against the door with her tits in my mouth, or bent over the couch, reaching around to stroke her slick, wet pussy while she moans my name. If you weren't here right now, I'd be eating her out and loving every second of it. Forgive my preoccupation. What were you saying about the album?

"Your voice is almost gone, huh?" He nodded at his own assertion. "No need to talk if you can't."

I stared at him, breathing through my nose, working to regain control of anything. This was why I hated the minutes and hours after a show. I wasn't thinking straight. I wasn't myself. It was a peculiar kind of madness.

Did I want to take Mona against the door or bent over the couch? Absofuckinglutely.

But did I want that—here, in this random room, sticky and sweaty after a concert with thousands of people just feet away, the constant risk of someone coming in, interrupting us—to be our first time together?

No.

But in my current state of mind, I would. I definitely, definitely would.

Gathering a deep breath, I forced myself to relax my hold on the tumbler. "It's probably best if I don't speak at all," I murmured, returning my attention to Mona. But this time, she was also watching me.

She wasn't smiling. Her gaze was direct, sharp, and—if I wasn't mistaken—hot. Mona lifted her hand toward me in invitation, mouthing, "Do you want to sit with me?"

I shook my head. The only way for us to sit together in that chair was if she sat on my lap. Bad idea.

Her hand dropped, a slight wrinkle forming between her eyes. She looked anxious.

So I lifted my hand and mouthed, "Five minutes," making no attempt to disguise my meaning.

Five minutes.

One way or the other—either they left, or we did—we were going to be alone in five minutes.

[13]

PLASMA PHYSICS

Mona

I checked my phone for the tenth time in two minutes, licking my lips, my mouth and throat dry.

Abram was looking at me, watching me. I'd felt his eyes on me earlier, but now I *felt* his eyes, the force of his intentions. I squirmed in my seat, my skin hot; the area between my thighs coiling, twisting, aching; my breasts heavy, sensitive. Unable to follow Allyn's funny story, or Marie's clever questions, or Matt's silly comments, just the act of breathing felt like a miracle.

Two minutes, twenty-two seconds left.

Twenty-one.

Twenty.

Nineteen.

There was a reason we'd snuck backstage before the last encore, and I'd been careful to bring others. The photos in LA of me—that everyone assumed was Lisa—were a sobering reminder that cameras were everywhere.

Hilarious in retrospect, I'd brought two condoms with me, just in case he wanted to do something here while we waited for the crowds to disperse, before we left for the hotel. I'd tucked them in the side of my strapless push-up bra and spent an inordinate amount of time reasoning with myself while getting dressed, trying to convince myself that I wasn't being presumptuous.

Therefore, in hindsight—now that I was here, and he was here, and I couldn't think straight, his eyes on me—my concerns about being presumptuous were hysterical.

I knew what he wanted as though he were speaking it aloud, over and over, whispering it in my ear.

The fine hairs on the back of my neck prickled and I rubbed the spot, checking my phone again. Two minutes, thirteen seconds.

I almost cursed. Was time moving backward? When would the five minutes end?! When would these people leave?!

Or, I debated, obviously not at all in my right mind, *we could just leave. Now.*

A laugh tumbled past my lips at the thought. Thankfully, it was well timed, as Marie had just said something to make everyone else laugh.

Then again, why not?

Why not just go?

Why stay if we didn't want to stay? Why care whether we were photographed? Why care who knew? Or when? Why not leave? So many questions, and I couldn't think of a single satisfactory answer other than *go.*

Go.

My eyes cut to Abram's. Collided. Crashed. He was still watching me, sipping something the color of brandy or whiskey. But it was *how* he watched me—like we were already alone—that made up my mind.

No more waiting.

I stood, in some kind of bizarre trance, seeing only Abram, and crossed to him. He watched me come. Someone, my brother, was talking to him. Wordlessly, Abram handed his glass off.

"Let's go," I said, taking his hand, holding it in both of mine as I walked backward, pulling him toward the door. He said nothing. Just looked. Just followed.

"Don't you want your shoes?" Allyn asked.

Abram stepped forward and, in one fluid motion, reached behind me for the door while using his leverage on my hands to twirl me, tucking me close against his side. He was strong and solid, and I loved it. He was also damp, and I loved that too.

"You guys." I heard Marie call to us. "It'll be peak crazy out there right now."

Too late.

He'd opened the door. People screamed his name—excited screams, not the killing kind—from somewhere to our right. The security guard stationed at the door looked to Abram, nodded once, and then turned.

"Follow me," the man said, walking down the mostly empty hall to our left. "Your car is ready."

Flashes went off. We passed people in the hall, too stunned to do anything but back up, stop, and gape. Echoes of the frenzied shouts and screams followed us. We encountered a broken bottle of beer and Abram scooped me into his arms without saying a word, his boots crunching over the glass, not breaking his stride. More flashes.

Then we were outside. The limo was there. New shouts. Fans catching sight of him and running toward us. Cameras going off, flashes, screams—still the excited kind—the thunder of a sprinting crowd.

Sights and sounds caught up with me, yanked me out of this strange daze. My heart in my throat as the guard calmly opened the door, Abram placed me gently inside, I slid down the bench, and he followed. The guard closed the door, the locks engaged, we were off.

Abram turned to me as the car lurched forward, threaded his fingers through my hair, his eyes darting over my face. "Are you okay?"

I nodded, strangely out of breath.

We're alone.

"Where to?"

BLARG! We're not alone!

"Old Town," I blurted before Abram could speak, announcing the precise address to our driver as I fumbled for the button that would lift the privacy screen. "Once you get there, drive around the block until we tell you to stop," I hastened to add before the screen completely closed.

But as soon as it did close, I turned to Abram, prepared to fling myself at him. I was too late. He'd already grabbed my arm, tugged me forward, and fused his mouth to mine. Off-balance, all I could do was hold on to his shoulders, open my mouth while awkwardly straddling his leg, and take the hot, ardent invasion of his tongue.

One hand pressed me forward at the small of my back, urging me closer. His hold rough, determined, his fingers digging into my hip, like he was worried I might disappear or flee. I felt the palm of his other hand on my thigh, equally rough and frenzied, pushing my dress up until it bunched at my waist, his fingers sliding between my legs and cupping me firmly through my lace undies.

I gasped. He cursed. The sound a deep, rolling rumble as he pushed the scrap of fabric to one side and stroked my opening.

"Your mouth tastes so sweet," he growled, biting my upturned jaw as I struggled to breathe. "Your skin is sweet." My hips rolled instinctively, seeking his circling strokes, his breath hot against my neck. "I bet this tastes like candy."

An overwhelmed, inelegant sound sprung from my lips as he entered me, stretching me with two fingers, making me pant, scattering my wits.

I couldn't think. I had plans, ideas, things I wanted, things I hoped for, but they'd vanished from my mind, leaving it blank. I'd become a creature of reaction. I wasn't used to this. Yes, the last time we'd done something, Abram had been in control. But in all my previous encounters with men other than Abram, I was used to calling the shots. I was the one who mapped out the course, set the boundaries and goalposts.

But this—the imbalance, the dizzying lack of control while he took and touched as he pleased—felt so good, so right and essential.

And yet, also mildly terrifying.

I loved it. I loved that I could smell him and me, his sweat and my sex. The fragrance pungent, and sweet. His mouth was at my breast, nuzzling, searching, and when he found my nipple, he caught it with his teeth, a sharp sting of pain making me cry out. And just like the last and only time he'd touched me, I was already close.

"Abram," I moaned, my brain paralyzed as I gripped his shoulders, frustrated with myself because I hadn't touched him anywhere. Yet my body was in motion, my back arching, pushing my breasts forward, my hips rolling, riding his fingers, everywhere heat, lava, fire.

And then his hand was gone.

"Come here."

"What? Where?" My eyes flew open. I hadn't realized they were closed.

"I want this off," he grunted to the strap of my dress, biting it and moving it off my shoulder, his stubbly beard scraping my skin. "Take it off."

Jerking at the hem, I pulled it over my head, only struggling slightly to free my shoulders before he was there, helping. I reached around my back for the hook of my bra and he covered my hands, stopping me.

I looked up and found his eyes on the swells of my breasts. Abram licked his lips. "No. Leave it. I like it, for now."

Moving me off his lap, he slid to the floor, opening my legs and kneeling between them. His mouth feasting on my neck, he reached inside the cup of my strapless bra with his index and middle finger to pinch and then pluck my nipple.

I cried out, surprised, and I felt him smile against my chest, bringing my breast completely out to soothe the offended peak with his hot mouth and tongue.

Oh. My. God.

"Abram."

"Hmm."

I cleared my throat, my body vibrating. "Will you do that again? Please?"

"What?" He tucked the abused breast back in my lingerie while reaching inside for the other. "This?"

Rougher than the first time, he pinched me, tugging harshly, and I gasped. Just like before, he soothed it with his tongue, drawing it into his mouth and sending churning, languid heat low in my belly, twisting between my legs.

Setting me to rights again, I whimpered, wanting more. He slid lower, holding my sides, kissing my stomach, swirling his tongue in my belly button and making my hips buck off the seat. Bracketing them, he used my position to pull down my underwear.

I tried to grab his fingers, but he was too fast.

"Oh my God, what are you doing?"

"I need you."

"Abram—oh—oh—oh God."

His hands had moved under my thighs, gripping my bare bottom and pulling me to the edge of the seat, his mouth there. Right *there*. Between my legs, licking, lapping, loud indecent sounds that made me wild.

Abram groaned, flexing his fingers on my backside and then slipping them from beneath me, down my legs to my ankles. He bent my knees, lifting my feet to the bench, spreading me wide, exposing me completely.

My fingers were in his hair, mindlessly grabbing and releasing, kneading and massaging his head and neck. I was so close, so close, *so close*.

"So close," I moaned.

Abruptly, he removed my hands from his hair and replaced his mouth with his fingers, a light touch. I heard a click just before the darkness was replaced with a flood of light.

"Open your eyes," he commanded as I blinked, endeavoring to adjust to the brightness, and caught the tail end of him pulling off his shirt, tossing it over his shoulder and advancing forward again, pulling me off the bench until I was kneeling with him on the floor.

His mouth fastened to mine, demanding, hungry. I tasted myself. I'd never tasted myself before and it made me crazy, making me feel reckless, naughty. Maybe a little vulgar. His hands moved over me, kneading, massaging and stroking my backside, lifting to unhook my bra and palm my breasts as it fell away. He groaned against my mouth, lifting the soft mounds.

"I'm tired of waiting," he said, a growl, and turned us both to set me on one of the long side benches that ran the length of the stretch limo. His touch grew frenzied as he grasped and caressed my naked skin. "I'm so fucking tired of waiting."

I wanted to say, *Me too,* but the words caught in my throat because his hands were everywhere and mine were fumbling stupidly for purchase. I reached for his pants, awkwardly unbuttoning and unzipping his fly, reaching my hand inside to cup him. Before I could feel the full, hard length, he pulled my hands away, freeing himself.

Abram shoved his pants down and I sucked in a breath, my hands hovering between us, not touching him even though I longed to do so. He was so beautiful. Thick and long and hard, his erection curved slightly upward, and—as a fan of anatomy—I knew that meant really good things. Really. Good.

My mouth watered in anticipation and a swirling heat pulsed between my legs. Entranced, I watched as he grabbed himself, rising above me, his immense, powerful shoulders and chest and arms filling my vision.

"Lie back," he ordered, spreading my legs with his knee, stroking my opening with his erection before guiding himself inside and thrusting.

I gasped.

Thrusting.

I gasped again. My body arched off the seat as he withdrew and then immediately pushed deeper, rougher. Repeating the motion, his fingers laced with my fingers and he held them over my head, against the leather of the seat, biting and sucking on my neck.

I felt like I was being devoured. Possessed. Dominated. It was all so familiar, but this time we were naked. This time he was inside me, deep inside, skin to skin, damp and slick, the sparse hair of his chest friction against my breasts. His hips rolling and pushing, stroking my body with his much larger, more powerful one, holding me down, covering me.

I can't breathe.

That same little fissure of fear ignited in my belly, making everything sharper, the sight of his glorious form brighter, more vivid. I loved it. I craved it. I welcomed it. He grunted, moving faster, the slap of his thighs against mine echoing in my ears, a purely carnal sound of sex and surrender. Taking, seizing, wild and rough, yet he moved with a skillful rhythm that matched my racing heart.

"You feel so good. Like heaven." His mouth was at my neck, biting and sucking, sending ticklish shivers down my spine just as he hit the right spot, the tight, aching center of my body, and I cried out.

I cried out, chanting *yes* and *please*, panting, splitting apart.

I cried out and the world disappeared except for where he moved, hitting the tender, twisting, secret place, my walls clenching, pulsing, until I completely shattered apart.

I can't breathe and it's so perfect and beautiful and wrong. You like this? What's wrong with you?

"Mona."

I barely heard him. He sounded far away, but I knew he was still there even as the stars continued to burst behind my eyes, even as the little whisper of fear became a louder voice of doubt, guilt.

You can't like this. You have no control, you can't like this.

Waves of pain and pleasure rolled through me as he moved faster, pushed harder, his body heavy, pressing me down.

"I'm losing my mind. I can't—I can't—" He groaned, tensing as his hips broke their elegant rhythm to pound deep, hard, covetous and mindless, and the force of his thrusts pushed me up the bench.

Abram's body curled, bowing forward, forming a cocoon of bronzed skin and sinewy muscle, and I breathed him in, raptly watching his face as he came, desperate to see his loss of control, tears pricking behind my eyes as I asked myself, if *he* can lose control, why can't I? Why is it wrong for me?

He's not afraid.

His eyebrows stitched together, he exhaled roughly.

Like it hurt.

Like it cost him.

"God. Fuck." His arms shook as he lowered himself to touch my forehead with his. "You're perfect. So perfect. I love you, I love you so much." His mouth crashed to mine and he released my hands, cradling my face, stroking my hair. Still inside me, he slid his hand lower, fondling my body, petting me.

"I love you," he said.

Or maybe I did.

I couldn't be certain.

154

"It's never going to be enough," I said.

Or maybe he did.

I couldn't be sure.

But I was certain that I sucked in a hitching breath as he gathered me to him and cradled me lovingly. And I was sure that the air I held within my lungs was to halt the beginning of a sob.

[14]

TIME AND SPACE IN SPECIAL RELATIVITY

Abram

S omething is very wrong.
        I'd held her, leisurely kissing the silky skin of her face and neck, fondling her luscious breast, enjoying the decadent softness and weight and the feel of her in my hand. The earlier desperation had morphed into elation, I was wholly and completely enamored. I'm talking fucking stars-for-eyes, cartoon-heart-beating-out-of-my-chest euphoric, convinced that this, being with her like this, so close, just us, exposed and vulnerable to and with each other was my heaven on earth.

In the moments after, thoughts of her happiness consumed me. I wanted and hoped I'd made her feel what I was feeling. I wanted her happiness, her laughter and joy, her contented sighs and smiles. But, almost immediately, it became abundantly clear that she *did not* feel what I was feeling.

She didn't push me away. She said nothing as I touched and tasted. In fact, she lay perfectly still. Even her chest didn't move. Slowly, much slower than I'd like to admit, I became aware that she was holding her breath, the beats of my heart ticking off the seconds.

I stopped kissing her, a prickle of unease between my shoulder blades. I waited, listening, certain I was being ridiculous. She'd been right there with me. She'd said *yes* and *please*, and when she'd come —*God*—she'd been so fierce, so beautiful.

Something is very, very wrong.

Abruptly, she breathed. Exhaling slowly, carefully, and then drawing in another breath to hold it. *What the hell?*

Lifting myself up, I searched her face. She wasn't looking at me. Her eyes were glassy, dazed, focused internally, her expression completely impassive. The warmth of euphoria was replaced with icy dread.

"Mona."

She seemed to give herself a little shake, her attention shifting outward, and she pressed her lips together. She was still holding her breath.

"Are you—what—what's wrong?" I wasn't going to panic. I wasn't. *I won't.*

"Nothing." She shook her head, her lips curving into an unconvincing smile, but her eyes betrayed her. They looked frantic. Sad, angry, confused, scared.

She was freaking out.

"You're lying," I thought and said at the same time.

The corners of her mouth turned down, her eyes shuttering, growing cold. "Can you give me a little space?" she said, her voice quiet and firm, laced with impatience, like I'd irritated her.

Space.

She wanted space.

She wants space.

I stared at her stupidly, feeling as though I'd just been slapped. The last time she'd asked for space, it hadn't been her. It had been Lisa. But since I hadn't been aware of that fact, I'd experienced the very peculiar sensation of feeling my heart fracture in real time.

This is all so familiar.

I remembered this. I remembered what this felt like, like being her garbage.

Except, this, now, this was her, and we'd just . . . I'd just . . . *shit.*

Stop. Don't panic. Just take a minute. Think.

Easier said than done.

Pushing myself off and away, I dropped my eyes to the floor of the limo, a balloon of confused dejection swelling in my chest, a rush of heat moving up my neck. I fought against both, telling myself to slow down. *Think.*

An object near her bra caught my attention and I squinted at it, something that looked like a piece of wrapped candy, or—*no.* Condoms. Two foil wrappers, glinting under the overhead light. I doubted they'd been left behind by a previous customer, the rest of the limo was too clean for them to be overlooked.

Mona brought condoms. Why would she bring condoms? Had she changed her mind about using a condom? Was that why she was upset now? Did I—*shit.*

I pushed a shaky hand through my hair. I'd been selfish. I'd been so desperate to have her. I must've pushed her or—

No. Wait. That's not how it was. She was just as desperate. What am I missing?

Mona was moving and I numbly lifted my eyes, watching as she searched the limo, her arm covering her breasts. Finding her dress, she turned away and pulled it over her head. Not looking in my direction, she held my jeans and boxers out to me, her eyes on the floor of the limo.

On autopilot, I took them, pulled on my pants, my preoccupied mind combing through the last twenty or more minutes, looking for a sign, for what I'd done wrong, or what I'd missed. *What the hell am I missing?*

Mona sat on the bench across from where we'd made love, frowning down at herself. She was moving her underwear between her legs, like she was trying to wipe herself off, like the evidence of what we'd done frustrated her.

Doing my best to ignore the flare of pained anguish in my chest, I spotted my shirt crumpled by her feet. I moved toward it, wanting to help, wanting to fix this, make it right. She turned her head at my approach, flinching as I came closer. The small action made me stop as a renewed wave of dejection filled my lungs.

I couldn't quite see. My senses weren't working as they should. My brain in disorder. All tools of perception were focused on the pain caused by every heartbeat and trying to figure out how to get through it. *God, this hurts.*

I cleared my throat, and I swallowed, and I moved back to where I'd been sitting, opting instead to tell her from a distance, "You can use my shirt, to—to clean up. If you want."

Mona stared at me, like she was trying to make sense of my words, and then she blinked several times, her back straightening, her mouth opening and closing. I watched her gather a deep breath, and then in the next moment, her chin wobbled.

Totally confused, but also absolutely fascinated, I studied her as she covered her mouth just as a sob escaped, tears filling her eyes and rolling down her cheeks. She shook her head. Her face crumpled, and she curled forward, bowing her head as she cried.

Stunned, I stared at her, completely at a loss. She'd just been so cold, aloof, composed. She'd wanted *space*. But now she was crying. *Crying.* Body-wracking sobs. My heart thundered between my ears, bouncing wildly against my ribcage, as though trying to reach her.

Did I hurt her? Fuck.

I couldn't breathe. I didn't know what to do, but I had to do something. I *had to.* I couldn't watch her like this from afar. I'd rather chew glass.

Carefully, slowly, keeping my eyes on her, I lowered to my knees. "Mona."

She hiccupped, shaking her head. "I'm so sorry," she said. "I'm so sorry. I ruined it."

What?

Fighting the instinct to just grab her and hold her close, I gathered an unsteady breath, as deeply as the ache in my lungs would allow, shifting closer. "Can I hold you?"

Instantly, she nodded. And then, before I could move, she flung herself at me, her arms wrapping around my neck, nearly strangling. Because I sensed she needed it, I held her tightly, leaning back to cradle her on my lap.

I second-guessed myself. I couldn't read her. I'd been wrong before. I couldn't trust that I knew what she wanted. Maybe she didn't want to be held tightly. Maybe she just wanted to hold someone.

"Hold me tighter," she demanded, as though reading my mind. "Please. Please forgive me. I'm so sorry."

I immediately complied, relieved for the explicit direction, and stroked her. "Is this okay? Can I do this? Does this—is this bothering you?"

My questions and uncertainty seemed to only make her cry harder, and then she growled, the sound frustrated. "Please, just touch me like you want. Don't—don't ask!"

I stared forward, my brain paralyzed by confusion. I was so confused. I wanted to ask her so many things, starting with, *WHAT THE HELL IS GOING ON?*

Instead, I swallowed them. I held her, stroking her back, kissing her shoulder, whispering words of reassurance.

And I silently simmered in the chaos of my mind and heart.

* * *

We drove around for at least an hour while she snuggled against my bare chest. Every so often, she'd squirm, like she wanted to get closer, and then she'd sigh, like she was frustrated by the limitations of our physical forms. But then she'd kiss me, my collarbone, my shoulder, my neck, and settle once more.

It did wonders to soothe my earlier dejection.

It did nothing to untangle my confusion.

It did a lot to increase my concern for her.

The hour was time well spent with my thoughts, reviewing every moment between us. Three in particular stood out as significant.

The first, when we were in Chicago during that original week and I'd found her in the dark, in the kitchen. I'd startled her, but her reaction at the time, even after she knew she was safe—sad, angry, confused, *terrified.*

The second, in Aspen, when I'd backed her into my room and stood between her and the door. The look in her eyes then—sad, angry, confused, *terrified*—reminded me of how she'd looked just after we'd made love.

The third, the last time we were in Chicago, in her sister's apartment, when she'd rested on the bed after I'd touched her, curling herself into a ball, her eyes vacant. Sad, angry, confused, *terrified*.

In the past, I'd wondered whether something had happened. What made her shrink from touch? But when she didn't recoil from me, when she'd seemed to welcome it, allow me to touch her freely, I'd— selfishly, stupidly—let the curiosity go.

But now.

Shifting in the seat, loathe to move her, I reached for the button to lower the privacy screen, cracking it an inch.

"Thanks, but you can take us to the address now."

"Okay, Mr. Fletcher," the driver said.

I lifted the window again, frowning at the direction of my thoughts and at the way Mona's body was now tense in my arms. I felt her swallow. She sniffed. She swallowed again.

"Are . . ." Mona started, stopped, cleared her throat. "Do you still want to stay with me?"

"Of course." But doubt had me asking, "Do you want me to stay with you?"

She exhaled a loudly, lifting her head to look me in the eyes, miserable, remorseful, overwhelmed. "I'm so sorry. I love you, so much, and I'm so sorry."

"Please." I cupped her cheek with my palm, stole a quick kiss. "Please stop apologizing."

She nodded, pressing her lips together to firm her chin, but then blurted, "I'll do anything to make it up to you."

My heart heavy with worry, I frowned at her misery, trying to make sense of what had happened earlier and what was happening now. But I couldn't, and I wouldn't be able to unless she told me.

Gathering a deep breath, I slid my palm down her arm and lifted her fingers to my lips, kissing the back of her knuckles. "There is one thing you can do."

"Anything."

"You have to promise, before I ask, that you'll do it. That you'll give it to me, whatever I want." It was a dirty trick, but I was at my wit's end here. I needed her to talk to me, and the ends in this case justified the means.

"I promise. I swear, anything. I'll do anything." Her eyes were so wide, she looked so earnest and scared.

I thought back to Marie's statements about adults who grow up with neglectful parents and subsequently felt even worse about this manipulation. Just like Marie said, Mona was eager to prove herself, and now I was leveraging that vulnerability.

I kinda hated myself in that moment. But I also kinda didn't care. I needed her to tell me the truth, so we could figure this out, together. As long as I lived, I never wanted to see that look in her eyes again.

So, I gathered a deep breath, bracing myself, and asked, "Mona, why don't you like to be touched?"

She stared at me. And then she blinked rapidly, her eyes dropping. She pushed against my chest. I let her go. Climbing off my lap, she moved to the bench where she'd sat before, crossing her arms at her middle, not looking at me.

"I just don't like unexpected—"

"No," I said firmly, shaking my head, disappointed she wasn't telling me the truth. "No. That's not it. You're scared."

Her mouth dropped open and she gaped at me. "I'm not."

"Tell me the truth. Please."

She flinched. "I am, I am telling you—" She sucked in a hitching breath, the beginning of another sob, and then she closed her eyes. Her head fell back to the leather of the seat and she whispered, "Damn it."

"Why don't you want to tell me?" I asked softly, aching for an answer.

She shook her head, a humorless smile on her lips. "Because it's so stupid."

"Whatever it is, it's not stupid. If it makes you check out after every time I touch you, it's not stupid."

Her eyes opened and they cut to mine, held, devastating. Deep, bottomless wells of anguish. "I'm sorry."

"Stop. Apologizing. Please. Just tell me what happened."

Mona's chest rose and fell, breathing faster. I recognized this. She was working herself up to admit something difficult.

"I don't want you to look at me differently. I don't want you to treat me differently. I don't want you to think I'm crazy."

"I won't."

"But you might. Because what happened—God, Abram. It's nothing. It's so minor, especially compared to what other people go through. Nothing happened, and yet—and yet, I carry it around with me, empty luggage, and I have no idea why." Her voice cracked on the last word. I wasn't used to her sounding so helpless, so lost. I hated it.

Impulsively, I moved to where she was, knelt in front of her, and held her shoulders as well as her eyes. "Forget about other people, okay? If you stub your toe, you're allowed to acknowledge that it hurts like a motherfucker."

She laughed, a tear rolling down her cheek.

"If you break your arm, knowing someone out there in the world is starving and suffering shouldn't numb your pain. People say comparison is the thief of joy when it comes to success, right? But it's also the thief of compassion when it comes to suffering."

Mona nodded, sniffling, swallowing. "Okay, okay," she said, just as the car pulled to a stop.

Gritting my teeth at the inconvenient timing, I covered her hands with mine and squeezed. "Listen. We'll go inside. You take your time. If you need to sleep on it, fine. But before we do anything again . . ." I paused at the panicked look in her eyes, how her hands spasmed in mine.

"Abram." My name sounded like a plea.

"This isn't an ultimatum." I licked my lips, choosing my words carefully, gentling my voice. "This is me being careful with you."

Her face crumpled and she sounded angry as she whispered, "But that's just it. I don't want you to be careful with me. That's the opposite of what I want. And *that's* the problem."

Mona's words were a puzzle I was nowhere near solving when a knock sounded on the door.

I was resigned to the delay. "Come on. Let's go up."

She nodded, wiping at her tears.

Unable to help myself, I hugged her one more time, silently promising both her and myself that this was the beginning. No matter what she said, no matter what darkness or trials waited for us, or what events in her past held her hostage, my feelings for her would never change.

Tonight was the beginning, not the end.

[15]
RELATIVISTIC MOMENTUM AND ENERGY

Mona

F rom the road, you would never know that the modest brownstone was an awesome twentieth-century Chicago-gangster themed bed and breakfast. Situated in a quiet neighborhood, with single-family homes, parks, and coffee shops and restaurants at each corner, it looked like any of the other brownstones.

And that was exactly why I'd chosen it. Well, that and the huge bathtub, the relatively reasonable off-season price, and the milk and cookies available in the kitchen 24 hours a day.

My embarrassment was a great distraction from all the feelings churned up during our limo ride, and I did my best to not make the situation any more awkward for our driver. He was nice enough to give us his jacket, his shirt, and act like Abram's request was perfectly normal. The shirt was for Abram since I'd used his as a towel. The jacket was for me since my dress was torn. I didn't remember it tearing. But, then again, fabric cohesion had been the last thing on my mind when Abram helped me take it off.

I muttered only one anytime-phrase, "So, it has come to this," while Abram held out the jacket for me to put on, his eyes glinting with reluctant amusement.

But I still didn't have any shoes. Therefore, Abram insisted on carrying me to the gate where I punched in the code, and then to the door, where I punched in the other code. Once inside, he didn't put me down, instead whisper-asking me where we were going. It was late, and the rest of the guests and house staff were definitely asleep.

First, we had to swing by the kitchen to pick up our room key where the owner had hidden it. He then carried me up two flights of stairs. Our room took up the whole of the top floor. Walls had obviously been moved during the remodel, sectioning off the stairs from the rest of the space, with only one door accessing the entire suite.

Again, once inside, he didn't immediately put me down. He seemed to pause, glancing at the sitting area with a dark brown leather couch, the small mahogany bar in the far corner, the big screen TV mounted to the wall, and the black-and-white picture of Frank "The Enforcer" Nitti.

The gangster looked slightly confused, his eyes focused someplace above the camera, his hair parted to one side. If I didn't already know he was a gangster, I would've guessed he was a butcher. Or a baker. But not a candlestick maker.

As though suddenly deciding something, Abram carried me into the bedroom, twisted left, then right, conveying us to the bathroom before finally placing me back on my feet.

"There. You probably want to . . ." He pulled his hand through his hair, looking unsure and frustrated with himself. "Or maybe you don't."

I caught him by the hand before he could turn to leave. Swallowing around a lump of uncertainty, I held him in place and waited until he gave me his eyes.

I told him the truth. "I want to be brave with you."

His gaze softened, warmed.

So I quickly added before I could overthink it, "Will you take a bath with me?"

Abram's eyes widened, and he held still, looking caught, torn. "Uh."

"We won't do anything," I promised, giving him a beseeching half-smile. "It's just, I don't want to be alone, and we're both impressively dirty right now."

He chuckled, his eyes shifting to the side, glancing at the bathtub. And then he did a double take, noting roughly, "That's a huge tub."

I nodded, hope fluttering in my chest. "Yes. It is."

"Fuck," he said on a breath, the word one of deep despair, making me smile.

"Come on." I tugged on his hand.

His eyes came back to mine, even more conflicted, and his feet remained rooted in place. "No, Mona. No. I'll, uh. I'll come in later, after you're done."

I stepped back to him, holding his hand tighter, fear constricting my throat. "Please. Please stay with me."

"I will. I promise. But I can't take a bath with you without wanting to make love to you again. And, I'm sorry, but you scared the shit out of me in the limo. Once you tell me what happened, then we'll—"

"I was fifteen," I blurted, suddenly tired—so tired—of this between us. My brain switched to autopilot. "He was my chem lab TA. He found me alone one night in the lab and grabbed me from behind. He made me think he was going to rape me, though he never said the words. He let me go and said it was a joke. When I tried to leave, he grabbed me again, pinned me against the wall until I started to cry."

"Oh my God." The words tumbled out of him as he rocked backward on his feet, his large, shocked eyes darting between mine.

"But he didn't. He didn't rape me. He didn't hurt me. I had no bruises. He laughed at me, again. Said I was gullible, that I was just a little kid, that I reminded him of his little sister. He let me go. And that's it."

Abram swallowed convulsively, and I watched as the surprised confusion behind his eyes was eventually eclipsed by outrage and anger.

It was strange, telling him this now, how distant and removed I felt. When I'd told Gabby, I'd been shaky, sweaty, my heart had raced.

But not now. Now, it just felt like a fact. An ugly tale that happened to someone else but wouldn't stop following me around, making itself relevant to my life, insidiously inserting itself into my decisions. I wished it never happened, for so many reasons. Mostly though, I was frustrated with myself and how much power I'd given an event that didn't matter.

And I'd allowed it to ruin our first time together.

"Did you report him? Did you tell anyone?"

Shaking my head, exhausted, and abruptly feeling every speck of dirt and grime on my body, I crossed to the bathtub, turned on the faucet marked *hot*, and engaged the stopper.

"Come take a bath with me," I said, allowing fatigue to bleed into my words. "Please."

Considering me with a thoughtful and distracted frown, Abram acquiesced. I allowed myself to feel mildly relieved. I'd been afraid that telling Abram what happened would make him not want me anymore, as irrational as that sounded.

Except, the truth was, I was still afraid. I was still terrified that everything between us was going to change. He'd look at me differently, treat me like I was fragile, or crazy. Or he'd think I was overreacting, blowing the whole thing out of proportion. He'd tell me to get over it, like I'd told myself a thousand times.

Visibly distracted, Abram's fingers came to the buttons of the borrowed shirt. It was too small for his shoulders and too big for his waist. Meanwhile, numb, I shrugged off the coat, pulled off my dress, and climbed in the tub, adjusting the cold and hot water until the right temperature was reached.

I caught movement in my peripheral vision and turned my head to watch him push his pants down his hips, sparks of heat dancing in my lower stomach. My body came alive at the sight of his body.

Shame was quick to swoop in, reminding me that I'd just told him about what Leo had called *a trauma*. And now here I was, lusting after someone.

But he's not someone. He's Abram.

It didn't matter. Something was wrong with me. I shouldn't have lustful feelings so soon after speaking about *the event*, I shouldn't want to be held down while he took pleasure from my body, moving inside me. I shouldn't crave being dominated during sex. I shouldn't love it, but I did.

I faced forward again, cupping my hand and lifting it, watching the water spill around the edges until equilibrium was reached, leaving just about a tablespoon in my palm. Ah, what a perfect allegory for life. No matter how much I tried to hold on, ultimately, it would eventually slip through my fingers.

I looked up just as Abram climbed into the huge tub, his boxers still on. His mouth a frown, his eyes wary, he took the spot across from me.

"You take a bath with your boxers on?" I tried to make my voice light.

Abram studied me for a long moment before saying gently, "Tonight I do."

"You're afraid I'll attack you?" *What are you doing, Mona? Trying to turn this into a joke?*

Yes. Yes, I am. Maybe if I made it a joke then it would lose its power and I could move on.

His eyes narrowed, telling me he didn't think my statement was funny. In fact, it seemed to anger and frustrate him.

I swallowed again, my throat tight, my heart fluttering pitifully, wishing he would . . . *what?* What did I want? Did I want him to treat it like it was nothing? As I had? Did I want him to try to kiss me and make it better? Did I want him to grab me and devour me as he'd done in the limo?

"Was I too rough?" he asked, pulling me from my unanswerable questions.

"Pardon?"

"In the limo, when we were together. Was I too rough with you? Did I scare you?"

I shook my head but stopped. He'd been a little rough, and I'd loved it. But thinking about things now, I found it difficult to separate my feelings at the time from the guilt at having felt them.

"I was too rough," he said, sounding angry with himself. "I should've let you tell me what you like. I shouldn't have insisted that we discover each other. I'm sorr—"

"No. No, you weren't too rough. And I agreed with you, if you remember. I want us to discover each other. I want to give us a chance to be good at this. We're already good at this, we're great! It's just that it's—it's complicated."

He took a deep breath. "Complicated."

"Yes. Because I love you." My eyes stung with new tears, but I determinedly blinked them away, pulling my knees to my chest.

"That doesn't mean I get to do whatever I want to you."

"But I want it too. I like it rough. I—" I laughed, because I didn't quite know how to explain without sounding crazy, or wrong in the head. Sniffling, I said firmly, "I'm going to be brave, okay?"

He nodded, his eyebrows still knotted.

"Here is the truth, and if this makes me disturbed, then so be it. I've always been the one in control, with all my past partners. Always. But not with you."

He opened his mouth like he was going to say something.

I held up a hand, blinking against the stinging in my eyes. "Wait. Let me finish."

Abram nodded, clearly agonized by this data.

I took a deep breath, needing to clear my throat of emotion before continuing. "I love how you make love to me. I love it when you hold me down. I. Love. It. It gets me so, so hot. I love it when you're above me and I can't move. I love it when you take control and tell me what to do, order me around. However, after, I feel guilty about it, ashamed, and I can't stop comparing what happened when I was younger with what I enjoy, with you, during sex."

Abram blinked, distraught, his gaze moving over my head for a long moment, during which I regained control of myself, successfully winning the battle against the urge to cry.

"Have you talked to anyone?" His eyes cut back to mine. "A therapist?"

I hesitated. "Leo gave me some numbers a few weeks ago." It didn't escape my notice that everyone—Leo, Lisa, Gabby, and now Abram—seemed to think that my touch aversion in certain situations was related to *the trauma*. I still couldn't figure out why I flinched sometimes, and at other times I didn't, even with Abram. "I spoke to one of them—twice so far—but I just . . ." I shook my head.

"What?"

"It's like, I don't know this woman, and I'm going to tell her everything about myself? It seems very strange."

His mouth twitched. "Mona."

"Abram."

"That's what therapists do."

"I know."

"That's their job."

"I know."

His gaze moved over me. "Will you please talk to a professional about this?"

Ugh. Crap.

"Fine."

"I'll go with you if you want."

I splashed water on my face, hoping to wash off some of the eye makeup that I was certain had smudged under my eyes. I probably looked like a football player. "I'll, uh, let you know, if I need you to go."

Wiping my face of water, I gave him back my gaze. The bathtub was almost full, but neither of us made a move to switch off the water. I was too busy mediating a four-way battle between longing, hope, fear, and shame.

I longed for his touch, for things to be like they were before, between us.

I hoped he'd still want me.

I feared that he wouldn't.

Shame . . . well, that was a dead horse. I'd beaten it enough.

We were silent for a long time, long enough for anxiety to swell in my chest, long enough for me to await his next words with both dread and anticipation. I was terrified of what came next. But tonight was a night for bravery and recklessness. I'd come this far, I'd revealed this much. Therefore, even though I was nervous, I decided to rip off the Band-Aid.

Balling my hands into fists, I lowered my gaze to the surface of the water. "I already had your bags moved here. But if you need some time or want to stay at your original hotel for the next few days, or somewhere else, I completely understand."

Abram chuckled, it sounded incredulous. The laughter drew my eyes back to his and I found them to be equal parts tired, concerned, and frustrated. "Oh, my Mona. Do you really have no idea how I feel about you? Do you not understand that, even as I sit here, worried about you, livid and plotting revenge on your behalf, I'm trying to figure out how to prove you can trust me? Always. I love you with every part of myself, you've invaded every corner, every secret place, and I only want—I've only ever wanted—your happiness. If you want me to stay, then with you is always where I want to be."

I blinked against those confounded tears again, this time battling misery instead of apprehension. *Why does his beautiful profession of love make me miserable?*

"What can I do?" he asked, worry adding an edge to the softness of the question.

"I just . . ."

"What?"

"I don't want you to see me differently," I confessed to the water. "I loved how you looked at me, like you were hungry for me, like you wanted me all the time, like you're insatiable. I looked forward to it. Does that make me superficial and shallow?"

"Look at me."

Bracing myself, I did. His eyes glowed amber. Hot. Full of such raw desire and affection, it drove the air from my lungs and most of the wits from my brain.

"How am I looking at you?" His question was a deep rumble.

I couldn't answer, the words stuck in my throat, viscous with lust, heart humming happily. *Harlot heart.*

"I'm looking at you the same way you're looking at me. If you want the whole truth, and not to put any pressure on you, because that's the last thing I want to do, I'm—selfishly—trying to figure out a way to get inside your pants without making you feel guilty afterward. I'm conjuring ideas, wondering how you'd feel about dominating *me*, tying *me* up."

I had to swallow, because *lust*. "But, would you want that? Is that something you'd like?"

"Oh yes." His mouth curved, a flash of teeth, his dimple deeper on the left than on the right. But I knew it would be. "Yes. I'd like that very much."

"Even though you wouldn't be in control?"

"Uh, sign me up."

I couldn't help it, I laughed, shaking my head at him. "You want to be dominated?"

"By you? I would *love* it. Just think, I sit back, let you do all the hard work, sounds amazing. We could even get a blindfold and some handcuffs. I'd like that, you teasing me, making me crazy."

I laughed harder, tears leaking from the corners of my eyes, shifting my leg to kick him lightly with my foot under the water. "Now you're just being funny."

"I'm not." His voice, tired and raspy as it was, dropped an octave and he caught my foot, his hand sliding up my ankle to my calf, his touch calming and soothing the part of me that had been frantic about losing him. "Please, have your way with me. You're so clever and sweet. I bet you would come up with some very interesting, and probably educational, carnal activities. I swear, I am a million percent serious right now."

"A million percent?" I twisted my lips to the side, crossing my arms.

His eyes darted to my chest and then back up. He held my foot on his lap and was massaging the arch with his thumbs. "I've never been more serious about anything in my life. Except that I love you."

I huffed another laugh, but—after inspecting him closely for another few seconds—I believed him. My body *definitely* believed him, but it was biased, so it didn't count. My brain believed him. Most importantly, so did my heart.

Endeavoring not to smile like the sex-with-Abram-crazed lunatic that I was, I said, "Fine."

His eyebrows jumped. "Fine?"

"Let's do it." I pressed my lips together firmly.

"Yes, let's." He grinned, his eyes dancing. However, seconds later he blinked, and his stare sobered. "Also, you'll call your therapist? Talk to her about everything?"

Trying not to groan, I settled on a sigh instead, the reminder submarining my buoyed mood. But—strangely—not by much.

"Yes," I agreed, earning me a bigger grin.

"Promise?"

"Yes. I promise. I'll call."

[16]

INFRARED, ULTRAVIOLET, X-RAY, AND GAMMA-RAY ASTRONOMY

Mona

I'm beginning to suspect that I have a tendency to overthink things (and don't roll your eyes at me, I CAN SENSE YOU ROLLING YOUR EYES!).

Take Abram and his desires, thoughts, and motivations as an example. It was morning o'clock. Or quite possibly afternoon o'clock. I couldn't be certain without looking at my phone or an actual clock, and this B&B didn't have one next to the bed. Anyway!

Here we were, nebulous time of day o'clock. In bed. Together. Except, when I woke up, instead of being tangled in each other like I'd been led to believe is standard for lovers upon waking, he was on one side of the bed, facing me, and I was on the other side of the bed, facing him. Also, we were both fully clothed in unsexy yet comfortable pajamas.

Uh, rather, let me amend that. Abram was always sexy. His Iron Man flannel PJ bottoms and no shirt were quite sexy. Whereas my pink cotton PJ bottoms with Albert Einstein sticking out his tongue rendered in cartoon, plus my baggy white T-shirt, were not sexy.

But back to nebulous time of day o'clock.

Blinking, I scowled at his handsome slumbering face. What, pray tell, did this bed distance and lack of tangling mean? Did it mean he'd changed his mind? Or that his subconscious didn't want me? Evidence suggested I ought to be in service as a femme pillow au extraordinaire. But I wasn't.

Were they not pillow material?

Twisting my lips to the side, I reached up, beneath my shirt, pushing it up, and tested my breasts. Grabbing and squeezing, I considered the value of a breast malleability quotient scale, where breasts could be tested and ranked for skin softness and general pliability.

Not that I wanted to give women another thing for society to tell them to fret over. But, if there existed women like me, who enjoyed having data to do with what they pleased, then I'd be very interested in a random sample normalized curve of bosom to suppleness ratio, and here is why: The last romance novel I'd read, and the seventeen before that, always included a scene where the hero and heroine woke up embracing, invariably with the man cradled against the female's chest.

Therefore, why wasn't Abram cradled against mine? Were they a non-pillowy shape? Not pliable enough? Where had they failed me?

First, an analysis was needed. Then a diagnosis of the problem. I squeezed and kneaded and inspected, endeavoring to think of words to describe them were I a heroine in a romance novel. Typically, racks were described as something like, *Her supple bosom,* but never something like, *Her jagged tits.*

Squeezing one and then the other, I closed my eyes and took a moment to diagnose.

Mona's malleable mounds.

No. That was just lazy alliteration, not an accurate reflection of my boob-truth.

"What are you doing?"

Tensing, my eyes flew open. I gaped at Abram's raised eyebrows and the sleepy, confused amber irises beneath.

A small smile curved his mouth and his stare brightened with suspicion. "Are you . . .?"

"I'm doing a breast exam." My voice was much higher than normal, so I cleared my throat, keeping my face impassive. "Always good to, you know, check out the—uh—good old mammary glands and whatnot."

His eyes narrowed, his lips somehow pursing but still smiling. "You're giving yourself a breast exam? Now?"

I nodded, trying on my academic face. "Of a kind, yes."

Abram seemed to be working harder to subdue his grin. "Okay, okay. That's cool." Taking a deep breath, he rolled to his back, pushed down the covers and his pajama pants to his feet, and gripped his morning wood.

I gasped.

I sensed him glance at me but didn't actually witness his eyes on my face. My attention was otherwise engaged. Watching him. Stroke. Himself. And, you know, panting. (Me. I was panting. The panting came from me.)

"Go on," his voice said. "Don't let my penis exam distract you from your breast exam."

I'd never watched anyone touch themselves before. Big, strong hand, long fingers wrapped around his thick shaft, smoothing down and up, down again in perfect rhythmic strokes, a sexy metronome. It was hypnotic.

Clearing my throat again, and obviously still panting, I nodded, rolling slowly to my back, eyes still fastened to his erection. My shirt bunching at my collarbone, I massaged and caressed Mona's suddenly sensitive malleable mounds.

I had to stifle a groan as Abram tucked his other hand behind his head, giving me a completely unobstructed view of his torso and chest. *So unfair.*

"Found anything?" he asked, his voice still deep with sleep and his efforts at last night's concert.

"No. Not yet," I panted (yep, still panting), my nipples now tight, hard beads against my palms, my stomach twisting and coiling and heating. "How about you?" I made the mistake of glancing at his face and found his eyes on my hands where I touched myself.

He looked almost angry, his eyes—sharp, feral—were at half-mast, his jaw tight. He licked his lips, his tongue darting out, and I had the most *intense* desire to shove off my pants and straddle his face.

Why don't you?

"Nothing yet," his voice scraped. "But I'm not finished yet." Then he groaned. "Mona, what are you doing?"

His eyes tracked lower, looking pained, and I followed his line of sight to discover I'd moved one of my hands to my stomach, the tips of my fingers skimming along the waistband of my PJs. My gaze flickered back to his, and I tested a reckless hypothesis, dipping my hand inside my underwear and pushing them down my hips.

Abram's breath hitched, ragged, unsteady.

"Pelvic exam," I said, just as I brought my knees up and parted myself with my fingers.

His eyes shot to mine, held, his head shifting forward on his pillow, like he was going to *do something.* But he didn't. He stopped himself. He glared at me, reminding me of a tiger behind the bars of a cage, making promises with his eyes. *If I weren't trapped, if I could touch you.*

I hoped my stare communicated, *Why can't you? Touch me!* I was so hot, wet, ready. I was *right there,* next to him. Why didn't he reach out? His lack of action clearly frustrated us both.

Instead, he swallowed thickly, his eyes drifting down again, first to my breasts, and then to where my fingers moved between my spread legs, heated, dazed. His jaw ticked. His breathing grew labored. He blinked. Hard. Like he was having trouble focusing.

And then, suddenly, Abram sat up, stood up, pulled up his pants, and left the room. A second later, I heard the shower come on, and my mouth dropped open.

!

So.

There I was.

In bed.

One hand on my breast, the other between my legs.

Bereft.

Listening to my gorgeous boyfriend take a shower by himself. *Probably naked*! Unless he wore boxers in the shower as well.

Growling, I also sat up, stood up, but I pulled my pants down. Whipping my shirt off, I marched after him into the bathroom, finding him—AH HA! *NAKED*—in the glass shower. I stopped short inside the door because his back was to me and his back was very naked, and I'd never seen a naked back like his before, if you don't count shirtless rugby players in spandex shorts (which I didn't).

Plus, this was Abram's back. Not anonymous sporty guy's back. Therefore, it was a spectacular force. Breathing hard, because I was turned on and angry, I placed my hands on my hips, and whisper-yelled, "Why did you leave?"

Abram turned his head, giving me just his profile, and then shook his head, turning away. "Give me a minute."

I took a step closer, so he could hear me better, not so I could get a better view of his ass because the shower was steaming up the glass. Not because worry had cut through the lusty fog in my brain and told me things between us were not functioning as per Mona-Abram relationship standards.

"Abram. Talk to me. Please."

He cursed, flipped off the shower, turned completely around while reaching for a towel to hide his glorious engorged erection. The action left me feeling uncertain, so I plucked a washcloth off the counter and used it as a fig leaf of sorts for my vagina, covering my breasts with my arms.

"Mona," he began, frowning at where I held the tiny square in front of myself. Shaking his head as though to clear it, he started again, "Mona. Last night, you shared yourself with me. I am so appreciative that you trusted me, thank you. And, because of what you shared, I'm doing my very best here, trying to keep my hands to *myself*. Which—" he glanced down at the tented towel at his pelvis " I am incapable of doing while you're next to me touching yourself."

During his speech, I'd opened and closed my mouth many, many times, mostly planning to object, or question the validity of his logic. Conversely, as I listened and I realized the truth—that he was trying to be respectful and save me a visit to shame town—I snapped my mouth shut.

Glaring at me like I was a roast beef sandwich he'd been denied (the most exceptional of all sandwiches), he cleared his throat, stretched his neck, and waited.

At first, I didn't know what to say. I mean, he had a good point. But on the other hand, no. Hadn't he been the one to suggest me taking the lead last night? So why was he—*Oh!*

"Ohhhhhh!" I nodded, my nods slow and exaggerated. "I get it!"

He gave his head a subtle shake. "What do you get?"

"You want me to dominate you, tell you what to do."

Abram flinched, sucking in a breath.

But before he could speak, because that was my job now, I tossed the washcloth back to the counter and once again stood before him proudly, hands on my hips.

"Abram, my love, please step out of the shower."

He lifted an eyebrow over narrowed eyes, his lips parting and his jaw shifting to one side, a spark of something in his stare that had me grinning. *Was that defiance?* How wonderful.

Eventually, he did it. He stepped out of the shower, letting the towel shift to his hip where he gripped it in one hand.

His eyes struck me as sardonic and so did his tone as he asked, "What now?"

"We're going back to the bed." I mean, obviously, right?

I watched as he took a deep breath, like he was steadying himself. With reluctant movements, he began using the towel to dry his skin.

"No," I said, frowning.

"No?"

"Don't dry off. I want you wet."

He blinked again, like my words landed somewhere sensitive. His grin a tad incredulous, but also amused, he nodded and placed the towel on the edge of the tub. My gaze dropped to his erection and I licked my lips, the electricity of excitement making me restless.

Crooking my finger as I backed out of the bathroom, I motioned to him. "Come on."

Turning, I didn't wait to see if he would follow and crossed to the bed, standing at the edge of it, waiting for him to appear and nervously worrying my lip.

With the males of my previous acquaintance, providing directions before and during intercourse had felt a bit like giving a lecture, or explaining how to make poached eggs. But with Abram, I was a bundle of nerves, wanting to make this good for him, wanting to make it amazing like he'd done for me.

The main impediment as far as I could tell was my libido. I was already so incredibly turned on. Therefore, I concluded, I would just have to take things slow, get him worked up with foreplay in order to ensure his orgasm was pleasurable.

Go slow. I nodded at the assertion.

He appeared in the doorway, and I straightened. Realizing I'd been twisting my fingers, I stopped, scratched the back of my neck, and then pointed to the mattress. "Lie down. In the center."

Saying nothing, Abram strolled to and stopped just two decimeters in front of me. His eyes on mine, making my heart beat like crazy, and I recognized something about myself. The fear was back. Just like before, it made everything brighter, colors sharper, my skin too tight, my breasts heavy, so heavy, sensitive.

Huh.

But before I could give this realization much thought, Abram's eyes dropped to my mouth, heated. He swayed forward, like my lips were magnetic. The way he looked—again, like a tiger pacing in a cage—sent a sharp thrill from the top of my skull to the base of my spine. I shivered.

I actually owned a pair of tiger-print underwear and matching bra, and I'd brought it with me. *Note to self, wear sexy tiger underwear today.*

His eyes cut back to mine. His jaw worked.

"Lie down," I whispered, holding his gaze.

He did.

He lay down. In the center of the bed. His body visibly tense. His hands balled into fists. His muscles flexing. And his gorgeous penis. *Sigh.*

Swallowing the thirst, I climbed onto the bed, now on all fours, and crawled to where he lay. Nudging his legs apart with one of mine, I placed a knee between his thighs, my hands on either side of his torso, and bent to lick the water from his chiseled abdominal muscles.

Oh yeeeeah.

Desire pooled low and insistent in my belly. He flinched, then groaned, his penis pressing tenaciously against my stomach, hard and hot, smooth like silk. I gripped it. He was rock hard.

I felt dizzy. My sex clenched around nothing, reminding me of how neglected it was, how empty, and—

Yeah, you know what? Forget taking it slow.

Impulsively, I straddled his hips and lowered myself, sucking in a relishing breath at the delicious, stretching invasion. This, clearly, shocked the hell out of him because his hands came to my thighs and squeezed.

"God. God. Mona—"

I bent forward, bracing my arms on either side of his head, and took his mouth. He groaned, immediately opening, chasing my tongue, obviously fighting the urge to take over as I rolled my hips, using him to rub just the right spot.

Abram's hands were moving, sliding up my sides, cupping my breasts, rolling my nipples between his fingers, and then tucking themselves beneath my arms to lift me higher so he could suckle one, and then the other, lavishing both with wet, hungry kisses.

Tingly, hot tendrils of electricity played tug of war between my pelvis and nipples, stretching, curling, making me slightly insane. The urge to sit up and ride him more completely was overwhelming. I needed him deeper, I needed more force, faster.

Placing my hands on his stomach, I straightened away, eliciting a frustrated growl from his throat, his eyes piercing as I shifted, using the hard plane of his stomach as leverage while also feeling him up.

"Say something," I demanded, because why the hell not? *He is mine to command*!

His lip curled into a feral smile, a baring of teeth, sending a renewed fissure of alarm down my spine to the back of my legs, making me hot. *So hot.* I was sweating with exertion and the thrill of uncertainty. I loved it and I was so close. I could feel the start of it, the deep ache teetering on satisfaction.

Abram's covetous eyes caressed a scorching path from my lips to my breasts and then further south, obviously watching us where we mated. "Thank you for the view," he said, his voice like gravel, his hands sliding to my hips. His fingers flexed into my bottom like he wanted to help lift me, help me go faster.

"Do you like watching?" I asked because I really wanted to know for some reason. It was *essential* that I know. Another shiver. I couldn't catch my breath.

"I like watching you." His hand came around to the front of my thigh, his thumb slipping between my folds. "I like this." He circled my clitoris and *OH GOD OH GOD OH GOD—*

"I like watching you come on my cock," he said through clenched teeth, sounding a little sinister.

His statement was well-timed because I was coming. So. Hard. My hips jerking, searching, seeking, needing to prolong the fullness and friction. My body igniting. I couldn't think, but intrinsically I knew he was coming too.

His hips pistoned, rolled, inelegant searching, just like mine. His head pressed against the pillow, exposing his neck, his powerful form in sharp relief. His hands moved away from my body, gripping the bedsheets and pulling. I heard a ripping sound. I ignored it, bowing forward above him, my hand on his heart.

Then I collapsed. I just freaking fell right on top of him, limp, my mouth at his neck, greedily gulping air as his hips still worked, seeking the last bit of his pleasure from my body. A moment later, I felt him go lax, also breathing like he'd just run a marathon. I felt fingers thread into my hair, grabbing a fistful to angle my head for a kiss.

Somehow, both of us breathing hard, our bodies completely spent, we were still able to kiss. Maybe because it was sweet. Tender. An unhurried, soft meeting of lips and tongue. Abram smoothed his hand down my back to my bottom, stroking it. He made a little sound in the back of his throat, something halfway between a growl and a hum.

Or maybe that was me.

No. That's him.

I fell asleep, right there, naked, on top of my purring tiger.

[17]

THE NATURE OF STARS

Mona

I. Was. STARVING! when I woke up. But I was also sticky and alone. The former wasn't a surprise, but the latter was.

Wrinkling my nose, as I'd once again awoken without an Abram on my bosom, I rubbed my eyes and searched for my phone to determine the time. Honestly, I had no idea where it was. The night before had been a blur.

While I scoured every surface that could be scoured from my spot in bed, I noticed a folded piece of paper on the side table, one that had been torn from a notebook. My heart gave a little leap. Pushing myself to a sitting position, I snatched it, and chuckled when I discovered he wrote *DO NOT BURN* on the outside.

Dear Mona,

First, I love you.

Second, Marie called and said your phone was left in the green-room last night. She picked it up for you so I'm meeting her now to grab it. I'm also picking up some food, because I'm starving.

Third, did you know this place has milk and cookies 24 hrs a day! I left you milk and a plate with oatmeal and chocolate chip in the mini fridge under the bar. EAT THEM.

Fourth, sorry I ripped the sheet. I told the owner and they'll send up a new one later today.

Fifth, I love you.

-Abram

PS I have to confess something. I watched you sleep while you were naked until my stomach growled so loud, I was afraid it would wake you up. Now, when I close my eyes, I see your naked body. Thank you for all the views. You are very sexy.

PPS I love you.

Smiling stupidly and reading the note more times than I could count, I eventually stood, refolding it carefully and tucking it inside my suitcase. On a happy cloud, I crossed to the bar, opened the mini fridge, and stood at the counter scarfing down cookies and gulping milk.

It was at this point I realized I was very naked. It felt a bit like Adam and Eve discovering their nudity, except without the creepy snake.

"What was in those cookies?" I mumbled to myself, hurrying to the bathroom and rushing through a shower, the promise of more food spurring my movements.

But when I finished and dressed—making sure to put on my tiger-print undies and bra—and Abram and the food still hadn't arrived, I was at a loss. The B&B's lack of Wi-Fi was supposed to be a bonus. No Wi-Fi meant less distractions. But I hadn't even brought a book! Without the distraction of my phone, access to email, or a book, I wandered around the large suite and inspected the photos of gangsters hanging on the walls.

After engaging in a staring match with a photograph of someone named Vincent "The Schemer" Drucci, an open notebook on the living room desk snagged my attention. Meandering to it, I peered down at the open page, recognizing Abram's handwriting immediately. I scanned the first few lines.

. . .

Your mouth tastes so sweet, your skin is sweet too
  Hold still, my love, and let me savor you
  Pushing lace aside I ask her, does this taste like candy, I wonder—

GASP!

I tore my eyes away and took a giant step backward, my hands flying to my suddenly hot cheeks, my skin—everywhere—breaking out in goose bumps.

It was sexy poetry. About *us!* Based on my body's crazy lava-like reaction to the first three lines—an explicit and direct window into his beautiful brain—I couldn't handle it. Catnip and love potion and a mixture of all aphrodisiacs in written word form and in Abram's handwriting.

Is this what life would be like with a poet? One minute I'm fine, minding my own business, and then the next I'm consumed by lava lust?

Good Lord. Have mercy. Amen.

"Oh no."

Startled, I turned toward the sound of Abram's concerned exclamation and I grimaced, my hands falling to my sides. "Ah! Sorry!"

"Who told you—wait, what? Why are you sorry?" Rushing across the room, he shut the suite door with his booted foot and placed three white plastic bags—of what I assumed was takeout—on the coffee table.

"I accidentally looked at your sexy poetry." My eyes moved over him, gobbling the sight of him up. He wore dark jeans and a black leather jacket over a button down dark blue shirt.

Oh jeez. I wanted him. Right now. Clearly, I was powerless against the power of suggestion where Abram was concerned, and especially when the suggestions were made by his poetry. If he ever turned his sexy poems into a song, I'd be ruined.

But Abram didn't seem to follow. "Sexy poetry?"

"Your notebook." I gestured to it, tangentially surprised it didn't burst into flames, what with all the hot, suggestive thoughts recklessly left on its pages.

"Oh." He gave me a distracted flash of his dimple, his eyes moving over me like he thought I was adorable. "No, that's totally fine. Read the whole thing if you want, it's all about you anyway."

"Oh my." My hands came back to my cheeks. *Lava-like lust.*

"Listen." Abram's gaze turned bracing and he encircled my wrist with his fingers, tugging me toward the couch. "Something's happened."

I allowed him to lead me. "What? What happened?"

"Last night, when we left the stadium, we were photographed."

"Oh. Okay." I twisted my hand so that our fingers tangled together, the smell of food finally permeating my senses. "Hey. Is that Mexican food? You didn't happen to pick up enchiladas, did you?"

He frowned. "Mona. This is a problem."

"Is it?" Now I frowned. "You didn't want anyone to know we were dating?"

"No. That is, I figured it would come out eventually, and I thought I was fine with it coming out now."

"But now you think everyone knowing is a problem?"

"Yes," he said emphatically. "Because it's not just about everyone knowing."

"Yikes. Did I accidentally flash someone? I knew that skirt was too short. So, Mexican food?"

He looked at me like he thought I was crazy. "No. You didn't—how can you be—" Abram growled. "Listen. This is important. You didn't flash anyone, most of the shots are blurry because it was dark. But they've got it wrong. They think it was Lisa with me, not you."

"Oh no." I grimaced. "I'll call and apologize to my sister."

"Mona. They—the websites, the newspapers, social media—they're having a fucking field day. They've dug up old pictures of Lisa, when she was with Tyler, and are making this into a shitstorm. Saying she's using me to promote his album, claiming that's why I've played his song."

"Obviously that's not true. How badly are they treating her? What did they say?"

"They're relentless, vicious. Saying she's not good enough for me, saying she's grotesque, ugly, saying she's a leech, a user, a gold digger and worse. It's brutal."

"Ah, crap. I'll call her now, let her know we'll get this all straightened out. Did you get my phone?"

He shook his head as though to clear it. "Yes, absolutely, we'll call Lisa, see what we can do to make this go away for her. She shouldn't have to go through this. But you're missing my point. If we tell everyone that it's actually you in the photos, that we're together, there's a chance you'll be ripped apart."

He lost me again. "Uh, yeah?"

Eyes flashing, Abram exhaled suddenly, clearly perplexed and frustrated by how well I was taking this. "And that's okay with you?"

Staring at him, comprehension slowly seeped through the barrier of my intimate familiarity with all matters celebrity. "Ah! I see. You didn't realize this was going to happen."

He seemed to choke on my statement for a few seconds before coughing out, "I thought, maybe, there'd be a few haters, outliers, whatever. But nothing like this. You were expecting this level of vitriol?"

"Yes. Well"—I waved my hand in the air—"not the Lisa part. And I can fix that for her. But the *Abram Fletcher's girlfriend being criticized for existing by news and social media* part? Oh yeah. I knew that was going to happen, and I knew it would be vicious. That's what always happens to women who date attractive male super celebrities."

Abram gaped at me like he'd never seen me before, and then he jumped up, paced to the other side of the room and ripped off his leather jacket with jerky movements.

Left alone with the food and an empty stomach, I slowly reached for the closest bag while keeping my eyes on him. I didn't want to be rude, as I could see he was going through a crisis of reality-fueled frustration, but I was extremely hungry, and my stomach demanded action. Reasoning with myself that I could be supportive *and* well-fed, I untied the top of the plastic bag, reaching inside to withdraw the first container of mystery takeout while hunting for utensils.

"I can't believe this." His hand was over his mouth and muffled the words slightly. "You wanted to be with me even though you knew this kind of cruelty might happen to you."

"Yes," I answered evenly, popping the container open. *NACHOS!* Licking my lips in anticipation, I dipped the cheesiest of the chips into a pool of salsa, and then shoved the whole thing in my mouth. Yum. So good.

Pacing back and forth, he scowled at me, quietly seething, "This is bullshit. You shouldn't have to deal with this. You shouldn't have to put up with being torn down simply because we're together."

"I mean—" Speaking around a mouthful of nacho, I had to swallow before continuing, "In a perfect world, yeah. This wouldn't happen. But this is just how it is."

"Why aren't you more pissed?" He stopped short on the other side of the coffee table, his eyes accusatory.

"Abram, I grew up around celebrities, rock stars, movie stars. I guess I'm used to it. You'll get used to it too." I meant my words to be comforting, hoping they'd make a positive impact.

They did not.

He exhaled. Loudly. If he'd been a dragon, I was certain I'd be on fire. His hands came up, his fingers stiff, and he shook them while making a growling sound. "This is so fucking *frustrating*!"

He paced away.

Surreptitiously, I quickly ate another nacho, chewing with haste and swallowing before he paced back. "Okay, okay. I can see you are very upset—"

"UPSET?!"

I rolled my lips between my teeth, standing and making a slow, careful approach. "And I appreciate you being upset on my behalf. But, my dearest love, I entered into this beautiful relationship with you knowing that, eventually, once we made our connection public, the peanut gallery was going to pick me apart. Everything about me will be public fodder. But that's okay, it always has been to a certain extent. I'll deal with it."

His eyes cut to mine, glaring at me like I was nuts.

"I'll let you in on a little secret." I took a few tiny steps closer. "The peanut gallery doesn't actually matter. All those haters? Who tear people down? They don't matter. And what they say doesn't matter. It'll just be more publicity for you, more noise. Your name will trend upward. My parents always say, 'All noise is good noise, unless it's mocking noise.' I don't think you'll be mocked for dating me, but I don't know for certain."

Abram shook his head. "I don't care about me, I don't care what they say about *me*. That's not the problem. It's what they say about you."

"But they don't matter."

"They shouldn't be allowed to say such hateful things."

"But since they don't matter, what they say doesn't matter either. It's like multiplying any number by zero. The peanut gallery is the zero."

He snapped his mouth shut, his jaw flexing. Breathing hard, his hands on his hips, once again he reminded me of a caged animal. But this time, it was angry helplessness I spied, not hunger.

I made a soft sound of compassion, closing the distance between us to place a hand on his scruffy cheek. "Oh, Abram. Please don't waste energy on this. Haters gonna hate, idiots gonna procreate."

He huffed a laugh, but his eyes looked sad, trapped. "I'm never going to be okay with this." Covering my hand with his, he brought my palm to his lips. "I'm going to fight the world for you." He sounded so fierce.

It made me smile. "Challenge all who besmirch my name?"

His mouth curved against my hand.

"You like that word? Besmirch? It's a great word, right? I dare you to use it in a song. You know another great word? Nachos." Turning my fingers, I caught his and tugged him toward the coffee table. "Come. Sit. Feast."

Abram allowed me to pull him back to the couch, and then he allowed me to gently push his shoulders until he was sitting again. Hesitating for a second but ultimately yielding to the impulse, I sat on his lap. Immediately, his arm came around me, one hand on my hip, the other on my thigh.

"I've never fed anyone before. Do you want me to feed you

nachos?" I lifted a chip toward his mouth. "I can make airplane sounds."

Eyes still sad, he laughed, and his forehead fell to my shoulder. Again, he made a growling sound.

"Or train sounds? Choo." He shook his head, so I ate the chip. Turning, pressing my chest against his chest, I wrapped him in my arms. "It gets easier to ignore people who don't matter. I promise. Like any skill, it just takes practice."

"But what about your career?" He lifted his head, leaning back to capture my eyes as his scowl returned. "I think Marie tried to warn me about this. Charlie too."

"Physicists—and the science community in general—don't pay much attention to the chatter of pop culture unless it furthers their own careers. Me dating you might be the cause for some minor curiosity, and I'll probably have to put up with a slight increase in snobbery and pretentiousness. Eventually, they'll go back to hunting for puzzle pieces to the universe and struggling to find grant dollars to fund their research. Remember who my parents are. I've been dealing with their shadow most of my life."

Abram leaned further back, his eyes moving between mine, questioning. "I thought you were worried about candid pictures of you being made public. You said they could destroy your career. And, for the record, I don't like the idea of being a shadow for you."

"Oh, depending on the picture, they totally could wreck my career, or derail it. If that picture of me in the lab coat were released, I'd definitely lose a few of my grants and would have a hard time finding any funding. At least, for a while."

Aghast, he stared at me. "Then why did you send it?"

"Because I thought you'd like it."

"Mona."

"Abram."

"We should delete them. We should delete those pictures now."

"No. We shouldn't. You were right. Other people shouldn't be dictating how I share myself with you, so don't let them dictate how you share yourself with me. I came to terms weeks ago with the futility of conforming to pompous ideas of what constitutes appropriate behavior."

"You did? When?"

"When I sent you that picture of me in a bikini. I even told you in the hospital, but you might've been too sick to hear me. And actually, futility isn't the right word. It's *damaging* to everyone who comes after. It's damaging for Mona DaVinci to sit quietly and let others dictate her —my—personal life. Then what good have I done? History—the good kind of history—is seldom made by those who keep their head down."

His dimple winked at me as his eyes gazed deep into mine, like he was a little mesmerized. "You're the most remarkable person I've ever known."

"Ditto, Mr. Harris." I stole a quick kiss, grinning down at his handsome face. "But don't get ahead of yourself. I haven't done anything yet. It's not like I'm going to hand out bikini shots of me at faculty meetings. I'm just going to act like myself, do what I want to do. I'm going to be *honest*." Tilting my head to one side then the other, I shrugged. "And if trouble follows, so be it."

* * *

I called Lisa while we ate the nachos. As I suspected, she wasn't too freaked out about the social media "shitstorm" as Abram called it, but she did surprise the Schrödinger out of me by offering to maintain the ruse.

"Just think about it," she said. A second later, I heard a microwave beep on her side of the call.

Abram and I swapped stares of disbelief, not because of the microwave beep, but because *what the heck?*

"Why would you do that?" I blurted, for obvious reasons.

"It's the least I can do for you after what you've done for me. And it doesn't bother me. We could just not comment on the pictures. It would buy you and Abram more time together without the press following you everywhere. Like I said, just think about it."

Abram frowned thoughtfully in a way that made me nervous. I

glared at him, wanting to deter any temptation he felt to take my sister up on the offer.

"No. No way." I said this for his benefit as much as hers.

"Can you give us a minute?" Abram cut in and put Lisa on mute.

"The answer is no." I crossed my arms.

"She makes a good point about giving us more time. And if she doesn't mind, why not?"

"You can't be serious. You were the one who came in here less than an hour ago, huffing and puffing about how terrible the news was treating Lisa."

He gathered a deep breath and, holding my eyes, he nodded. "You're right. It's not fair to Lisa, and it's obvious she's trying to be a good sister here. I have to give her credit for that. But it's just, I love you. And I'm worried about you. You're more sensitive than people think, and you feel so deeply. I know you said you're prepared for this, but I'm worried. *But*, I also trust your judgment. If and when you want to go public, I'm all for it."

I understood his concern, and I wasn't looking forward to the glimpses of hateful pomposity I'd get from my place on the periphery, but I wasn't going to let Lisa be my stunt double, or my red herring.

Of note, as I inspected him, I sensed his worry, absolutely. But I was also picking up on some other vibes, like—despite his apprehension—he was relieved and happy I was opposed to Lisa's suggestion. *Weird.*

Anyway, in the end, we turned down Lisa's offer.

I then called my therapist's office and scheduled a new appointment. Since I'd now fully committed to the idea, I decided to make a list of items I wanted to discuss. For example, the flinching, why did I do it with Abram sometimes? I loved it when he touched me, so why would I flinch away at odd intervals? Also, if I felt fear both times we'd made love, why did I feel shame after he was on top, but not when I was on top? That made no logical sense. This therapist was going to have her work cut out for her. *FOR SURE.*

And then, since I was in a list making mood, I navigated to a few websites looking for some tips on dirty talking. I'd never done it before, but after reading three lines of Abram's sexy poetry and experiencing an electromagnetic burst of incalculable desire, the impulse was one I couldn't ignore. Dirty talking was clearly an electromagnetic force.

Now, all four atomic fundamental forces had been identified: his body made me weak (weak force), the urge to smell him was always strong (strong force), my feelings for him impacted time (gravitational force), and Abram's sexy poetry/his brain (electromagnetic).

While I composed my lists, Abram spent the next hour or so of the —early evening? What the heck time is it?—on the phone with his record label, and then his publicist, and then a conference call with his record label's publicist. They all promised to hammer out a press release for our perusal by tomorrow morning.

At one point they wanted to know if my parents' team needed to be brought in the loop. I shook my head, making a split decision based on the need for expediency.

Plus, my parents had a great committee of people looking out for their interests, and that was the problem. I wanted Abram's interests to be the priority, not theirs. If they got ahold of the story, they'd spin it to their own benefit somehow. Therefore, *no*.

When he finally got off the phone and we were able to sit down properly with our Mexican feast, I discovered that he had procured enchiladas and I fell a little bit more in love with him.

Over dinner, or lunch maybe? Whatever. Over food, conversation flowed easily, as expected. Whenever we'd spoken on the phone over the last several months, time had run out too quickly, our conversations never seemed finished.

Presently, he was finishing up a story about how one of the roadies showed up for pre-show rehearsals in his bathrobe and nothing else.

"He'd used the hotel sauna—the hotel was across the street from the venue—and forgot his room key, locking himself out of his room."

"Oh no."

"Oh yes. And when he went downstairs, the front desk wouldn't give him another key without his ID, which was in the room."

I laughed at this poor man's misfortune though doing so made me feel like a jerk.

"So he waited in the lobby, in his bathrobe, until someone with the show happened to be walking by, which was me, but I was already running late for an interview. So we decided to go to the venue—I got him in no problem—and see if anyone had extra clothes he could wear until we could make it back to the hotel and sort out the key issue."

"And?" I leaned forward, way too invested in the story.

"No one had any extra clothes. The poor guy had to do the sound checks in his bathrobe, and it was a windy day." Abram lifted his eyebrows meaningfully.

I covered my mouth, feeling badly about my laughter.

"But he took it in stride. I ended up giving him my T-shirt and just wearing my jacket."

My eyes widened, contemplating the kind of stir that must've caused. "How did that go over in the interview?"

Abram made a strange face, like he was trying to smile, but couldn't quite manage it. "It was fine." He pushed his rice around with his fork.

"Hmm. That sounds like a falsehood."

Rolling his eyes, he released his utensils and leaned back in his seat, saying as though bored, "The interviewer asked if she could touch my stomach."

I wrinkled my nose. "That's gross."

He shrugged, like it wasn't a big deal. And yet, something about his display of apathy felt off.

"How do you deal with it?"

"What's that?" Abram leaned forward again, picking up his fork and spearing a piece of enchilada.

"All the attention. My parents love it. I think nothing thrills my dad more—at least when I was younger, and I saw him interact with fans—than when a strange woman tells him how sexy and handsome he is. He honestly eats it up. But every time you and I talk about this facet of your job, it seems like you—"

"Hate it?"

I nodded.

"I do."

I frowned. "Except—and no judgment—why did you do those underwear ads?"

Abram's chest expanded with a deep breath and his gaze lifted to the ceiling. "You have no idea how much I wish I hadn't done those ads. It's like, especially since I did them, people assume I'm brainless. Or, they don't assume, they just don't give a shit. We have a few PAs who seem nice, but they make me uncomfortable every time we're in a room together. Always brushing against me when they walk by, even if there's a mile of space around us. I no longer go to VIP ticket holder meet and greets after this one woman—uh . . ."

His eyes widened and he blinked at me.

I lifted an eyebrow. "This one woman?"

He made a resigned sound. "Drunk, she offered to go down on me in front of a room of other VIPs, which inspired more people to make the same offer. Nothing happened, though. I just left, no big deal."

"God," I croaked, and I did my best to ignore the sour taste in my mouth. "I'm sorry."

He shrugged. I didn't like how much he was shrugging, and I'd almost convinced myself the tight feeling behind my eyes wasn't jealousy. Well, not really jealousy in the classical sense, because I trusted Abram. It was more like second-hand distress on his behalf.

A thought occurred to me, a worry, unsettling my stomach a little. *And maybe next time don't have so many jalapeños.*

"What's wrong?" Abram covered my hand with his. "Honestly, don't worry. It's nothing. It's like, what can I do other than avoid the PAs and ignore the VIP sessions, right?"

"Abram, I am going to worry. People shouldn't put their hands on you without your consent. That's not okay." In truth, it also made me uneasy because he sounded like me.

It's nothing.

Nothing happened.

No big deal.

He squeezed my hand. "The tour won't last forever. It wraps up this fall, and then I'll be done."

"Done? Aren't you already working on another album?"

"Yes, but we're not signed for two albums, just the one. I'll stipulate in my contract that I don't want to do a tour next time."

My mouth dropped open. "You—you don't want to do another tour?"

Abram shook his head, looking both determined and tired. "No. No more tours."

"I—I can't believe it."

"Believe it," he ground out, releasing my hand and reaching for his beer.

"This fall." I said the words like I could conjure the time jump just by reciting them. "Where will you go? Do you need to live in New York? To record the next album?"

"No. I'll go wherever you are." He said this easily, like it was already decided, like it was obvious.

And it made me giddy, so I grinned and spoke without thinking, "We should get a house!" *Ah!*

Immediately, I wished the words back.

But he was also grinning. "Yeah. Sure. Where? In LA?"

Now I was out of breath, because I hadn't expected his answer. "Are you serious?"

"Yeah. Why not?" He shrugged, like it was no big deal, and my heart deflated.

Bah. Of course. He wasn't thinking of a house like I was thinking of a house, as a place to raise a family, as a home, a future, stability.

"Yeah. Maybe. No big deal." I forced a smile and nodded, my attention focusing on my rice. "We'll see."

[18]

THE INTERIORS OF STARS

Abram

Feeling a little cooped up after a day spent inside, and craving Stan's donuts, Mona convinced me to walk with her down to the donut shop. I didn't require much convincing.

When we made it to Stan's, after we'd ordered, after we'd sat down across from each other, I swiped some of her donut.

"For old time's sake," I said.

Scowling at my laughing eyes, she held the remainder to the side, supposedly out of my reach. "You are never invited again."

That just made me laugh harder. Excusing myself, I returned a few minutes later with six chocolate cake donuts, handing her one and explaining the rest were for tomorrow morning.

"By the way, what time is it?" she asked, patting herself down. "Shoot. I left my phone in our room. I keep forgetting to check the clock."

I shrugged. "I don't know. It's not time for you to leave yet, and that's all I need to know."

"Yes. We still have *two days*. Can you believe it?" She grinned at me, dancing happily in her seat.

I grinned back, pleased to see her mood had improved, but thinking three days wasn't nearly enough. I also wondered when she was going to tell me why she'd grown so quiet after dinner. She'd seemed preoccupied, but not distant. A little sad, a little resigned.

"I have plans for tomorrow," she said, pulling me from my thoughts.

"You do? Tell me." I picked up my own donut, toasted coconut, and took a bite.

"First, we'll go to Andersons and we'll do some leisurely book browsing. And then, dinner at that Italian restaurant where we had our first date."

My eyebrows ticked up an inch. "Our first date?"

"Yeah. You know, right after Andersons you took me to that place, and I had the lasagna."

"You're counting that as our first date?"

She looked at me as though I were odd. "Of course. Activity plus dinner makes it a date."

I laughed. "Mona, I think your hindsight is not twenty-twenty. That was the night you told me I was behaving inappropriately."

"So?"

"So, if it had been a date, then me making the moves wouldn't have been inappropriate."

She opened her mouth, lifting a finger, seemed to reconsider whatever she was going to say, and let her hand drop. "Okay. Good point. Then that means we haven't technically had a first date."

"What about tomorrow?"

"Now there's all this pressure. The *first date*." She made a face. "What did your parents do for their first date?"

"Um, let me see." I glanced over her head, trying to recall the story. "Ah, yes. The way my mom tells it, she *fancied* my father, but he was very quiet, shy. So, one day after a football game—he was on the team in high school, but his parents were really poor and all the money he made from his job went back to the family, so he could never go out with everyone afterward for food—she met him at his car with a picnic. She told him he could take it and eat it on his own, if he wanted. Or, they could eat it together. They ate it together."

Mona sighed. Deeply. "That's so wonderful."

I grinned, liking how her eyes were unfocused and dreamy. *She's such a romantic.* But then, so was I.

Before I thought too much about it, I asked, "How about your parents?"

She blinked rapidly, her eyebrows pulling together, and straightened in her seat. "I don't know."

"You don't know?"

"No. I never asked. They never said. I don't know. Anyway." Mona broke off a piece of her donut and popped it into her mouth, chewing and swallowing. "Did they tell you about their second date?"

She was attempting to change the subject, but I'd made myself a promise to ask her about her family more often. She needed to know she could talk to me about them, good or bad.

"Mona, why don't you talk about your parents?"

Her eyes dimmed. "There's not much to say."

"They're not interesting?"

"Oh, they're very interesting." Under her breath she added, "They're the most interesting people they know."

Hmm. "Would it bother you if I asked questions about them?"

"Why are you suddenly so interested?"

"It's not sudden. Not really. You never talk about your family, and in my experience—with my own family—they're a fundamental part of who I am. I'm interested in you, everything about you. By extension, I'm interested in your parents, how they contributed to who you are."

"Not every family is like yours, Abram. Not everyone's parents are directly involved with, or even interested in, their children."

"I find it really hard to believe your parents aren't completely fascinated by you. I mean, you're fucking amazing."

"As we've established." She flashed me a grin, there and gone, but her gaze remained troubled, or perhaps already exhausted by the subject of her family. "They're not interested in me." She took a deep breath and shook her head. "And that's okay. They're very busy. I understand that they have a lot of responsibilities and demands on their time. Being who they are, I consider myself lucky to—"

"You don't believe that," I cut in, because she was using her academic voice. It was the one she seemed to employ whenever she wanted to distance herself from the information she was sharing. "Why are you saying things you don't believe?"

"I'm—I'm not."

"You are. You don't believe anything you've just said. It's like you were reading from a script, saying the words you feel like you should say, even if they're all false."

She swallowed thickly, her eyes cagey, like she'd been caught.

I didn't want her to feel trapped, I wanted her to know she could share this part of herself with me and be honest. Gentling my voice, I tried to reach her. "You can say they're assholes, Mona. You can say they neglected you, if that's the truth. Or you can say they didn't neglect you, but that they weren't what you needed, if that's the truth. But trying to make the best of a situation in retrospect by telling lies about what actually happened, trying to reframe it, that's like—God— that's like putting a two-by-four in a fancy vase and trying to pass it off as a floral arrangement."

Her mouth twitched, and then she laughed a little despite looking like she didn't want to laugh. But she persisted in silence, saying nothing.

"What I'm saying here is, don't put someone else's spin on your life. Be honest, not just with me, but with yourself. Yeah?"

"Yeah." She nodded slowly, swallowing again. "That makes sense."

I waited, watching her, hoping my small smile was encouraging.

But she wasn't looking at me. Her gaze moved around the restaurant. She scratched the back of her neck, her cheek, the bridge of her nose. She twisted her fingers and sighed, taking another deep breath just to sigh again.

And I waited.

Eventually, Mona cleared her throat, and then blurted, "They're disappointing." Huffing a laugh, she leaned her elbow on the table, her forehead falling to her hand. "They navigate the world very well. They live firmly within it, and are praised for always saying the right thing, being upset and outraged at the right time. They set trends, are edgy but not foolish, and their charisma is suffocating. I don't actually know them very well, as people, but I don't think they know themselves either."

"What do you mean?" I kept my voice soft even though I ached for her and instantly despised them.

"I started to suspect, when I was in college, that my parents are more a product of the world than they are truly themselves. Every decision is made by a committee of experts—what they say, what they wear, who they're photographed with and where—and their interest in me—or Leo, or Lisa—is heavily dependent on how their committee votes. Sometimes I'm the right person for a photo spread, depending on the message they want to convey to the world. But sometimes I'm not."

Mona lifted her head, giving me her eyes back. They were tired, resigned, and I hated that Marie had been right about Mona's parents.

"Do you think that they might change? If you asked them for more of their time, that they might try?"

"No," she answered immediately, no hesitation. "They won't change. But you know what? Nothing changes."

"What do you mean?"

"Nothing changes. Not really. I mean, everything changes. Change is the only constant in the universe. Except, nothing really changes. Case in point, in undergrad, in my philosophy class—which I hated—the professor handed out a list of issues that were supposed to be problems with the world today, and they were spot on. Except, they were written thousands of years ago by a Greek philosopher."

"Huh. What do you think that means?"

"I guess . . ." Her eyes shifted up. "I guess, what's wrong with the world never changes. Selfishness, greed, brutality. There will always be stupid, brutal people. There will always be intelligent, brutal people too. And that's depressing."

"But what about the flip side to that?"

"The flip side?" She picked at her donut.

"Don't you think, if what's wrong with the world stays constant, then what's right with the world—love, compassion, honor, generosity—is constant as well?"

Staring at me intently, her breathing changed. She was doing that thing I was beginning to recognize as the precursor to discussing or saying something difficult.

I'd already braced myself for a big announcement by the time she said, "Abram."

"Yes, Mona?"

"I want a house."

I lifted my donut for another bite. "Okay." *Was that it?* Why would she get herself worked up about that? She'd already mentioned it.

"And a picket fence."

"A what?" I asked around my bite, frowning, certain I'd misheard her. It sounded like she'd said, *And a picket fence.*

"And a garden with roses. And a flagstone path leading through it. And a room—with a piano—that's big enough to also house a Christmas tree between Thanksgiving and New Year's. I want a dog and an alarm system. And a flag on a flagpole that's lowered to half-mast during national tragedies. And dinners together every night at six. And enough bedrooms so that, as my kids get older and need more space, I won't have to bunk them together anymore. But they should definitely share a room when they're younger so they can learn how to compromise. And I want to help someone with their homework and help them win the state science fair."

I blinked. Hard. "Wait. Slow down. Back up. You want—you want—"

"Kids. Not right now, but before my eggs begin to disintegrate. I could freeze them, true. But I'd prefer not to, for a variety of reasons."

I lifted a hand, laughing lightly and studying her sweet, earnest face. "Hold on."

"I'm not saying this dream of mine is a foregone conclusion. I'm not saying I expect you to want the same things I do. I'm just, you know, communicating what my dreams are, should you wish to have them as a data point."

"Mona. Stop. Let me ask something, okay?"

She crossed her arms. She uncrossed her arms. She glanced at her donut and began tearing it into crumb sized pieces. And then she nodded. "Proceed."

"Thank you. First of all, you want a picket fence?"

Her eyes narrowed, like it might be a trick question. "Yes."

I shook my head, making a face of distaste. "Why?"

Statue-still, Mona continued to regard me with doubt. "Because, I guess, I like the way it looks?"

I made a soft sound of disagreement, wiping my hands with a napkin. "We don't want a picket fence, believe me. They typically use pine, because you don't paint cedar, and then you have to keep repainting, and the wood rots, or the sections fall over. It's a real pain. We should get metal fence, aluminum, if you have your heart set one, and assuming it's not for security reasons. I mean, a picket fence isn't going to keep anyone out. Aluminum is low maintenance and it looks nice."

Now she was looking at me like I was crazy.

I held up both hands. "If you don't believe me, just ask my dad. He doesn't talk much, but he'll have a lot to say about fences. And I'm sorry, but I'll never live it down if we get a pine picket fence. He'll be out there painting it every time he comes over."

She made a strangled sound. "Abram!"

I crossed my arms, giving my head another shake so she knew I was serious. "I'm not budging on this. You don't know how my dad is about home construction and landscaping. Every conversation will start with, 'Hey, so, can we talk about the fence?'"

Her hands came down on the table and she leaned forward. "After everything I just said, *that's* what you want to talk about? The fence?"

"Yes."

"Why?"

"Because it's the only thing I disagreed with," I shrugged, giving her a small smile.

Mona blinked like I'd blown dust in her eyes, and then leaned back in her chair again, her pretty lips parted. "You want to have a family? Kids?"

"Absolutely."

"And a house? In a quiet, suburban neighborhood?"

"I honestly don't care where we do it, but we can't have a picket fence."

She wrinkled the bridge of her nose, blinking again. "It's not about the fence. But you said, when we were in Aspen, that you hadn't given marriage much thought."

"I haven't. But you don't need to be married to have a family, children, a home."

"Do you don't want to be married?"

"Are you proposing?" I grinned, lifting an eyebrow.

She made a face, clearly trying her best not to laugh, and asked, "Since when have you wanted kids?"

"Since forever." I scratched my beard, busy imagining what this dream of hers would entail, and I couldn't help but think about my own childhood. Moments I'd witnessed between my parents, how they'd shared their struggles and joys. Of course I wanted that.

Things hadn't always been easy for my family. My parents had struggled financially to make my dad's business work, and we'd had lean years. But I'd watched my mom and dad fight to make their marriage work, fight for my sister and me, fight for each other. Apparently, Mona wanted it too, presumably with me.

No. Obviously with you. She wouldn't have told you if she didn't want it with you.

Indulging my imagination, my mind drifted to scenes from our future. What would that be like? A house, kids, a home with Mona? *Beyond heavenly.*

Her gaze softened. "I had no idea."

"Well, now you do." My grin grew because she was smiling at me, her eyes dazed and warm and happy, and I lost myself a little in her gorgeous whiskey gaze. Truly, she was breathtaking.

I could get used to this, making Mona happy on accident, just by being myself.

Speaking of which.

On a sudden impulse, I blurted, "I need to tell you something."

She nodded eagerly. "Yes. Of course."

"So, I'm worried about you and what happens when the press release goes out tomorrow."

"Abram—"

"No, wait. Listen. I'm confessing here." I didn't believe this admission would make her happy but being honest felt important.

"Okay. Fine. Proceed." She didn't roll her eyes, but she looked like she was tempted.

I wavered for a second before admitting, "I'm glad you turned down your sister."

That got her attention. "Glad?"

"Yes. Relieved. Happy."

"Really?"

"Things are going to be significantly more difficult than I thought they would be. I'm going to fight the world for you. But part of me—the selfish part—really wants everyone to know."

Her smile wide, Mona reached across the table and entwined our fingers. "That we're together?"

"Yes. I want them to know that you're mine." I lifted the fingers I loved so much and kissed them, one at a time. "And that I'm yours."

* * *

We were most of the way back to the B&B when Mona said, "It's frustrating that people can't use the same adjectives to describe men that are used to describe women, and vice versa."

I glanced at her. "What? What do you mean?"

"Like, graceful. You call me or parts of my body graceful. And even though they apply to you, I wouldn't say so aloud." We stopped at the gate for her to enter the code.

"Why not?" I didn't see a problem with being called graceful.

"I wouldn't want to, I don't know, make you think I—bah!" The gate buzzed.

I opened it for her to walk through. "Do you think of me as graceful?"

"Y-yes," she said, stumbling on the word while we climbed the concrete steps.

"Good." We paused at the keypad for the door. "Because I am graceful."

Mona lifted her chin and grinned at me. "Yes. In so many ways."

Her eyes seemed to grow hazy and hot, and I didn't need to guess what was on her mind.

I shoved my hands in the pockets of my jacket. Not touching her was hard. In fact, when she looked at me like she was looking at me now, a lot of things were hard.

Clearing my throat, I withdrew one hand to open the door to the bed and breakfast. "Then tell me I am. It's a beautiful word, with a beautiful meaning, no matter how it's applied, unless it's ironic or sarcastic. I think you should tell me how you feel, what you feel about me, and not worry about baggage that comes along with the adjectives."

"Beautiful?" She looked over her shoulder, waiting for me to draw even with her before continuing to the stairs.

"Thank you. I rather am, aren't I?"

She chuckled, her gaze sweeping down and then up. "Yes, you *rather* are. Let me see, what other terms, words, and labels can I apply now that the entire vocabulary is open to me?"

I bent and whispered in her ear, "Luscious?"

She almost missed a step, her grin wavering. "Absolutely."

"Sweet."

Her smile returned. "Yep. And kind."

"Thank you." That was a good one. Really good.

"Gentle," she said thoughtfully, just as we made it to the top landing. Adding in rapid succession just as I unlocked and opened the door, "Brilliant, lovely, tender, sexy, competent." She strolled into the suite.

I followed, shutting the door and leaning against it. "Competent?"

"Yes. Competent." She turned to face me, her hands on her hips. "And, honestly, I feel like it's the greatest of all compliments. So few people are actually competent."

I nodded. "Okay. I'll take it."

"How about curvy?" She turned her head to one side, walking toward me in a way that seemed more like a prowl, while watching me out of the corner of her eye.

"Am I curvy?" I shoved my hands in my pockets. The urge to always be touching her would be my undoing. *She needs space, and time.* I had no doubt we'd work things through and come out on the other side stronger. But for now, keeping my hands to myself was the only way to stay sane.

"Oh yes." Her eyes dropped, moving over my body slowly, stopping somewhere around the vicinity of my hips.

I grimaced. There was no mistaking the *curviness* in the front of my pants. "Want to watch a movie?"

Mona's gaze cut back to mine and she grinned, but also looked perplexed. "What? No. I'm appreciating you, and your superior exterior. Including all your curves." Slowly, so slowly, she stepped forward. Her stunning eyes hot with intent.

My lungs filled with fire. "Mona." I groaned through gritted teeth.

Her lips parted, her lashes fluttering, her body surging forward firmly. "I'd like to help you with that."

"We should do something else." I shook my head, balling my hands into fists inside my jacket, trying not to lose my mind.

She shook her head in a contrary movement. "What? No! In this economy?"

I exhaled a laugh but sucked in an abrupt breath as she fit her hand between us, stroking me over my jeans. "Let me help. I really, really want to."

Encircling her wrist, I pulled it away and behind her back. She quickly replaced it with her other hand, reminding me of an octopus. The next stroke more aggressive, she lifted her chin to place biting kisses on mine.

"If we only have two days left, we should make the most of it."

I pulled the second hand away and fought the consuming impulse to turn her and take her against the door. "But we'll have more than two days the next time." Unable to help myself, I stole a quick kiss from her soft lips. "A movie?"

"The next time is so far away." She nuzzled my neck, lifting to her tiptoes to suck my ear in her mouth. "I don't have a lot of experience with blow jobs, but I'd *love* to suck your co—"

"Mona!" No way was I going to let her finish that sentence, but I shivered as her tongue worked in my ear, and my brain finished the sentence for me. "It's not a good idea." My voice cracked. At this point, I didn't know if I was talking to her or myself.

"Abram." Her hot breath spilling against my neck pulled another shiver out of me, her hand somehow managing to break free to stroke me again. "I bet it tastes like candy."

I wanted to touch her, but I didn't trust myself. My hands hovered over her upper arms without making contact as hers unzipped my pants, reaching inside. *Oh—*

"Fuck."

"Maybe a little later." Her sexy chuckle slid over me, making me dizzy. "I miss you. I want you. And I want your big dick in my mouth."

I couldn't think. Words failed me. Her hand was now on me, tugging, massaging. I fully admit I was not strong enough to say no.

Mona rubbed her body against mine as she shoved my pants down my hips, lowering herself to her knees as she held my eyes. "Don't you want me?"

"Yes." It was really the only word in my vocabulary at this point. My next song would just be the word *yes*.

Hot, electric sparks of anticipation ignited at the base of my spine and I licked my lips, near panting, watching her, devouring the sight of Mona on her knees. Her hot, wet, sweet mouth an inch from my dick. She kissed the head and I clenched my jaw, flattening my palms on the door behind me to keep from fisting them in her hair, but—*oh how I want to.*

In the next moment, her lips closed over my cock, her hand sliding from my pelvis to my stomach, pushing my shirt up for her eyes. I took it off. And then I grabbed her hand, pressing it to my skin as her mouth sucked, so hot, so fucking soft.

I cursed, my fingers closing around hers. But then I released her hand, not wanting to hold her too tight. I was already so close. It felt like being on the edge of a blade, so frustrated by my inability to make this last, I physically hurt. But also greedy for the promise of a happy ending.

"Mona. I'm going to come. I'm—" I pressed the base of my palms into my eye sockets, trying and failing to control the jerking of my hips as I pumped into her mouth, falling off the razor's edge into an abyss of ecstasy.

So good. So fucking good.

I couldn't catch my breath.

My heart was pounding like mad.

And she was suddenly gone.

Opening my eyes and leaning heavily against the door, I heard a faucet run in the other room. *The bathroom*, my brain told me. I gave myself a minute to calm. The whole thing, from first stroke to finish, must've lasted less than three minutes, but I felt like I'd sprinted a mile. Eventually, my heart slowed, and I bent to gather my jeans.

"What are you doing?"

I lifted my eyes and did a quick double take. Mona had taken off her shirt and pants, leaving her in—no lie—a matching tiger-print underwear and bra.

Weakly, I straightened, unable to tear my eyes away. I choked on a spike of raw hunger, a powerful, visceral, scorching ache thrummed below my skin, everywhere. She advanced, and I held a hand out to stop her, wanting—no, *needing*—to see her this way.

Messy ponytail, eyes hazy, red swollen lips, neck flushed pink, black lace along the top curves of her breasts leading to the white, orange, and black animal print. Her chest rising and falling. The same black lace was at the waist of her underwear, and I think I blacked out a little as my eyes moved down her long legs.

"What?" she asked, her tone breathless, but also vaguely uncertain.

I blinked, my eyes cutting to hers. "And thus, I die."

She grinned, looking happy. *So happy.* "Come on, tiger." Like before, she crooked a finger, daring me to follow. And like last time, I had no choice. I would follow her anywhere.

"Take your pants off and come to bed."

* * *

We were naked.

I'd just taken her from behind—at her direction, and careful to keep my hands *only* on her hips, though the temptation had been strong to roam and stroke and grab as well as smack her glorious ass—and now I was sure I'd relive this day in my dreams every night for the rest of my life.

213

Tangled together, her head rested on my chest and her body pressed along mine. One of my hands was on her bottom, the other covered hers where it lay on my ribs. We were quiet. Neither of us had spoken for several minutes, each navigating our own thoughts, and I was reminded of that night in Chicago. The last night.

The first night, my brain corrected. I smiled, because it was. It was the first night we'd slept together and the first night she'd listened to my heart. I'd been so frustrated, but I'd also been concerned, determined to give her the space and time she needed to figure things out.

Just like now, except much less frustrated.

Mona stirred, her leg sliding higher on mine. "What are you thinking about?"

"Chicago."

Her arm on me tightened. "After The Blues Brothers?"

"Yes."

"Me too." I felt her smile against my chest, her hand curling on my body. "I wanted you, very badly."

I chuckled. "You have no idea."

"Uh, I think I have some idea. I mean, I was lying there trying to figure out how to cross dimensions and locate one where I didn't have to lie to you, one where we could be together."

"And now we're here." I dipped my chin to my chest as she lifted her head, our gazes meeting. "So I guess you did."

Now she smiled, her attention flickering to my left cheek and then back to my eyes. "Yeah. I guess I did." Resettling, she snuggled closer, inhaling deeply. "And your heart is just the same."

I bit my bottom lip, liking her compliment, and thinking back to Aspen, to the night she'd asked to listen to my heart. It had been a critical night for us, the first time she'd heard "Hold a Grudge," and she'd given me her letter, but I'd—

I frowned. "Hey."

"Yeah?"

"What was in the letter I burned?"

Mona was quiet for a beat, and then she busted out laughing, shaking her head and turning to hide her face in the crook of my shoulder.

Another automatic smile claimed my mouth at the sound of her laugh, but—suddenly, given her reaction—I really wanted to know. "Hey. Tell me." I rolled to my side, making her roll to hers, and I pushed my fingers into her long hair, angling her chin to give it a soft kiss. I then moved to her lips. Whispering against her mouth, I beseeched, "Tell me."

She grinned, her eyes bright. "I told you in Aspen, when you burned it. It was the truth."

"About what? About what happened in Chicago?"

"About how I felt. About what I wanted."

"What did you want?"

"Uh, interdimensional time travel, and—" Her hand on my ribs slid down to my hip and then up to my chest. "This."

Not following, my eyebrows pulled together. "What? Me naked?"

"Yes. Always. But mostly—" Her fingers over my chest flexed. "—this. This is what I wanted. This heart."

I swallowed around a sudden thickness and tightness and depth and breadth and gaping cavern of inescapable craving, tripping headlong into her, knowing I'd always be her fool. This time, I welcomed the notion.

"My heart is yours, Mona." I kissed her nose, my voice like sandpaper. "Always."

Her brilliant eyes moved between mine, glassy with emotion. She feathered her fingers into my hair, her touch gentle, cherishing.

"And my heart is yours, Abram Harris," she whispered. "Infinitely."

EPILOGUE
THE CONTINUOUS SPECTRUM OF LIGHT

Abram

W aiting for Mona's plane to land at Heathrow, I paced back and forth in front of the arrivals exit, tapping my fingers against my leg while I pretended to be on the phone. I'd cut my hair short and shaved my beard the day after the tour ended last week, and I'd been careful to avoid being photographed since.

I also wore a suit, hoping it would aid in my quest for anonymity, and because tonight was Marie's rehearsal dinner. I likely wouldn't have much of a chance to change by the time Mona and I made it to the castle.

So far, while I paced, I'd received a few interested double takes, but no requests for an autograph. Nowadays, this felt miraculous.

Mona was flying in for my sister's destination wedding. Years ago, Marie organized and planned her friend Janie's wedding. Now, Janie Sullivan had decided to return the favor. She'd called me with the idea a few months ago and I'd immediately offered to pay the hotel and food bill for all guests. Janie covered the air travel (she owned a private jet, long story) and flew everyone over to London. She also organized the Harry Potter themed bachelorette party last weekend that Mona attended, but for which I was—happily—absent.

Don't get me wrong. I liked Marie's friends, but all together in a group, they could be overwhelming. Especially her friend Sandra.

Matt, my soon-to-be brother-in-law, picked up the bill for everything else. Except the dress. My parents bought Marie's dress, mostly because it was the only thing we'd let them pay for.

When my sister had discovered what we'd done, she called me up crying. "You're crazy. Why did you do this?"

"Because I can," I said. "And because I love you. Don't make a big deal out of it, Hufflepuff." All the planning had been worth it, to make Marie happy.

I checked my watch and glanced at the arrivals board. According to the sign, the flight from Geneva had landed twenty minutes ago, and I knew she had no checked baggage. Since she'd flown over last weekend, her bags were still at the hotel. Assuming no holdups at customs, she should've been exiting the arrivals door, any minute.

Any minute now.

My phone buzzed in my hand, catching me off guard. Lowering it to check the incoming number, Mona's face filled the screen.

I answered immediately. "Hello?"

"Hey! How are you? How is Marie? Is she excited? Where are you? Are you here?"

I grinned, the sound of her voice taking the edge off the cold, granite block of missing her I carried whenever we weren't together, and wherever I went. After almost a year of mostly separation with short windows of meeting in random cities, I'd grown accustomed to the ache. What I hadn't grown accustomed to was the loss of breath each time we met again.

Or, as Mona would say, each time we met for a *rendezvous*.

The last six months had been full of highs and lows, with the worst weeks coming right after we went public with our relationship. I hated many of Redburn's fans' reactions to the news, how they talked about Mona on social media, how they picked apart her appearance, interviews she'd given in the past, making memes out of her pictures, and how they felt entitled to message me with their "thoughts."

But a few months ago, my producer, seeing that I was struggling not to feel betrayed by my fans' vitriol, said to me, "Be consumed by your art, Abram. Not the people who consume it." That had made all the difference. Like Leo's words about softness, it was one of the truest things I'd ever heard.

"Abram? Are you there?"

"Sorry." I was still looking for her in the sea of faces. "I'm here. Are you past customs?"

"Yes. And I'm past the arrivals exit. Did you get the bag I left at the hotel?"

"Yes, I have the bag you left last week. It's still at the hotel."

Mona had flown out last weekend, two days before I'd arrived, but hadn't been able to stay for the entire week. She was so close to the end of her tenure at CERN and couldn't spare the time. I couldn't leave the States until after several New York meetings about the new contract and album.

"Great! Glad you have the bag. Did you pick up the car?"

Frowning at a woman with long dark hair who was not Mona, I turned toward the elevators, searching for her there. "Yep. I have the car."

"I don't see you yet." She sounded distracted. "Should I wait on one of the benches?"

My forehead wrinkled as I twisted my neck, hunting for her. "Wait, are you in terminal three?"

"Yes. Terminal three," she confirmed just as an announcement sounded over the loudspeaker. I heard it echo on her side. Mona was definitely nearby.

"You don't see me?" I scanned the mass of people. The crowds in every direction would've made it difficult for a shorter person to see, but I was easily the tallest person in the arrivals area.

"Wait, you're here? I don't—ah! I see you!"

Turning in a slow circle, I shook my head. "I still don't see you."

"Now I'm hiding because I'm drooling. Good Lord, that suit."

I straightened, pleased, sliding a hand down the front of my jacket. "Do you like it? I had it made in New York."

219

"Do I like it? Does each action have an equal but opposite reaction?"

"Nerd."

"Sorry. Newton. Not the fig kind."

I laughed. "Mona. Where are you?"

"I'm here, but I need another minute to admire that to which I aspire."

"Nice rhyme. Come here."

"Not yet. Do that circle spinning thing again."

"I'm feeling a little objectified right now," I teased.

"Then your feelings are spot on."

I turned quickly, because I heard her voice in stereo that time— over the phone and nearby—my attention skimming the crowd, focusing on those closest until I found a woman staring at me. Except—

Wait.

"Mona?"

She wore a mischievous grin and fire engine red lipstick that matched her short dyed hair—no, not her hair. A wig. Her eyes were lined in thick black makeup, her body encased in a tight black shirt, a leather skirt, and black and white striped thigh-high stockings. On her feet she sported combat boots. Around her neck was a leather choker with spikes, and in the center of her nose was a ring.

"Hey, handsome."

Officially speechless, I stared at her. One hundred percent sure it was Mona, but still disbelieving my eyes, I unabashedly devoured this unexpected but not at all unwelcomed sight.

Her grin widened and she strolled closer, hooking a leather jacket at her shoulder over her black backpack.

Biting her tongue playfully, she wagged her eyebrows. "Looks like you're not the only one in disguise, Wall Street."

* * *

I couldn't stop staring at her legs. A big problem since I also wasn't used to driving on the left side of the road.

When Mona flew up last week for the bachelorette party, she'd taken the train out to the countryside and back to the airport without much issue. She'd been photographed just twice at Heathrow as she arrived, and only once in the Underground.

But this time, as we would be together, we'd implicitly agreed on renting a car. Once the news of our relationship broke last March, it seemed like traveling together on any public transportation—or even walking together on the street, no matter where we were in the world—ultimately led to mobs and disaster.

"Watch out," she said for the tenth time because it was my tenth turn. "Are you sure you don't want me to drive?"

"You can drive if you want." I shrugged, clearing my throat and struggling not to stare at her thighs again. Something about the combination of the thigh-highs and the leather skirt—*something about all of it*—made me want to do very, very bad things. "But then my hands will be free, and we might not make it to Marie's rehearsal at all."

Mona laughed, sounding delighted. "Okay, subject change. How are you? How's the new album? How's the band?"

"Great, now. We're almost ready for the studio. Charlie and Ruthie are looking forward to spending Christmas in Geneva, and you'll get to meet Broderick." After the wedding, I would be flying back with her to Switzerland and that was it. No more tour. No more concert dates on the calendar. No more meeting in random cities for only days or hours and then parting for weeks. We would be living together from now on. *Finally.*

I didn't blame Mona for deciding to stay at CERN through the fall semester. The work she did sounded exciting—well, she made it sound exciting—plus every time she stepped foot in the USA she was mobbed by paparazzi. We'd hired her a bodyguard the last time we'd met up—in Miami—but, honestly, I didn't want her traveling in the States unless we were on the same plane.

Where I went, the band and support personnel followed. The new album would be recorded in Switzerland, with pickups and final mastering in LA after Mona and I returned to the States.

"How about you? Work? Grants? Those assholes still withholding your funding?"

One of the deepest lows came two months ago. According to Mona, the funding for three of her grants—which were fully awarded through the remainder of the fiscal year ending in June—had been suddenly halted, the grants managers claiming they required rereview of her progress reports.

That was bullshit. She insisted it could be anything—maybe she'd pissed off someone during the London symposium over the summer, maybe she'd irritated an important person at CERN, maybe one of her thesis advisors was frustrated that she hadn't returned to LA yet—who knows?

But I assumed the culprit was our relationship. She received the notice one week after we were photographed together in Rome having a romantic dinner at the Piazza Navona. She'd worn an unbelievable red dress and the press had gone nuts, calling her the "Philandering Physicist."

Philandering? What? Fucking idiotic nonsense. It didn't even make sense.

Currently, Mona sighed. Shrugged. Sighed again. "It doesn't matter. I figured out a solution. I should be able to defend my thesis in the spring without funding issues."

I glanced at her, surprised. "You got the Darwinger grant?"

"No," she ground out. "It went to someone else."

Motherfu— "Then how . . .?"

She scrunched her face, looking cute and indecisive, but finally admitted, "I'm using the fun money account my parents set up. I'm funding everything with that."

My hands tightened on the steering wheel as I absorbed this startling revelation, but I was careful to keep my expression and voice serene. "Oh?"

We'd been dating almost a year and I still hadn't officially met her parents. But I had been photographed with them. Twice. DJ Tang and Exotica had attended several of the same industry events as me, and we'd been photographed on the red carpet together—both times their publicist approached my publicist and said, *Let's make this happen*— but they didn't actually talk to me.

Although, her dad mumbled, "Smile like you mean it."

They'd swooped in, posed for the photos, and left without a back-ward glance. The next morning's headline read, *"One Big Happy Family."*

It was the strangest. When I told Mona, she hadn't seemed at all surprised, but she was embarrassed. I told her not to worry.

"Yes. I'm going to use the money." She exhaled the words, like they pained her. "I know you suggested it two months ago as a stopgap, but I needed to think about it. The thing is, as you know, my therapist and I have been talking weekly, and so I told her about the idea." Mona's therapist was one of my most favorite people in the world. But I'll get to that later. "Anyway, she and I were talking about stressors in my past, my parents, the nature of neglect in all its forms, and whatnot, and how I was so tense about the grants. And, well, she pointed out that we—all of us—are born with a different set of resources. Like you, for example."

"Me?"

"Yes. You came from a family with an abundance of love, but not always an abundance of financial security. She asked me which I thought was more important and if it made sense for you to reject your parents' love because other children—i.e. me—grew up neglected."

"Huh." See? The woman was amazing.

"We went back and forth for a while, because the issue is obviously not that simple. Money buys advantages that love cannot, and—anyway—after we discussed the nature of merit-based reward systems, bias in peer review grant awards, the problems with inherited wealth and so forth, I made a decision to use the money to finish my thesis, and I've committed to not feeling gross about it."

I wanted to say, *Hell. Yes.* But instead I simply nodded and said, "Okay."

Since Mona had started talking to Dr. Kasai last spring, she'd become so much more comfortable in her own skin, so much more willing to appreciate a moment rather than look for reasons to second-guess her enjoyment of it.

As an example, she loved being tied up. She loved blindfolds and handcuffs on either or both of us. The distinction Dr. Kasai had made clear for her, which Mona told me about when we'd met in London early over the summer, was the difference between giving control and losing control. Mona loved the idea that she was giving something rather than losing it.

"It's like, in my dream best-case scenario, I win the Nobel Prize in physics," she muttered fiercely, obviously still thinking about her funding situation and giving me the sense she was speaking to herself. "And the Darwinger Institute can choke on a dick because they then can't claim any credit."

I almost choked on air, sending her a surprised look. "Choke on a dick? Where'd you pick that up?"

Mona's smile was small but impish. "Your sister's friend Sandra used it last week during the bachelorette party. I've heard Gabby say it in the past. But after Sandra used the phrase, I warmed up to it."

Ah, Sandra. She was a handful.

The rest of the drive passed uneventfully, which was good. A few times, I caught myself staring too long while she talked, or glancing too often at the band of skin where her short skirt hit her legs. I'd also been distracted by my generous imagination, considering how best to make use of our disguises before the rehearsal dinner. . . since we were making such good time.

But when we arrived and were crossing the lobby on the way to our room, she stopped, squeezed my hand, and gave me a kiss on the cheek.

"Okay, I'll see you later."

"Wait. Where are you going?"

"I have to meet the other bridesmaids for rehearsal." She gestured over her shoulder with her thumb.

"The rehearsal isn't for another hour."

"Oh, no. I'm not talking about the wedding rehearsal. Well, I am. Sort of. It's a—but, well, you'll see tonight."

I caught her arm as she turned away again, disappointment landing on my shoulders like a shove. "Wait, wait. Mona, wait." I slid my hand down to capture hers again, staring deeply into her eyes. "Don't you need to change first?"

She grinned a slow grin at my obvious hint, and then she giggled, sounding gleeful. Stepping forward suddenly, she threw her arms over my shoulders and kissed me, her nails scratching the back of my neck, her tongue a hot, hungry slide against mine.

Before I could react the way I wanted—carry her off to our room—she caressed her hands down to my bottom, gave it a double pat, and then leaned away to break the kiss.

"See you tonight," she said, wagging her eyebrows. "Don't change the suit."

Turning once more, Mona left me to stare after her. I was too distracted, enjoying the view of her backside walking away to say anything else. She gave great view.

But as soon as Mona turned the corner, I shook my head, coming back to myself, and decided I'd try to find my parents, see if I could help with any last-minute arrangements.

Pulling out my phone, I sent my mom a text. But just as I finished, a flash of color caught my eye and I glanced up. I did a double take. And then I took a step back.

My cousin Anna, and my sister Marie, and all of Marie's close friends were walking across the lobby, and they were all attired in black leather, bright neon spandex, and various random wigs. Even Marie's friend Ashley, who was visibly pregnant, was similarly dressed.

I braced myself, straightening my spine, especially when Sandra—the handful—caught sight of me and smirked.

"Whale, whale, whale. Look who it is." Elizabeth Moretti stopped in front of me, her hands on her hips. She was wearing an insane amount of blue eyeshadow and what looked like a David Bowie wig.

My sister stepped forward first to give me a hug, pressing a kiss to my cheek and then using her thumb to rub off excess lipstick. "Did you get Mona? I was just about to text you."

"I did. She went that way." I tilted my head toward the room where Mona had disappeared and then turned to greet Anna, giving her a tight embrace.

Sandra rubbed her hands together. "Excellent. Excellent."

As soon as Anna and I separated, Janie Sullivan—who wasn't wearing a wig, her naturally curly red hair styled like she'd just survived a tornado—gave me a searching look. "There's something different about you, Abram."

"His hair?" Fiona Archer pointed to my head, looking me over with the disinterested attention of a mom surveying one of her kids' friends.

Janie narrowed her eyes, inspecting me. "No. His hair is the same, isn't it?"

I tucked my lips between my teeth. For all of Janie's brilliance, she was terrible with faces and features.

"Can we talk for a moment about the devastating loss of his glorious beard?" Ashley Winston Runous pointed to my jaw with one hand and rubbed her belly with the other. "Damn shame, Abram. Damn. Shame."

I chuckled at her, rolling my eyes.

"It's not his face." Janie scrunched hers as she said this, scrutinizing me. "But it is his face. There's something . . . different."

"The suit?" Anna tried, straightening my tie. "That's a nice suit, Abram. You look very handsome." My cousin gave me a big smile before adding, "Almost like a real adult."

"Har." I elbowed her.

"While we're on the subject, can I have the name of your tailor?" Sandra piped in. "You and Alex have the same build. It's hard to find suits that fit those shoulders. I agree with Janie, though. You look different, kid."

Lifting an eyebrow at her use of the word *kid,* especially since her husband was younger than me, I was about to make a charming joke and then excuse myself when a quiet voice said, "He's in love."

All eyes turned to Kat Caravel-Tyson O'Malley, who was wearing a black leather dress, a blue wig in long ponytails, and a small, knowing smile. "That's why he looks different. He's happy."

* * *

Apparently, even before Janie decided to throw my sister a destination wedding, The Bangles tribute band had been in the works. It was revealed just after dinner that the bridesmaids had been meeting over Skype on Tuesday nights, Chicago time, and Mona had tried to make the virtual practices whenever possible. She'd been reteaching herself the piano.

I knew Matt was a *huge* The Bangles fan. He'd even corrected me once when I'd said, "So, you're a huge Bangles fan?"

Matt had grimaced, shaking his head quickly, seeming to struggle for a moment, and then blurted, "I'm so sorry I have to be a jerk right now and correct you. It's *The Bangles.* You can't just call them *Bangles*, that could mean bracelets. I have nothing against bracelets. I'm just not a big fan of them like I am of The Bangles. Or someone might mistake your meaning as—*God forbid*—the Cincinnati Bengals."

He looked at me like he was pained, like correcting me physically hurt him, but he simply could not stop himself. And that's when I realized Marie was right. Matt and Mona were basically the same person.

Honestly, I was okay with that.

The ladies had their final practice in person. It took place during the hour prior to the rehearsal dinner itself. Marie and Ashley sang lead and harmony. Mona played the piano, and Anna—who was also the maid of honor—was on the drums. The rest of Marie's friends rounded out the band in various roles. Janie and Kat didn't play an instrument, so they played the part of backup singers with tambourines.

We all saw Marie and the rest of them in their getups during the actual rehearsal for the wedding. Matt and us groomsmen attributed the outfits to some kind of bridesmaids bonding ritual. When the real plan revealed itself after dinner, we were all shocked and awed.

The great thing about having so many people in the tribute band was that they could take turns. Elizabeth Moretti also played the piano. She took over for Mona so that she could dance with me. Ashley sang lead vocals so that Marie and Matt could spin around the dance floor.

Later, much later, Matt requested a non-The Bangles song—"Careless Whisper" by Wham!—earning him a particular kind of look from my sister. But Ashley, Ashley's husband Drew, and I stepped up, making it happen for the couple.

By the end of the evening, it was pretty clear who the musicians were, but everyone had a great time pitching in and helping out. It was my favorite gig in forever.

"Such a great time." Mona used my hand to twirl herself. I carried her boots and she carried the rest of her champagne in her free hand. "What kind of tribute band do you want?" She glanced over her shoulder at me.

This time, stay.
Let me usher you to bliss.
Nothing else for me here
Just you gone, only memories remain to reminisce
Telling tales of your skin, your eyes, your mind, your kiss
Gasps and sighs and soft greedy sounds,
Amazes, razes, dazes, and astounds.
You
Never
Stay.

"Hey. Buddy. Eyes up here," she whispered.
I didn't lift my eyes. "In a minute."
Mona laughed quietly and continued pulling me towards our room.

I twist and turn and ache to touch
I promise I won't hurt you, I hope you won't hurt me much.
I see only you,
I know you want me the same way
The pull, the push, but too soon it's over.
I
Never
Stay.

It was late, but I didn't know why she was whispering. The entire hotel had been reserved exclusively for the wedding. The only guests on this floor were us, and most of the other guests were still dancing in the hall.

Whereas Mona and I had left just moments ago, after I'd bent my lips to her neck and whispered a few lines I'd been thinking about all night in her ear.

"No taste of you will ever be enough,
I try to take things slow, but you tell me you want it rough."

She'd shivered, her breathing changed, and—grabbing the lapels of my jacket—she pulled me off the dance floor mumbling something like, "VOILA! Electromagnetic desire."

Finally, we arrived at our door. Releasing her hand, I unlocked it, opened it, tugged her through, dropped her boots, shut the door, and pushed Mona against it.

Your eyes betray you, how they search for and find me
Burns in dreams, singes reality
Stealing my breath, my thought, my sanity
A moment without you, an endless eternity.
We
Never
Stay.

"Hello." I braced my hands on either side of her head, liking my view.

"Hello, Wall Street." Mona sipped champagne, and then decided to chug it, watching me over the rim. When she finished, she smacked her lips, dropped the plastic cup to the floor, and smiled. "What are we doing?"

An unhurried grin took my mouth, and my attention drifted to her lips, the neckline of her shirt, the swell of her breasts. My hands fell away from the door, lowering to the mesmerizing skin between the hem of her skirt and the tops of her stockings.

"I like these stockings." I fingered the band at the top. "You should wear them more often."

Mona bit her bottom lip, her hand sliding inside my jacket. "I like this suit." She tugged at my shirt. "You should take it off."

I smiled at her bossiness, getting ready to lift her skirt and play my part. But then I stopped, and I looked at her, and I committed to memory how divine of a moment this was. Here we danced on the precipice of something new.

After tonight, a tomorrow with Mona, and a day after that, and a day after that.

So this time, don't leave.
This time, tell me you'll stay.
This time, don't let life steal you away.

"Mona, my love." I kissed the tender skin below her ear.

"That's me." She tilted her head, giving me more access, her hands sliding under my shirt.

"No costumes tonight." I covered her left breast with my hand, seeking her heartbeat beneath. "I just want you."

Her fingers lifted to my jaw, angling my face just far enough away so that our eyes could meet and dance. Staring with me, she nodded, and lifted her chin for a sweet kiss. I gave it to her.

We would have opportunity for costumes and lady rockers and Wall Street tycoons later.

But not now.

Now, we finally had time.

~The End~

ABOUT THE AUTHOR

Penny Reid is the *New York Times*, *Wall Street Journal*, and *USA Today* Bestselling Author of the Winston Brothers, Knitting in the City, Rugby, Dear Professor, and Hypothesis series. She used to spend her days writing federal grant proposals as a biomedical researcher, but now she just writes books. She's also a full time mom to three diminutive adults, wife, daughter, knitter, crocheter, sewer, general crafter, and thought ninja.

Come find me -
Mailing List: http://pennyreid.ninja/newsletter/
Goodreads: http://www.goodreads.com/ReidRomance
Email: pennreid@gmail.com ...hey, you! Email me ;-)

OTHER BOOKS BY PENNY REID

Hypothesis Series

(New Adult Romantic Comedy)

Elements of Chemistry: <u>ATTRACTION</u>, <u>HEAT</u>, and <u>CAPTURE</u> (#1)

Laws of Physics: <u>MOTION</u>, <u>SPACE</u>, and <u>TIME</u> (#2)

Fundamentals of Biology: STRUCTURE, EVOLUTION, and GROWTH (#3, coming 2021)

Irish Players (Rugby) Series – by L.H. Cosway and Penny Reid

(Contemporary Sports Romance)

The Hooker and the Hermit (#1)

The Pixie and the Player (#2)

The Cad and the Co-ed (#3)

The Varlet and the Voyeur (#4)

Dear Professor Series

(New Adult Romantic Comedy)

Kissing Tolstoy (#1)

Kissing Galileo (#2, read for FREE in Penny's newsletter 2018-2019)

Ideal Man Series

(Contemporary Romance Series of Jane Austen Re-Tellings)

Pride and Dad Jokes (#1, coming 2019)

Man Buns and Sensibility (#2, TBD)

Sense and Manscaping (#3, TBD)

Persuasion and Man Hands (#4, TBD)

Mantuary Abbey (#5, TBD)

Mancave Park (#6, TBD)

Emmanuel (#7, TBD)